GW00535868

ROGUE FLIGHT
Part One

A Novel of World War One Aviation

By

Fritz Wintle

Grosvenor House
Publishing Limited

This book is published by
Grosvenor House Publishing Ltd
Link House
140 The Broadway, Tolworth, Surrey, KT6 7HT.
www.grosvenorhousepublishing.co.uk

This book is a work of fiction. Any resemblance to
people or events, past or present, is purely coincidental.

A CIP record for this book
is available from the British Library

ISBN 978-1-80381-073-7
eBook ISBN 978-1-80381-074-4

Dedicate to

Jenna, who encouraged me to look to the skies,
and my children who have kept me grounded

*'Love of the skies, Respect of the enemy,
Contempt of the war.'*

He stood alone and forlorn as he leant over the handrail, and was wrapped in a heavy overcoat shielding him from the biting wind. Lost in thought, the piercing blue eyes idly watching the dolphins leaping from the water, using the bow wave of the ship to frolic. Guilt and relief battled for supremacy in his mind. He stared at the water, and wondered if there were any submarines lurking underneath. It would be ironic he thought, if he were to be killed by his own side.

His shoulder ached like the very devil. The wound would heal in time, but he was doubtful if he would ever fight again. This anonymous individual kept to himself, and avoided unnecessary contact with any of the many men, many wounded men, on the ship returning home.

His batman and friend, was an English veteran called Norman Smith, who was recently invalided out of the services. He was tasked to discretely ensure his charge was not bothered by anyone at all, and ensure his immediate needs were catered for.

Smith found him easily enough in his usual spot by the rail on the quarterdeck, "Dinner is ready for you sir in your cabin. I've managed to find a little bottle of something too."

He turned towards Smith and smiled, His German was atrocious, but he did try. He followed him back to his cabin.

In his jacket was a newspaper featuring an elaborate funeral generously organised by the English Army. It was in recognition of being the most celebrated and feared aviator of the time. In fact it was supposed to be his funeral, but he was instead thousands of miles away, and heading to the new world.

Chapter One

An Arrival

It was a good knock from Wentworth who nonchalantly left the field with a respectable thirty-seven runs. It wouldn't be enough to change the result, but at least they gave the opposition a run for their money. An impromptu cricket match between the cavalry and the Royal Flying Corps had been organised solely by Major General David Caddell, who had managed to cobble a scratch team together, against the cavalry who boasted a team that comprised of county cricket regulars, as well as a couple of internationals.

Adrian Wentworth discarded his pads and acquired a gin before slumping himself into a chair, next to the General sitting on the veranda of the pavilion.

"The cavalry will be crowing about this day for weeks David, and I suspect some of our team wouldn't know one end of a bat from another."

The General smiles benignly, and fidgeted with his pipe, he crossed his legs and leaned forward to watch the game. In truth he wasn't much of a cricket fan himself, but that wasn't the reason why he had invited the cavalry along in the first place.

He was relatively young for a General, and quite a small man. He had only grown his moustache in an effort to make himself more imperious and commanding. In contrast the young pilot sat next to him represented the very essence of an RFC officer. Adrian Wentworth was tall for a pilot, of slim build with dark unruly hair. He would be considered handsome apart from having a tendency to wear a protective scowl when in company.

"I understand that you are in a bit of bother again Adrian, something to do with disobeying orders?"

Adrian gazed out on the green where his replacement batsman, was readying himself on the crease. There was something familiar about him that distracted him from the conversation with the General. The batsman was certainly at ease with himself, and carried his bat with an air of confidence. The first ball confirmed Adrian's assessment, when he stroked the ball cleanly back pass the bowler for four runs. Finally, he turned to the General, "Just a misunderstanding David, I promise. I knew what I was doing, the flight leader didn't. Instead of acknowledging that I made a better decision, probably saving the neck of a new pilot, he puts in a reprimand. Bloody pillock"

David chuckled quietly while sipping on his Pimm's. "You are a fine pilot Wentworth, one of the best, but you never fit in, never settle. That's why your here today, apart from your batting prowess"

Adrian acknowledged to himself that the General's criticism was well founded. He was dismissive of authority, especially military authority, which he admitted was largely down to his precarious upbringing.

Once again, the General interrupted his thoughts. He waved his pipe airily in the direction of the cricket square. "Do you recognise the new batsman b' chance? His score is up to sixteen already."

Adrian screwed his eyes up against the pale sun. The batsman had just take a single, and was casually leaning on his bat. He was smaller than himself, and his hair was darker than his own. It was his complexion that caught his eye, which was at first sight, often mistaken for a dark tan. Recognition came as a lightning bolt.

"That can be but one man, by God. The one and only John Singh-Smythe, am I right?" David slapped his own thigh and laughed. "Singer Smythe in the flesh. Oh bad luck Dickie!"

Smythe's batting partner had just been caught for a duck.

"And what about him, chap who's now leaving the field? Never mind, I don't expect you to know him, That's Dick Watson, one of the lesser known pilots of the RFC, but a promising aviator, nevertheless. Found him languishing in training school as an instructor "The General turned to face the Lieutenant. "You know that 'Singer' is reputedly the best we have, with what, twenty plus kills."

Adrian snorted back. He was well known to have no truck in keeping score of his 'kills'. "I have heard that he's made a point of never claiming any kills or probable's. He has a point you know, after all the men he has killed have mothers and fathers, family, just like himself. It's done bugger all to endear himself to his superiors though."

The General ignored him and continued, "I am of the opinion, that young Watson has the potential to be as good as, if not a better pilot eventually, which is really why you are all here today. I'm told he can also speak passable German too, quite the accomplished chap, coming from his poor working-class background."

Adrian scrutinised the man in question, but was still unimpressed. "Hope his flying skills are better than his batting" Adrian's scowl had returned.

It was a win for the cavalry, but a narrow win. The General was familiar with Singh-Smythe's pre-war formidable all-round cricketing skills, which would have been his choice of career if the war hadn't intervened. His spin bowling also accounted for five of the opposition wickets, which almost carried the day.

The cavalry finally left with hearty congratulations for both sides, which left over twenty personnel now assembled in the adopted pavilion mess. General Caddell was flanked by John Singh-Smythe and a certain Herbert Rhys Jones.

Herbert was not a pilot, nor was he fit enough to fight. This was due to a hereditary defective leg, which gave him

4

a permanent limp. Jones was a large bluff Cornishman, who genius was the recruitment and management of ground crew. A talent largely taken for granted in established RFC circles, but Jones was an essential element in Caddell's planning.

Adrian was sat with the General and Smythe around a small table. David addressed Adrian directly. "John here has agreed to assemble an independent flight for specialist missions. All the men you have seen here today now belong to him." He pointed out several men milling around. "Each of these men are the very best we have. Engineers, fitters, riggers and so on. They will help you to make your machines better than the factories can. As we are only the size of a flight, so we have no room for normal military etiquette. You will work together, and you will mess together, which I think you in particular," he looked at Adrian, "will approve of."

John interceded, "With better pilots, we need the best support, and for that, they deserve, and will get our respect as equals."

It was an impressive pitch, and in his own mind Adrian had already decided his immediate future lay here.

John continued, "The General assures me to make it happen, we will need keep ourselves invisible both to the enemy, and the British military establishment."

Adrian cut in, "Thanks Singer but I was sold as soon as I saw you were leading the flight." John looked at his new recruit. "Call me John, Singer belongs only in the cockpit"

Adrian stood up stiffly and leaned forward to shake his hands. He may have finally found his calling after all these years.

John saved the best news until the last. "Our General here has managed to make sure we are the first to get the latest scout machine out of the factory, which we are told is as good as anything the Hun has in its arsenal. Its known as the Se5a, and I have one for each of you"

As they made to disperse, the General took Adrian's arm to pull him to one side. "Your father often asks after you m' boy. I think he'll be pleased for you on your transfer."

Adrian said nothing in reply. The scowl across his face was enough to convey his anger at the mention of his name.

*

A few days later found John with Herbert at Hendon airfield. The last to arrive for the gathering was Adrian, and it was typically dramatic. A squeal of tyres followed by a hurried farewell to the driver. The others invited were stood in a small group by a Bessoneau hanger looking on in amusement.

He had to stop the car again, just as it was moving away, and reached inside for his jacket. John stood impassively as he made his way toward them.

Dick missed the entire theatre, he was impatient to see what lay within. He was the youngest of the three pilots assembled and had never met or heard the name Adrian Wentworth.

He would soon though learn and know tales of the celebrated Wentworth, notorious in society circles back in the capital. Herbert stood next to John, leaning on his cane. he was the only one here who wasn't an aviator, but a handpicked engineer, who also had been asked to attend.

Adrian was now struggling to put on his jacket, which was in fairness needed, as the morning was dry but decidedly cold.

"Apologies one and all. Can't blame the maid now can one? bad form, eh? Had the devil of a trip, the poor driver couldn't find the bloody place. Still charged full fare though." He stopped in front of them uncertain why he had been summoned in the first place. By deduction he chose John as the most likely candidate, "Hello again John, Wentworth reporting as ordered. Not another cricket match I hope."

John nodded briefly, "Good of you to join us. Have you lost your uniform?"

Adrian made to look down at himself. "Ah well um. Uniform is still in the barracks Sir, which is where I didn't find myself this morning. Would you like me to change?"

The elaborate entrance was typical of the man, something the General warned him of. John just held out his hand, "John Singh-Smythe, this young fellow behind me is Dick Watson"

Adrian of course knew of the reputation of John 'Singer' Singh-Smythe, although he had never heard of Watson, he did however politely shake hands with him. "I'm sure we can find you some overalls to protect your civvy attire, perhaps I should have mentioned you are here to fly this morning"

Adrian looked over his shoulder to the offending hanger, which was probably why he was invited here, he thought.

Herbert led them into the hanger, where two scout type planes were sat side by side. The atmosphere changed in an instant, with Dick looking into the cockpit, and taking in the internal set up. Adrian ran his hands down the side of the fuselage. He walked slowly around finally settling to stand at the front. He put his hands on his hips and pointed at the square nosed frontage. "Not the prettiest bus I've ever seen," What say you Dick, Dick?"

But Dick was too busy playing with the ailerons and rudder to answer

"This my friends is the Royal Aircraft Factory Se5a. The latest and best we have to take the fight to the Boche," John announced.

Adrian whistled. "What can she do?"

John turned to Herbert. "Could you find some good fellows to push the crates outside. I think the boys here want to play. He turned to Adrian, "That's what you are about to find out. I'm told she's fast, robust and very responsive. but I need your personal assessment."

John shouted across the hanger. "Herb! don't forget the overalls."

John sidled up to Adrian, "I'm letting the boy go up in the other one, he's a bit green mind you. Perhaps you could show him how a veteran can fly, if you know what I mean."

Adrian's face creased into a cruel smile. "Happy to oblige Sir."

As Adrian went to change to fly, John found Dick underneath the machine. "What do you think of her my lad?"

Dick jumped up enthusiastically. "She's a beast Sir, a proper thoroughbred. May need some tweaks on the rudder, and the harness I would change. Won't know until we get up there." John put his hand on his shoulder. "Well get yourself ready lad. You will be among the first to fly her. Oh, by the by, our friend Wentworth there doesn't know of your flying prowess as I do. I believe he may try to show off a tad, at your expense. Just a heads up"

9

Dick smiled malevolently. "Not the first time is it sir. I'll be ready."

The ground crew pushed the two scouts out into the open with Herbert and John looking on. "Get some chairs for us will you Herb, I think we're in for some entertainment."

They took off side by side. Adrian pushed the throttle forward, and in no time took off smoothly, Dick in contrast had an erratic start with several bumps and some wing wobble before his bus finally took to the air.

Adrian thought he would leave the lad alone for a while before he would tease him. He took the SE through its paces, and he was immediately impressed. He was soon in amongst the clouds, where he had enough height to throw it around a bit. In the meantime, Dick had decided that the pantomime was over, and he too concentrated on familiarising himself with the capabilities of the new scout. Dicks sharp eyes though never left the other SE.

Adrian had learnt enough to know that the plane had some very good qualities he liked, and he knew it would take more flying hours even for an experienced flyer as himself to discover its full potential. "Right then," he said to himself. Where's the sprat with the bloody stupid accent"

He found him flying straight and level skirting a cloud. He was but a couple of seconds away from placing his machine right on Dick's tail, when suddenly it's right wing snatched vertical and he disappeared out of sight.

Adrian thought for a second that the poor boy had panicked and got into a spin. He looked frantically around, only to find the tables were turned, and Dick was sat behind him, in a perfect firing position. "humbugged" he swore to himself, as he threw his SE into a vrille.

The dogfight went on for over half an hour, with both pilots pushing themselves and the scouts to the limit. On the ground John became worried, He may have over egged it he thought to himself. It would be disastrous if his little jest resulted in the loss of a valuable plane, or pilot.

In truth both men were having a time of it, both were evenly matched, although Adrian had to concede his opponent's tactical awareness was the better.

The engine in Dick's machine gave a shudder, and oil began to pour out and along the fuselage. The controls became sluggish and unresponsive. Dick turned off the fuel tap and killed the engine. He was happy he had enough height to glide safely back to the aerodrome.

Adrian looked on with concern at the developing emergency and fired off a warning flare before Dick had time to.

He followed the SE down. Dick calculated the glide path and proceeded to position himself on a parallel course to the grass runway. He looked over to see Adrian flying alongside and gave a friendly wave to assure him he was alright.

Adrian waved back, 'bugger me but he's a cool one,' he thought.

Herbert had quickly assembled a truck and some men to stand ready. In the end the plane landed smoothly, and rolled up slowly almost at the exact spot they took off from.

Herbert came back alone now, his men surplus to requirements. John heaved a sigh of relief. "This is where your people come in Herb. We have to make that machine better than it was. Faster, stronger, and more reliable"

The two pilots walked together side by side in animated conversation about the flying qualities of the SE, as if nothing had ever happened. Such was the way of aviators. He pointed to the two men. "Y' see those two there Herb, with your able assistance that is the core of my new flight, come on let's go join them in a drink"

*

It was a dull, sullen day, with a light westerly breeze, typical of the time of year. The incessant thunder of guns rumbled in the background with whistling shells of assorted calibres, accompanied by the crump of exploding ordnance, this created a continuing symphony of background clatter, that most people over time, quite strangely got used to.

The aerodrome near Vignacourt was already occupied by a British squadron of scouts and reconnaissance machines. A single scout plane came to a standstill on the far side of the field, at the farthest point possible from the assorted types of planes of the two established squadrons already stationed there.

The squadrons concentrated around a clutter of tents, buildings and hangers. Scattered around were various scout types and two-seater observers, mostly ageing Be2s and Fairey111s. The arrival and departure of machines of all types was fairly routine for one of several aerodromes dotted behind the front lines. Whoever chose this particular place for an airfield obviously knew what they were looking for. A fairly remote spot far from the front, to enable the pilots to get enough altitude before reaching the front-line trenches. The airfield was flat and quite large in comparison to normal airfields, and was screened on all sides by trees, making it difficult to locate unless you were looking for it. Ramshackle huts and tents, mixed in with barns and a ruined farmhouse hugged the perimeter on three sides, making it ideal for more than one squadron to operate there.

This arrival did attract some attention, as it was of a type not seen before. It was a square nosed scout, which arrived unannounced, and curiously made its way over to a deserted corner of the field.

The new arrival caused something of a panic for a while on the ground. Although the Hun rarely made any visits over allied skies, except for reconnaissance, it was first thought to be an enemy raid. The stranger carried no identifying markings, and even its roundels were deliberately faded. Harry Loutham and a few other curious pilots who looking on, sauntered over to the intruder at the far end of the field. Harry casually filled up his pipe, as he made his way over. The captain was irritated at the peculiar place chosen to park, which was the furthest area possible from the resident squadrons.

By the time they had reached the newcomer, the engine was stilled, and the pilot was fussing over the airframe. He turned to look on at the approaching men, as he removed the layers of protective clothing. He took off his helmet revealing thick black hair which waved freely in the wind. He finally removed the last of the scarves around his chin revealing striking, almost exotic features and a distinctive tanned complexion. His dark eyes taking in what would be his new home for a while.

John greeted his welcome party with an easy smile. He was used to this kind of initial reaction from his fellow flyers. John Singh-Smythe's sultry features were the product of a long love affair between an officer stationed in Cawnpore, and a daughter of a prominent local merchant. He grew up around military barracks in his early years and enjoyed the unique lifestyle on offer.

John's mother was the most capable human being he had ever known. While his father was focused solely on his military career, she used the advantages of her upbringing into settling well into the country life. Such was her determination for her son to be successful, she brought her considerable talents to ensure the family, and especially her son, had every opportunity to grow to fulfil his potential. He returned to England with his father following his transfer back to England when he was but still a boy.

Growing up, his favourite pastime was polo, in which he excelled. Unbeknown to him at the time, this opened doors to the cream of English society, and he became a firm favourite amongst the more notable names at court. Cricket and polo remained his passions, but it wasn't long before he found a new love of flying. It was a natural part of the evolution of many of the young gentleman during his university days in the years before the war.

A few short years later found John wrenched from the tranquil Buckinghamshire countryside to an obscure field in France, ready to fight for the mother country he had adopted as his own. Now he was an established flying ace, flying his new favourite machine. In the last eighteen months he had flown many planes, some were faster, others more manouverable, but this one in his possession, was his plane of choice. It wasn't something he could put his finger on, but in the short time he had flown the Se5a, he fell in love with it. With the assistance of his crew they would in short order, make adjustments to the airframe and engine plant, to make it even better.

"Welcome to France," Harry said. "Are you by chance lost? Or indeed in need of help," the Captain ventured.

John held out his hand. "Unless my navigation has gone awry, may I assume this is sixteen Squadron?"

Harry was visibly bemused, but took the proffered hand.

From behind the Captain one of the more observant pilots chipped in. "Sir, the insignia on the side of his plane painted out, can't really see them unless you look close up. It belongs to 'Singer' Smythe. Is that you?"

Harry turned his eyes to the fuselage to inspect the offending marks. John laughed briefly, flattered at the recognition.

The pilot effused back to Harry. "Sir if I'm correct this is 'Singer' Smythe MC, one of our very first air aces. He names all his planes the sewing machine. Not sure what this one is though, never seen this type before."

Harry politely shook hands with John. "Welcome er Smythe, would you care to repair to our mess for refreshment."

The whisky and biscuits were very welcome after the long flight. The general conversation in the mess was animated and boisterous, with everyone wanting to know what 'Singer' Smythe was doing in their neck of the woods.

John politely suggested they retire to the CO's office to clarify why he found himself on this part of the front.

Harry led him into the CO's office. The Major wasn't in, so it was up to Harry to manage the situation. "So you have been assigned to our squadron." He looks down at the form laid on the desk. "Captain John Singh... Smith?" he reads out very slowly.

"Not quite sir, typing error again," John replied. "It's Singh-Smythe, recently transferred from headquarters on assignment, the Singh bit being the colonial heritage I carry."

Harry mused for a while at the recent arrival, and looked somewhat perplexed at his new charge. "Oh I see Captain, well, welcome to the sixteen, please take a seat. From my experience the way you landed your plane would suggest you would be someone of note, and your description is common knowledge, if you don't mind me saying so".

"Thank you Major, I am the vanguard of a small flight of new types being assigned here, together with our own ground crew and supporting personnel."

John paused for a while, and stared out of the window, not sure how to explain his arrival without offending anyone. "We are under the command of Major General Caddell. He has put together a small flight of experienced battle-hardened pilots assigned for special duties. We have our own specialist ground crew and support, being independent of any squadron." John paused to gauge the reaction of the Adjutant, whose demeanour remained neutral.

Harry reached for his pipe, giving him time to take in the news.

John continued. "The Good news for sixteen is that we are here to help, support and stiffen your ranks, which I hear, alongside others, are taking a bit of a pasting recently"

Was he being overly arrogant? Haughty even to suggest the squadron needing any more help than anyone else? He started puffing with intent to get the pipe lit.

Captain Harry Lougham was both perplexed and amused with this news. life in the squadron had been dull, repetitive and wearing in recent months. The monotony of daily missions over the German lines, and the ever-changing weather which seemed to frustrate all and every attempt to effectively challenge the superior Boche formations. Worst of all was the casualties, which was not outwardly spoken of much, but the losses had a depressing way of affecting morale for everyone in and around the squadron.

New pilots were the worst. They came and went without making a noticeable contribution, and in many cases no one even remembering their names.

Harry shook his head in resigned bemusement. "May we offer some accommodation until your flight arrives. As you may surmise, most of the squadron are out on patrol, and not due back for a while."

More refreshment was at hand, this time in the form of sandwiches and tea. It was taken in what was a rudimentary mess, which was as depressing as the surrounding area of operations, being a ramshackle collection of farm buildings. It was clearly the remains of an abandoned home, supplemented by makeshift walls of timber, and lighting provided by candles. The only saving grace was an old, embossed cast iron family stove used for cooking, and more importantly heating.

The heat radiating out of the old basket filled the room with warmth, giving lie to the squalid damp conditions permeating through the larger building.

"Tell me Captain, what precisely is it you are actually doing here. I can tell you, the CO will not at all be happy to have his little kingdom here disturbed by your presence"

At that moment, the distant throb of engines could be heard in the distance to announce the return of the mornings patrol. One by one they made their way out into the murky gloom of a winter's day. Together, they all looked west for the sight of the first planes back. A daily ritual for all the engineers, crew and ground crew who spent all their working hours in those same machines week after week.

John went outside with the others to watch the return of the flight. It comprised an array of scout aircraft, Pups, Spad's and DH2's. All capable airframes, but hopelessly outclassed by the like of Albatross D111 especially when flown by the more experienced *Jasta's*.

The planes circled the adjacent fields until a lumbering two-seater, obviously in trouble was able to land. Smoke was pouring out of the front, but luckily no flames were visible. It may have been that the pilot was wounded, but he was far too slow and too high, when the plane seemed to sigh, and simply fell, with not enough height to even spin. it simply dropped to earth and crumpled into a heap on the grass. The wreck was quickly surrounded by ground crew who carefully extracted the two crew. They were quickly removed from the scene of the crash, and dispatched in a makeshift ambulance, their immediate fate unknown.

The rest of the flight came in fairly quickly thereafter. They were two planes short, following an encounter with a flight of AEG and Albatross scouts. John observed the flight leader from outside of the mess. and recognised the slow walk and resigned look on his face. The ground crew fussed around their fledglings and pushed them into their allotted spaces next to the large line of hangers.

Squadron leader Sam Cohen made his way slowly to the office to make out his report. The patrol was a fairly uneventful affair, which how it was supposed to be, which was a simple familiarisation of the local front for the new pilots, with some much-needed practise in formation flying for the new arrivals. Tiredly he walked over to the huts to report the unfortunate clash that took place over no man's land

John watched the planes land one by one, and then decided to retire to his quarters, feeling like an intruder, as the flight had clearly had an eventful day.

Harry had been fretting on informing the CO on the latest losses, activities, and the unexpected intrusion of John Singh-Smythe.

Major Cecil Barrington stepped into the mess from his office, and was manhandled gently back to where he had come from. Mildly amused at his friends bizarre behaviour, he allowed himself to be eased backwards, while Harry shut the door behind him.

"Sorry Cecil need a private chat, and its news I don't think you are going to like." Harry paused, "We had an unannounced arrival today, and from what I have been told, we are expecting more," pointing to the window. "Over on the far side is a new type of scout that has been partially assigned to us." He paused again, "For a while, sort of, ad hoc, um, but not in the sixteen"

Cecil paced over to the window and searched the horizon for the strange apparition lurking on his territory. "A new type you say?"

Harry nodded.

"My guess is that's Singer's crate," The CO laughed briefly. "Relax Harry, I have been expecting Singer's flight for several weeks now. Orders came through on a need-to-know basis. Sorry to keep you in the dark."

Sam turned towards his desk and began to lay out two glasses, and pour two generous measures of whisky, handing one over to his old friend. "Thought you would be mad sir, you know, having some part-time interlopers in our area"

Cecil flopped down into his chair and sighed, and his chin rested downwards as if to grasp his thoughts. "Do you know how many pilots we have lost this week Harry? Bearing in mind we are supposedly on routine patrols in a quiet part of the lines?

"You know we are trying to get our new boys used to flying in some sort of formation, and get them used to the lie of the land?" He continued before giving Harry time to reply. "Three... three. One through engine failure, and the silly bugger landed in Boche country. Payne, I think his name is. Been here less than a week. Then there's Sanderson, who crashed on landing earlier, and a pilot whose name I can't recall arrived yesterday, lost us in the clouds, shot down over Saint-en-Rouge. How he found himself over there God only knows. Reported in by a nearby artillery battery." He took a gulp of the whisky "Poor sod. didn't have time to have his first breakfast."

Harry nodded sympathetically, "Sorry Sir, but it's not the first time. Why do they keep sending new pilots, all with less than fifteen hours flight time under them. They have no chance up against a decent opposition" He shook his head "We need more time to get them adjusted out here. At least to give to then a fighting chance. We need to give them more hours to learn basic tactic, learn the terrain, damn it and learn to fly."

Cecil slowly stood up and put his hand on his friends shoulder. "Which is why I have no problem of having four of the best pilots in the RFC on my field, even if only part time, as you say. I'm putting you in command of them Harry, just to take care of the admin side."

Harry was surprised but said nothing. "I must say I'm looking forward to meeting 'Singer', and I'm even more curious to know the identity of the other pilots with him."

The Major was a large affable man, who was the oldest in the squadron by some margin. He was also pragmatic, and understood the men under his charge needed help, and maybe, just maybe this would be the answer to his prayers.

They found their new arrival standing alone in the mess, looking distinctly uncomfortable. John hadn't felt this way since his first posting what seemed a lifetime ago, as a new pilot in training school. He clocked the Major making his way over to him, and was impressed to see how he stopped repeatedly to address his pilots, with gestures of sympathy, encouragement and the odd smile, finally standing in front of him, with Harry remaining deferentially some distance behind.

"By the living God's if it isn't the one and only Singer Smythe," while shaking his hand firmly, "You are very welcome to the sixteenth. Harry would you kindly get the drinks while I get to know our new recruit."

Harry left the Major to do the honours, while trying to avoid the eyes of his fellow pilots who were understandably endeavouring to quiz Harry, on the mysterious new arrival. Hands reached out, pulling his sleeve, to which Harry studiously ignored while enjoying the frustration of his colleagues desperate for news.

He returned with the drinks to find the two in deep conversation around a table in the corner of the room. With reluctance he deposited the drinks and left them to themselves. At that moment he would have given anything to be part of those deliberating whispers.

John was warming to the acceptance of his presence in what was a cauldron of air warfare. The familiar smells and sounds of the pilot's mess, which was comforting to him. Two comfortable armchairs, left courtesy of their previous occupants, were vacant which they found a good place to converse. He automatically reached into his pockets for his Wild Woodbines to settle himself further.

"I am very relieved to have someone happy to see us arrive Major. This is new territory for us as much as it is for you. I'm sure we can work together and make this situation beneficial to all parties"

He was relieved to find his host amenable, and was very interested in the flying and fighting qualities of the Se5a.

It was going to be an early start in the morning with a dawn take-off scheduled. At the suggestion of the Major, John agreed to tag on to the morning's flight.

He had little to do until the other pilots arrived, together with all the ground crew. These were scheduled to arrive piecemeal in the coming days. His own plane would not be ready for the morning, after the long flight, and would need considerable work undertaken until she was combat ready.

The long day was beginning to catch up with John, and so, making his excuses he retired early. The entire mess followed suit shortly afterwards in preparation for tomorrow's activities.

*

The trucks began to arrive shortly after dawn. It took some time to convince the gate guard that they were expected, but after some time they let the convoy in. The only clue as to where they were supposed to start setting up was the location of Singer's plane sitting alone, away from the concentration of planes and buildings at the other side of the field.

Sergeant Herbert Rhys Jones watched the proceedings with a practised eye. He stood leaning with the help of his stick and puffed contently in his unlit pipe. One of the charismatic and unusual officers in the RFC, and close friend of John Singh-Smythe. A well connected and intelligent man, Herbert had previously struggled to find his niche in this war, due to the inherent weakness of his leg. It was here he found it, with these few select men, many chosen by himself.

At the commencement of war, Herbert took it upon himself to identify and recruit the very best ground crew in the RFC. He personally selected the most talented mechanics, riggers, fitters and specialists he could find. He was determined to give his pilots the best equipped planes, adapted and tweaked to give his pilots the edge.

Herbert offered his team exclusively to John, and with the able assistance of the General they contrived to team up with men as selected by John himself.

He took this as an indicator that this is where they should set up, starting with a cursory inspection of a disused barn adjacent to John's SE.

They received several visits from various sources to enquire if they required any assistance or fuel, perhaps some additional manpower. However, the crew in tow were a singularly independent group, who politely turned down all offers of advice or help.

It appeared that Singer was 'out on a jolly' with an early flight and would be back in time for breakfast, within the next hour or so. Herbert had the experience and confidence to organise the entire operation himself, and duly set about putting their new home into good order.

Within minutes of their arrival, the crew had started to unload the lorries and began to erect tents in a set formation outward from the old barn, which was unoriginally renamed 'The mess'. All the infrastructure layout of a working flight was in Herbert's own head, and he took to this task with relish.

Many of the sixteenth looked on with some amusement at the ant-like endeavours of their new neighbours. It seemed as though an entire village apparition unfolded before their eyes. It became quite the spectator sport to look upon this novelty. Lorries continued to come and go, and amongst all this visual chaos was the Sergeant directing affairs as beautifully as a conductor does to his orchestra.

CHAPTER TWO

Rogue Flight

John considered himself very fortunate to be loaned a Spad for the flight. A bi-plane he was familiar with, and like most aircraft of the time she had her attributes and her weaknesses, but in the hands of a skilful pilot, it was a match for anything else the enemy could put up against it.

He was flying sentinel at a respectable eleven thousand feet, above and behind the two flights. John wanted some time and space to get used to the local landmarks and general lie of the land, which he observed studiously. Despite the cold, he felt very much at home once more. He loved this environment, and always had, despite the slight tension, fear maybe? The freedom of time and space was as food to his soul, and he could not but smile within himself as they flew steadily eastward.

Sixteen was sensibly flying an erratic 'ducks and drakes' course, but to one purpose, to make as difficult target as possible for the anticipated Archie thrown up by Boche artillery. Today's patrol was simply to take the fight to the enemy and wrestle command of the air above the trenches.

Singer automatically settled into the routine of scanning the sky in all directions for any sight of movement. For once the sky was largely clear of clouds, which on the positive side made it easier to spot the enemy. On the downside there was no place to hide from hostile planes, and the ever-present German artillery. As if on cue the bursts of Archie announced their arrival over the front. It also gave notice to enemy formations that may be lurking, that the British are here, and this is where you can find them!

Archie was, in its own way, less of a threat that encountering a hostile squadron coming out of the sun, nevertheless it was mighty unnerving to the novice pilots. Even the more experienced pilots duly changed course and height consistently to throw off the ground gunners aim.

John was on the verge of bursting out in song, and had to check himself, and question if he was getting slightly giddy with the lack of oxygen. This was his element, his natural place to be, despite the black puffs of smoke erupting below and behind.

*

"It's not right Corps, not right at all" Jacob was old school, and very proud of his place within the squadron. He worked hard and was always conscious of making sure his planes were looked after, cherished even, to the extent for his officer pilots to have the best chance in his making it safely home again after every flight. Jacob was devoted to sixteen squadron, and loved the sense of order both in terms of operations and etiquette. Anything less than a strict order of rank was almost blasphemous.

Word had spread like wildfire that the as yet undesignated neighbours operated in a totally different way to every other flight in the entire British RFC.

"It's as I am telling you," he announced. "Them there grounds crew did tell me themselves direct. Its rotten I'm telling you, nothing more than rotten."

Word had spread around the crews that this lot had amongst them some hand-picked pilots for 'special duties' which in itself was not the issue. What did not go down well was the set up in their flight was nothing short of revolutionary. No officer mess, no segregation of personnel off duty. In effect they all messed together, together! As equals. It was a very frightening and yet exciting prospect that had never been witnessed from any squadron from either side of the conflict.

"That actually makes sense to me" A voice not immediately recognised by those assembled around the pit fire. It was young Jeremy, a quiet lad, who has never been known to contribute to a general large-scale conversation. The old lags, all turned to face this new development. Jeremy looked down into his empty tea mug and forced himself to finish his point.

"You See... the officers get all the attention, and we know they get pampered... strut around with fancy nicknames, and all the bloody medals, right? But it's us stupid sods that does all the work, keeps them all alive, and wipes their arses night and day" A reverent silence hung over for what seemed an age. The boy had clearly made his point.

Standing at the bar was Herbert who had availed himself of their hospitality, and was enjoying a beer, with one of his own next to him. Herbert had been listening to the discourse for some time and decided to take up the young lads stand.

"My General wanted the best engineers and crew to look after his planes. What we do every night by servicing those planes, keeps them young men alive, and I ain't talking about your routine maintenance or fitting. I'm talking about many man hours going over the engines to get a couple of miles more speed out of them" He looked at his captive audience almost one by one. "Those adjustments the pilots want to suit them, be it a remodelled joystick, or a part from a completely different plane" He thumbed at the young man standing behind him "Young Matthew here."

He nudged the lad standing next to him. "He spends most of his hours checking and oiling the bullets one by one. Our boy's guns never jam, never," he paused. "Almost never," he said, with a wink. "We love them boys and it is us that keeps them alive," he repeated, "and they give us the respect in turn as brothers in arms. We eats together, we drink together, and boys, as someone who is older than all of yer here, I'm a proud man, with the best pilots in the air."

Jacob remained unimpressed, "Bunch of Rogue's the lot of you," was his final say on the matter. The name stuck, Rogue flight was born.

*

It was no coincidence that the ground crew were of a different breed you would expect in an RFC flight. The General himself was a keen engineer, amassing an extraordinary amount of hours in, underneath and around engines. He appreciated the technical expertise of those early pioneers of auto engines, which was still largely a dark art before the war. Furthermore, he was astute enough to further appreciate the rare skills of the engineers, and support staff who were entirely responsible for keeping his aircraft in the sky.

Among the assembly of the flight's ground crew fitters, riggers and mechanics were Joe Reynolds and Albert (Nosy) Naismith, who were gifted riggers, and who were forever experimenting with engine modifications, paints, wiring, tail and elevators configurations, anything to give their pilots an edge. Recently the General had abused his position to 'raid' the ground crew of the independent American Lafayette Escadrille squadron. An engineering genius from Detroit. Eugene (Genie) Carpenter was coerced into transferring on the General's word alone. He was a Black American, looking for adventure and some escape from the tyrannies still embedded in his country's social make up. The 'Genie' was referred amongst the pilots and ground crew as someone who could make engines sing, whatever the type, and squeeze some more miles out of them, which was always welcome by the airmen.

In every way he was ordinary looking, being of average height and weight, but he had a grace and air about him when he walked. This with his exotic skin colour and melodious accent made him a firm favourite with the local girls, when they did adventure out to the local bars and cafes.

*

A and B flight turned to the right and began to climb. John followed the track to see what caused this. He quickly spotted the reason for the change of course. They were over the German lines, which for today did not sit well with the enemy. Eight dots were at about a thousand feet above the two flights, and judging by their manoeuvres it was a clear indication that they were spoiling for a fight. It was always at this time when the more experienced aviators would analyse and decide the next course of action. All the unknowns were in play. What were they up against? What machines? What *Jasta*? Play or run away was the motto John had adopted from his old friend and mentor Lanoe Hawker. By god he missed that cantankerous bugger!

John had evidently not been spotted, circling around from the sun side. It was a common mistake of most pilots, they get 'blinkered'. So focused are they on the prize, they inevitably forget the golden rule, to forever scan the skies!

John cleared his guns briefly again. At this height, the cold could have a catastrophic effect on the delicate firing mechanisms on the Vickers. Now it was his time, as if a bird of prey he waited for the optimum moment to strike. The two flights met each other at about the same height. As ever the novices in the ranks flagged their arrival by firing far too early, without any effect. They simply waisted ammunition, and to add to their misery trumpeting their woeful inexperience in battle. To any German this was an open invitation to latch on the newbie for an easy kill.

Despite all the expectations, the drills and looking out for the appointed charges, the fight quickly degenerated into a frenzied melee of assorted machines. To the uninitiated it looked like a complete free for all, with men and machines desperately twisting and turning to get in a killing burst.

This was the time when the ethos of Singers battle strategy came into play. John circled lazily above watching and waiting, and it was some time before he made his move. Planes were already falling from the sky, which inevitably announced the death of another brave aviator. John continued to dispassionately observe the melee, and after some time, finally took his machine down to enter the fray. Another Bristol was in trouble with two Huns on his tail, one slightly above and one directly behind. It was as if they were savouring the anticipation of the kill, Without warning, the nearest or the two Huns only found out he himself was being stalked as a line of bullets made its way up along the fuselage and into the cockpit, with the unsuspecting pilot being killed instantly.

It was one of those occasions that the plane itself having no further input from the stricken pilot continues onward until the laws of nature takes over, and makes its own somewhat beautiful and mournful last flight down to Mother Earth.

John didn't have the time to witness his first kill of the day. His momentum of the dive had to be used to latch onto the second enemy machine. The Albatross was being flown expertly by its pilot, who threw his bus around with multiple manoeuvres to throw his aim off, and at the same time trying to keep his own prey in his sights. John mimicked his opponents' movements, and came within thirty yards of his target, still scanning the sky around for threats. The Hun fired short, accurate bursts into and around the Nieuport, as the tracer rounds confirmed. He was but seconds from getting into the optimum position from where he couldn't miss.

'Singer' managed to put a two second concentrated burst into his engine before looping out to get height once more. Looking down, the sky was empty of planes except for the last machine he had hit, which was making its way eastward, with smoke pouring from the engine, but clearly still in controlled flight. He silently wished his adversary a safe passage, and turned way for home. That is if he could find it! The entire theatre being completely alien to him.

*

As he flew into his final approach John witnessed for the first time the efforts of Herbert and the crew manifest itself below him. He parked close to the rest of the Nieuports and handed the plane back to its rightful owners. He was on the ground for just a few seconds, and was somewhat surprised to be met by two people, and each with a distinctly different take on the mornings patrol.

Pilot officer Richardson, a tall balding Londoner greeted him with a broad grin and took John's hand. "Bloody hell Captain, thought I was in for it then. Bless you, bless you," he repeated.

"Happy to help," John replied, and then nodded to Harry approaching from behind. "I think someone wants a word with me."

Richardson turned and stepped away. "I'll see you in the mess later. The drinks are on me."

John smiled ruefully and waited on Harry to arrive. He had a quizzical look on his face, and seemed reluctant to instigate the conversation. "Congratulations John. Two kills on your first flight. I've got flyers who have been here two months, and haven't got as many, and there's you, not even flying your own crate."

John appreciated the gesture, and he also knew was what troubling the Captain. "Actually, it was just the one. Only managed to wing the second. That's not why your here though, am I right? You want to know why I took my time up top," he stated flatly. "Why I didn't attack and engage earlier?"

Harry was embarrassed. "Well, yes really. I thought for a while that you had the wind up, and then you go and take down two of them in the blink of an eye."

John rested his hand on to the wing of his adopted plane, and rubbed his chin. "It's what this flight is all about Harry. We are going to fight this war differently to the way you do. Look, you have nine kills so far with some more probable's right? Do you know how many I have?"

Before Harry could respond, John held out his hands wide. "I've no idea, I don't count any more. Ever since I inflicted my first 'flamer' on an old Rumpler, I had no appetite for the numbers game." He pointed towards the planes grouped closely nearby. "All the pilots from all the squadrons on all sides it a fucking numbers game, not with my flight. The reason I was stayed above for that time, I was not looking for the nearest target, or the easiest kill. I was scoping for their best to show themselves. My crew are also trained to pick out the finest the Germans can put in the air, and put them out of the war. Thinking being that this will quickly demoralise the enemy and be a more effective strategy than counting the dead. How about a drink"

They both began to walk towards the tents in silence, giving Harry some time to take on board what John had told him.

"Those flyers that had so quickly got on your chap's tail. They weren't new to this game, and flew their planes with competence. Probably why they were so quickly behind your man." He paused, "and if I remember correctly, one was carrying streamers of a flight leader."

Harry opened the door to the mess where the pilots were slowly gathering. Harry hesitated at the entrance. "Makes Good sense John. Got any other surprises for us?"

*

The weather turned for the worse over the course of the day and all flying was cancelled, and if the weather had any pattern to it, it would remain the same for the rest of the week. The mist started to come down, and it was assumed by many, that it would mean the arrival of the rest of the flight would be delayed.

Richardson was as good as his word. He was happy to foot the mess drinks tab for the evening however his single subject of conversation was the flying prowess of Singer Smythe. Richardson himself was just happy to still be amongst the living at the end of this day. The evenings dinner was particularly raucous, knowing there was no chance of any flights tomorrow, more of the officers were taking the opportunity to unwind. From somewhere in all the hilarity it was unanimously decided to 'officially' name John's flight 'Rogue' as a nod to the peculiar and anarchic set up of their neighbours.

After dinner it was freely decided to head out for an evening's frivolities. The nearest town was not a popular choice, as it was currently crammed with Canadian soldiers with too much money in their pockets, and it would have been impossible to get any sort of decent service. William 'Billy' Reynolds knew of a village tucked away just a couple of miles from the airfield, that no one knows about. It was reputed there was a decent estaminet in the village square, with wines that are cheap and plentiful, and food to die for, if you had an adventurous pallet.

A truck was commandeered for the excursion, and it was mostly the younger pilots who piled into the back.

"Not tempted to go with them John?" Harry enquired.

"Early night for me Harry, I have my pilots arriving in the morning, and it's going to take some time to get them in some sort of order."

Harry scratched his head in bewilderment. "Didn't you hear the forecast earlier. Nothing is flying tomorrow. High winds, low visibility and rain all day."

John looked up skyward to confirm his friends gloomy assessment, and turned to walk to his billet. "Oh aye I've heard the forecast, but you see, my boys have called to say they'll be here tomorrow and if they say they'll be here. Then be assured, they will be here."

*

Le-Rouex

The loud noise of the truck announced the arrival of possible guests, plus the awful noise of untrained voices singing loudly, confirmed they were English, or Canadian? Claudette could never tell the difference. Wiping her hands on her apron she walked outside into the empty jumble of chairs and tables. She was one of two sisters, together with their mother who ran the cafe. All the men in the family being on active service, or dead, and two younger boys who were shipped further away from the front to family in Nantes.

Claudette had the dark features, dark hair and eyes typical of all in the family. She would never consider herself outwardly attractive, but she had grace and wit, which caught many a soldier's eye. At the age of just twenty, she was the oldest of the sisters and already a widow. Her husband was listed colloquially as 'missing'. That was over a year since. The reality was that he was one of countless others whose body lay beneath the mud of Verdun never to be recovered. The surviving members of the Faure family collectively ran this little estaminet, and in some ways were perversely reliant on the war to bring enough trade to survive, and even modestly prosper.

Mama Faure had already instilled into them all the folly of forming any of attachment with any of the many young men, be they infantry, cavalry, privates or officers, and all from many nations, "You have to remember" she instilled in them, "They will all die," just as her husband died, just as Claudette's husband had died. These wise words were qualified in the sense that it did no harm for business to be especially nice to them, and yes even flirt a little if it kept the wine flowing a little longer!

Claudette called out to Chloe, her younger sister, to be ready for business as the men piled noisily out of the back of the lorry, with the normal chaotic scenes of a scramble for the best seats. They started ordering wine and food, in English and very poor French. Mama as usual played the mother hen role, by going from table to table, trying to put some sort of order into the proceedings, while the daughters busied themselves smartly going from table to table, whilst studiously ignoring the appreciative glances from their guests. One of the airmen remained on his feet. It was Lieutenant 'Billy' Reynolds, whilst not the best of the flyers in the squadron, he was certainly one of the most popular. He was a newly appointed flight leader of B flight, which came as something of a surprise to him, as he had always felt there were others more qualified.

In social circumstances such as this, he was a born leader, and considered by the squadron as one of the more eloquent orators of them all. "Gentlemen, gentlemen," he almost whispered. With a supporting tap on a glass with his knife. The din died down in reverential silence. Brian turned with his hand outstretched to the café, and the fervent activity of the Faure family in attending them. "May I introduce to you, my friends, your hosts, the proprietors of this fine establishment, whose particular charms are evident before you."

A little cheer went up.

"Gentlemen, please, it was my considerable scouting prowess that discovered this oasis amongst the carnage all around. He hesitated, "A warning shot though my dear fellows, I implore you not to attempt anything in your minds anything of these ladies but friendship, with courtesy and gratitude, and nothing more. Lest you incur my wrath, or that of our dear Mama".

An appreciative cheer went up, and Billy duly bowed and sat down, satisfied that the message had been satisfactorily delivered.

The cafe became busier as the evening went on, with a smattering of soldiers, mostly Canadians, with elements of a Scots company and a few surly French engineers. All of which added to the distinctive bohemian atmosphere of a gentle summer's day.

Tucked away in a dim lit corner inside of the estaminet sat a couple seemingly intent on keeping as much distance from all and sundry, in an effort to remain anonymous. A pretty young girl from a nearby village called Gabrielle, who was no stranger to latching on to foreign officers, especially those who were of means. Opposite her sat a Young Captain from staff headquarters, who was in every sense unlikeable. He had a taste for talking down to anyone he thought inferior, which included those of all ranks not attached to the Staff.

This evening it was the turn of the RFC to particularly annoy him with the noise and uproar these types made. More so it distracted him from giving all his attention to the delightful Gabrielle, with whom he was completely enamoured.

"I'm so sorry m' dear if those bores outside are annoying you." That Captain was a certain Peregrine Cotter who took great pride in own turnout, which by design was meant to impress. "My love, would it please you if I had those gentleman removed from your presence"

Gabrielle smiled sweetly at the Captain and lent forward deliberately just enough for her suitor to look down to her slightly revealed breasts. "Oh, please my love, do not bother yourself just for me. An important man such as yourself should not be distracted so." She put her hand over Peregrines, who blushed with delight at the touch.

"As you wish my love, nevertheless I will speak with the Adjutant General in the morning of this"

She continued to look into the Captains eye's, and said nothing. Nor did she have to. This stupid young officer had no concept of discretion, and with little encouragement from herself, would expand on his relationship with his General, the staff, his own inflated opinion of his importance within, and the valuable snippets she extracted from him on military matters around Vimy Ridge.

Drinks were ordered at a pace by Gabrielle, which had the dual outcomes of further extravagant mumblings from Cotter on the inner workings of HQ and, as she gulped at her wine, it would help her endure the odious bedroom fumbling's from him later in the evening.

Chapter Three

Active Duty

Two fresh faced airman stood to attention outside the Adjutant's office. One of them fiddled nervously adjusting his tunic, the other was rehearsing in his mind, any questions that may be asked of him. They were ushered in by the duty Corporal, and stood immobile before the Captain. If they was expecting any sort of welcome or friendly greeting to this new posting, they were in for a shock. They stood before the desk still as statues for what seemed to be an age before Harry deigned to look up to his replacement pilots. Eventually he looked up to the young men with a look of mild disgust.

"I would welcome you both to the sixteenth gentleman. I would ask how many hours you have flown?"

The two new arrivals looked at each other for mutual support.

"Normally I would give you the courtesy of asking your names."

Before they could respond, Harry bellowed out for his aide, and the Corporal hurried into the office. "You will please take these 'gentleman' to their billets. You will then present them to flight leader Richardson for flight training. I want these men up all day, every day until next Sunday." He turned to Corporal who was by now quite familiar with the pantomime. "They will learn how to fly, where to fly, and how to not crash the planes for fun! Until then these Gentlemen are not operational, nor do I need to know their names until that time"

Adams and Taylor meekly removed themselves from the office, chastened and humiliated, not appreciating that the adjutant was doing the very best to keep them alive, at least for the next few weeks.

As expected, the early dawn was dull, with low cloud and rain. A general lie-in was expected by all stationed in the field, and those in the surrounding area. Above the desultory artillery fire from both sides, there came the familiar drone of aircraft engines approaching. Herbert's crew were noticeably already active, in readiness for the new arrivals. This was in contrast to the absence of movement from the other squadrons around the area from where the sixteenth operates.

Three planes forlornly lost height on spotting the airfield at last. Even by their standards it had been a challenging flight in terms of the weather, and more so, in navigating to this obscure backwater of the war. In truth they had to land some miles away at another airfield to get their bearings, but that snippet of information would stay with themselves for the sake of appearances. Two of the planes landed with minimal fuss, with the wheels gently brushing the ground without fuss and parked the machines with quiet efficiency. One however went for a tour around the field, and then made a very loud low-level pass to let all and sundry know they had arrived.

The aircraft were noticeable by their lack of identification and markings. No numbers or letters on the fuselage or tailplane. Even the roundels appeared to be faded. The colour schemes were not the usual one you would expect on RFC machines, as the camouflage altered subtly from top to bottom.

The three planes were taken under cover from the elements, and were seemingly swamped by the crew. Engine, framework and cockpit disappeared under the bodies of its attendants. The planes were all of recent design and not yet in many numbers on the front. Two were Se5a's scout planes, the other one was a two-seater Bristol F2b reconnaissance fighter machine.

It was one of the SE's that announced his arrival by 'stunting' over the airfield, which John had witnessed, and had already guessed the perpetrator! John walked the length of the field to greet his team. By the time he had traversed the ground, the pilots were waiting in some sort of line to meet their flight commander. It was almost comical to witness, four individuals swathed in a combination of heavy leather or fur coats, assorted boots and headgear. An antithesis to any military cohesion.

Dickie Watson, the Brummie was one of the pilots flying an SE, and the most accomplished pilot John had ever seen, but with questionable navigation skills.

A young man of average height and slender frame, his hollow brown eyes bore sentiment to the poor diet he had endured in his early life. He was a working-class city boy who by chance and favour found himself embroiled in the enthusiasm of the early pioneers of flight. Dickie happened to be in the right place at the right time, starting from his first flight as a benevolent gift, he went on to be amongst the first aviators of his generation.

To his right, the smartest of the ensemble stood, leaning nonchalantly on his cane was the notorious Lt Adrian 'Addie' Wentworth, an affluent bastard son of a prominent Lord. Ex cavalry, gifted pilot and the company's de facto banker, thanks to his father's generous allowance. Adrian had known privilege all his life. He carried a head of unruly dark hair and clear complexion. He had an easy smile, as well as his habitual scowl. He had learned that it was his inherent charm that usually opened many doors. Adrian oozed the confidence of his class. Before the conflict began, he had little interaction with anyone but his own kind. This war had completely opened up his eyes to the wider world, and he found himself growing up all over again. John's eyes finally settled on the 'twins' as they were affectionately known. Although not twins, they were cousins, the two diminutive individuals on his right were inseparable, Jules Rice, and his observer Mario 'Wally' Wallengburg. Both of whom were of Romany extraction and damn fine airmen. They both held an understated air about them, which belied their dangerous traits.

It was the background of the twins that was the most colourful, being multi-talented acrobats come entertainers, originating from European travelling shows. The very fact these two diminutive athletes were well versed in flinging themselves through the air, and having a superlative sense of balance, made them natural born flyers. One other unusual aspect of this partnership was they could readily interchange between pilot and observer, both equally proficient with both roles. Jules in particular was extremely intelligent and wise to the ways of the world which was due their extensive travels over Europe. They were fluent in French and German and possessed a unique neutral view as to the nation states either side of the conflict

After shaking each of their hands, they collectively decided to repair to the mess and buy the ground crew's drinks for the evening, in thanks for the hard work they had put in in making their new home habitable, and in some ways much more comfortable. Joe, Herbert, Ernie, Albert and Terry were already inside ready to be re-united with their colleagues, and a collective jeer went up from the crew as the pilots made their entrance into their new communal home. Adrian made a show of inspecting the interior

"Nice job Boys," Adrian teased. "Be nice when its finished."

Even so they were visibly impressed with the layout of the mess, which was considerably plusher than what the sixteenth had. A good size bar was set out on the left, and a large pot fire opposite, complimented with a colourful array of soft furniture and a surfeit of battered pillowcases, often used in late night skirmishes between the men. All this courtesy of Adrian's 'bank', which funded everything down to the decanters and pipe tobacco on tap for them. John used the time to get an appraisal from the crew as to the readiness of the planes, despite extensive adjustments and modifications, the demands of the pilots were never ending.

Dickie sought out Albert and pulled him to one side. "Cheers Albert. Good to see you again."

They clunked cheap glasses together in a toast.

"Was wondering Albert, if it was at all possible you could have a look at the sights on the Vickers? I did a test fire on the ground and thought it wasn't calibrated how I'm used to it."

Albert smiled benignly at the young lad from Birmingham, his accent endeared him to everyone, especially he being the father figure of the ground crew. "Already taken care of Sir."

He was very fond of this boy... man who has come up from the slums of the city, and with sheer will and single mindedness. He was not only a fine pilot, but a very decent young man.

"Fifty yards, as you like it, and a goodly numbers of 'Buck's Fizzers' as you likes them too." Albert was referring to the Buckingham incendiary bullets, that were particularly effective in downing the enemy.

A little-known story comes a few years after the war, in Paris, when Adrian recycled the name to use on a champagne-based cocktail invented during that time.

"I've also taken the liberty, if you don't mind, in enlarging the rudder somewhat and shaved its backside."

He looked back at Albert with sudden interest.

Albert went on "We think this will turn your beast a bit tighter than the standard fin from the factory, we hope," he qualified.

"Cheers Albert. If it doesn't work I'm sure I'll let you know."

John was satisfied that they were in readiness at least for a familiarisation flight first thing tomorrow, and after letting them all know of his intentions, they were left for the rest of the evening to get settled in.

Harry stared in wonderment as to the relative opulence of Rogue flights mess, when he later joined them. John guided the Major around introducing everyone on first name terms irrespective of rank or social standing. He looked on with unconcealed curiosity at the relaxed interaction of everyone. He met Dickie the exponent of the Se5, who John had added that this pilot had the keenest eyes in the RFC, or so he believed. He was impressed with his down to earth quiet demeanour. Harry knew pilots, and he could disseminate from the quiet, and the quiet dangerous types. This pilot in his opinion was clearly of the latter.

Then he was confronted with the ebullient world of Lt A.D. Wentworth DSO whose grace and style oozed charm. Harry had the distinct feeling that under the skin he was being scrutinised even dissected by this disarmingly charming gentleman.

Adrian carried on with his story, which some of his audience had heard once or twice before. It involved an encounter on leave with a '*Jasta*' of French chorus girls in Paris. It was a desperate affair whereupon he was outgunned, but went down fighting in a blur of champagne and oysters, missing presumed asleep! As this improbable tale was being imparted to the captive audience, it suddenly occurred where Harry had heard the name of A.D. Wentworth. Turning aside to his left was one of the crew, his name escaped him, but certainly one of the more prominent crew who, it was reported tinkered endlessly with the diverse and problematic engine modification demanded of the flight.

"Forgive me for asking, where have I heard the name of your pilot before, the name is very familiar?"

The recipient of the enquiry was Ernie Winters, whose weathered, tanned face, a product of a harsh urban upbringing, which made him look a lot more seasoned than his modest twenty-three years of age. Ernie theatricality put on a sombre face and leaned towards Harry in a conspiratorial manner. "That'll be very incisive of you sir, if I may say so."

As Ernie had not called anyone 'sir' in six months, it would have been a clear signal that sincerity was the last thing on his mind. To add to the charade, Ernie put on his native cockney accent to add to the authenticity of his response. "Nineteen Fifteen I believe it was. Young Wentworth here buzzed some staff officers in their car several times. Put the wind up them proper like. Went down like a stone. Talks of court martial, disgrace, firing squad even." Winters shook his head as if in disgust. "He would have got away with it, except of the fact his bus had his own design of noughts and crosses painted on it, Whispers are his Lord almighty Daddy pulled a few strings, not that I'm judging ye see?" He winked conspicuously. "Reckon that's why they paint the machines for invisibility you see."

It was then that Harry remembered the story now firmly embedded in RFC folklore. The irreverence the pilot showed was quietly cheered through the ranks as an act of defiance in the generally agreed incompetency of the General staff.

*

Three Flights of Sixteen Squadron crossed the British lines shortly after sunrise looking for trouble, including Taylor and Adams, the latest additions to the squadrons, on their first operational flight. Pilot numbers were still coming up short, so they were reluctantly drafted in for the patrol. Above them were elements of Rogue flight, with Singer, Adrian and Dickie at a couple of thousand feet above. Harry sat about a quarter of a mile behind at the same height. It was himself who decided to add to the numbers, even though he hadn't flown operationally for some time.

The Nieuport scouts continued flying on an erratic course eastward, and some eight thousand feet above the thick carpet of Cumulus clouds. Nothing visible was in sight ahead or above, but at least they weren't suffering the incessant attentions of Boche artillery, who were busy enough pounding the Canadian trenches which were unusually close to the German lines.

Sam Cohen estimated by flying time that they were now a couple of miles behind the lines, and decided to take the squadron down below the cloud line, to find out where they were, and who else might be about. He pushed the stick of the Nieuport forward and built-up speed, the rest followed their leader down into the unknown.

As they cleared the cloud in a steady downward angle, it became apparent to Sam, that they had drifted further south than they anticipated. The ground below was unfamiliar to the extent that there were no discernible visual references to fix their position, so he adjusted course to compensate. What was familiar was the brown desert of undulating treeless murk interspersed with ruined buildings and water filled trenches. All that was taken in in an instant by the experienced flight commander. It took a couple of more seconds to attune the eyes to a large number of dark specs, like them, flying just under the cloud cover. A few more seconds and they were recognised as a larger number of Huns slightly above, and to the right flying almost parallel to the squadron. Sam waggled his wings and turned towards this new threat, and led his group up into the cloud layer towards the enemy.

They were now roughly at the same altitude, and the EA turned to meet them, with no time to manoeuvre except to meet them head on.

Three of the Sixteenth turned away and down, back to the British lines. They were the new arrivals who were under strict instructions in such a situation to avoid any contact and dive back west as quickly as they can. They had no business in being in active combat, with their woeful lack of flying experience. They reluctantly but dutifully flew away from the combat zone, leaving their comrades, depleted in numbers to face the enemy alone.

That left six planes in line astern facing eighteen to twenty planes operating well within their own side of the lines. Confidence amongst the Germans would have been high. An eclectic mixture of German machines approached in three separate layers. Pfalz's, Albatross D1 and a few ageing Fokker Eindeckers, which in truth was still a formidable plane in capable hands. The two adversaries closed in on each other at a combined speeds of over two hundred miles per hour.

Singer saw the plethora of planes closing below him. He kept Rogue out of the line of sight by using the cloud cover which was at levels from three thousand feet upwards

The SE's came around to approach the Boche from abeam, Singer wanted to stay out of sight until the last moment, when hopefully the enemy would be focused on the squadron. Dickie took himself off further to port for more air space, and Adrian decided to follow suit.

The aerial battle had just commenced with both sides settling for a frontal attack. Singer has singled out a brightly coloured Pfaltz scout adorned with streamers, which was turning tightly to get in behind one of the Nieuports. He never saw the SE angled down behind him. The first realisation he was in trouble was the sparks of bullets striking the engine in front. He instinctively threw the machine on its side to dive out of trouble. The engine stalled halfway over, presenting his underbelly to the stalking SE. Another quick burst stitched a line of bullets from the cockpit and fuselage. Singer didn't have time to see if it was a definite kill. His momentum had taken him on to another enemy scout, that was threatening to exact revenge. He reversed course, and inverted his machine, and seconds later he was easing into position behind.

Dickie watched intently the skirmish with seemingly unfathomable turns, spins and aerobatics unfolding before him. Before long he was able to anticipate the likely flight paths of likely targets of opportunity. An albatross with a distinctive yellow colour scheme complete with a badly painted bird on the fuselage, was below and to starboard. The Se5 turned in anticipation of a left-hand turn, and he pointed the nose downward. It came as no surprise to Dickie to find the Hun flying directly across his sights. He put in a long burst along the length of the machine, which immediately fell way either to escape further punishment, or be fatally wounded. It flew into a lower cloud canopy, its final fate remaining a mystery. Adrian had the luxury of waiting a few more seconds for the second scout, following his comrade, to present himself in his sights.

From this range Adrian couldn't miss, and two bursts in quick succession rendered the scout dead in the air. The struts on the nearest wing failed, and the wings crumpled. Slowly it fell onto its back snapping the longerons along the fuselage, As it fell, the other wing detached. The disintegration continued all the way down, scattering in pieces as it fell. Adrian hoped that the pilot was dead, and wouldn't suffer further.

Several Hun machines had managed to turn back into the fight and were now manoeuvring to inflict some harm themselves. At two hundred yards several of the remaining German machines opened fire. The salvo had no visible effect on the flight, except to confirm that at least a few of the Boche pilots were inexperienced flyers. Singer targeted an albatross stationed on the top echelon who hadn't yet fired his Spandau's. His first ranging burst was from less than thirty yards and passed on the port side and above. A quick kick of the rudder, and firing a longer three second burst, and gratefully saw a concentrated number of hits to the wings and struts, confirmed by the tracers which impacted on the wings and tail. The apparition of a numerically inferior machines causing so much carnage on the first pass, caused panic amongst the entire Hun formation, who started to peel off in all directions. Seconds later two more allied planes seemingly came out of nowhere, which only added to the confusion and fear. One British Nieuport scout was seen spinning slowly, with fire and smoke coming from the engine. back towards the cockpit. The unfortunate pilot, if he was still alive, still minutes away from certain destruction, as the doomed craft tumbled earthward.

The *Jasta* was now in complete disarray each desperately looking to escape eastward away from the carnage, several with smoke or steam bellowing out behind them. The squadron didn't have it all their own way, as well as the one Nieuport lost, another one was later found to be missing. Harry took his squadron back to the aerodrome to rearm and refuel, and hopefully grab some breakfast. The squadron had two more flights on the same day, which of the only result was to tire out the pilots and wear down the machines.

*

The twins were not with them that day, as they were busy elsewhere flying low around another sector on a reconnaissance specifically requested from Staff HQ The twins in the 'Brisfit' were successful on taking photos in and around the railway sidings close to the German front lines, and were only subject to some ineffectual machine gun and rifle fire from bored German infantry.

They had landed sometime previously and were seen in overalls stripping the engine of the machine alongside the ground crew. They preferred to fly alone, despite the apparent weaknesses in their plane of choice. It was never immediately apparent to their adversaries that in the experienced hands of Jules (or Mario) at the controls, and Mario (or Jules) on the twin Lewis guns astern, they were a match for anything in the air. Either of them could throw the plane around like a scout, and the other situated in the observers' seat would be well versed with its remarkable manoeuvring capabilities.

The result was that Mario was capable of putting down bursts of extraordinarily accurate fire, that for most observers was unthinkable. In the observers' cockpit they had previously installed a simple but effective harness designed from their experience in the high wire acts they grew up with in the circus, where at even extreme angles, the observer was safely attached to the plane, and left him able to concentrate on traversing and firing the Lewis.

It was the end of a very long day, however and as soon as all of Rogue flight had parked their buses, they mirrored the twins actions in going over there machines in detail. Looking for damage, which was usually the case. Inspecting the wings, struts, wires, and guns. Some adjustments were ordered on the temperamental interrupter gears, which was a mechanism that enabled the pilot to fire his guns through the propeller, without hitting his own blades.

*

It may have been the free ale on tap that evening that resulted in Rogue flights mess being standing room only, whereas the Squadron mess remained deserted. Animated conversations of the day events reverberated with claims of kills, probable's and a share of kills where more than one plane shot down an enemy plane.

The loss of a pilot though was never far from their minds. It was Lt David Freer who was the unfortunate flyer last seeing going down behind enemy lines. It was a shame as Freer had made it through the first two months of operational flying, which was generally considered to be the most dangerous period for new pilots, and he was considered to becoming a very able airman.

The missing pilot was Reynolds, who had phoned to report he had landed in a field on this side of the lines with a dud engine. It would take some time to recover both pilot and plane.

Cecil Barrington finally tracked down his errant squadron after finding the mess empty. On walking through the door he was impressed with interaction of all the airmen, who seemed to be getting along well with the new arrivals. He sought out Harry who was debating with his engineers about the feasibility of painting the undersides of his plane to match the weather patterns of the sky on any particular day, to render it invisible from the ground.

He was beginning to see the merits of the breakdown of barriers between the ranks, especially if it helped morale, and reduced casualties. He would need to talk to John some more about this. This type of informality clearly would have no place in the established Army and Navy structure. God no! But with this very new method of technology which was changing month on month? He left the question behind, and talked to Harry on more mundane matters.

*

It was a relatively quiet evening at the cafe, Claudette and Chloe were sat inside waiting on some trade to arrive. It was usually quiet on Tuesdays, and they were speculating as to allow Mama a welcome break. It was on those occasions she liked to gather flowers around the village, or by the woods, and around the pond. She would meet with other widowed women from the parish, and decorate the inside of the church, to soften its austere appearance. It was a cold evening and so the fire was lit to take the chill out of the air. Only a few customers were in at that time, which was why it was something more unusual to see Gabrielle visit again, this time all alone. She quietly took her usual spot in the corner tucked away and ordered some wine.

Claudette and Chloe were keen people watchers who spent idle hours speculating as to where people came from, their occupations and backgrounds. Peoples clothes were scrutinised in detail as well as their demeanour. Wickedly they would make up background stories as to their honour, love lives and occupations, invariably never in a good light.

Gabrielle was a prime target for this type of assassination.

"Isn't that delightful Gabrielle again?" Chloe quipped. "She was here just a few days ago with that handsome young officer, you swore was too short for her."

They giggled conspiratorially.

"Bet she's here to meet him again for a tryst," Claudette replied. "And it's because she is married, oh! *an affair*."

They continued to speculate on the condition of their guest, and on the imminent arrival of the English officer who was seducing her. It was another half an hour into the evening when Chloe espied the young ladies companion, and surprisingly it wasn't the supercilious soldier from before. The new arrival made his way straight to the corner of the room, looking neither left or right but sat down opposite Gabrielle. They indulged in desultory conversation and smoked. The sister grew quickly bored of this non-event, and moved on to more entertaining victims for their game.

*

The artillery continued to pound in and around the German trenches of Vimy Ridge, which for all protagonists, was a prelude to an impending assault. It was hoped that the enemy would be so demoralised, and the defences smashed to pieces, before they were ordered to the attack. Surely this time it would be a piece of cake! From the Generals to the lowly privates they knew that it was probably a forlorn hope. This time though they would have new types of artillery shells designed to cut up the dreaded enemy barbed wire. They would also have a smattering of tanks, which to date has mixed results thus far, in obtaining the crucial breakthrough. The Canadians had several well-trained divisions for the purpose of taking Vimy Ridge. Harsh lessons in trench warfare had been paid by the blood of thousands of soldiers from both sides of several battlefields. It was at this time that Rogue flight were withdrawn from supporting Sixteen squadron, for the first of special missions they were set up for, much to the chagrin of the remaining pilots of the squadron. It was surprising how quickly they had all bonded, and to some extent how they had become reliant on support they had become used to in the two short weeks.

A briefing was undertaken by John in his office. They all squeezed into the relatively small room. John waited until Jules made his way into the room already crammed with bodies everywhere.

"Gentleman, make yourselves comfortable, or as best you can." He gestured to a couple of chairs. Adrian and Mario had perched half a cheek of bottom on the Major's table, just enough to not obscure the photo's laid out.

"Before you are a series of photo's, you might have to take it in turn to examine closer." John put his forefinger on one of the photos. "This one was taken months ago behind the lines of Vimy Ridge, these here," indicating a couple of photo's adjacent, "Were taken by our very own Jules and Mario a few days ago. Please take a few minutes to study then before I go further."

There was an unedifying surge towards the desk, with some pushing and shoving. They all eventually getting the time necessary to examine the photos closely.

"These ones were taken a month ago, we are fairly certain it's an ammunition dump not far from the railway sidings, here, and here." He looked over the room. "This one is of the same ground that the twins took. Any ideas?"

Silence followed as they, studiously compared the photo's. It was Adrian who first ventured an opinion.

"Clearly the second one indicates that the ammunition dump has now gone." He rubbed his stubbled chin. "And it looks as though they have just left a number of large calibre shells behind"

John nodded. "That's what we thought at first. Nothing to see here. Look again at the photos, bearing in mind, the twin's shots were taken some five hundred feet lower than the first ones."

Dickie jumped in excitably, he picked up a photo and stared at it for some time. "It's still their sir. The ammunition I mean. It's camouflaged, very well camouflaged, but there are very faint straight lines, here, and here, which is in the same spot as the originals. The only difference is, are the shells that Mario found."

John tapped his pipe on the side of the desk. "Very Good gentlemen, very good, and almost right" He used the stem of the pipe to indicate vaguely the photos on the desk. "The ammunition is in exactly the same spot it was last month, but someone has gone to a lot of trouble to make it invisible. He left the question in the air, almost enjoying the drama being unfolded before them.

"Why?" He barked, and waited for some insight. The quietness of the moment was palatable. "Look once more at those artillery shells." He again waited until they had finished. "See, here, look. Not shells. Not artillery, but tubes, cannisters if you will, Gas cannisters. You will note gentleman, that the cannisters seem to have disappeared. "However, staff intelligence." John waited until the giggling had dissipated. Ordinary soldiers being well versed in the long-held belief that staff and intelligence in one sentence was a contradiction in terms

With some patience he continued, "Staff intelligence, believes that the gas cannisters are still there, hidden under the camouflage. It's location here, makes for easy transfer up to the front-line trenches.

The atmosphere in the room sobered up immediately. Everyone loathed gas, hated its use, its users, and hated what it did to the flesh and lungs of men, whatever side of the trenches you were.

John pressed on. "Our task gentlemen will be to blow up the ammunition dump, and destroy the cannisters at the same time."

Mario put up his hand involuntary as if in school to ask a question John acknowledged the gesture. "Would the explosion from the ammunition destroy the gas?"

John looked down to the desk once more. "I'm afraid not. We have to attack when the wind is blowing easterly, which will be away from our lads, but unfortunately in the path of the German reserve trenches. "A general murmur of dismay reverberated. John raised his voice to be heard. "Gentlemen, Gentleman", he repeated more loudly. "It's a rotten job I know, but let me make it very clear, it's a job we are tasked to get done, and I don't want to hear any more on the subject, is that clear?" An awkward silence ensued, confirming it was the end of the matter

"You will now study the terrain, you will study the weather, the air cover, any intelligence of flight patterns, and finally, your proposals for the attack."

He started to leave the room "One more thing Gentleman, the Canadians are preparing to launch an attack to take the ridge very soon. You know, the Canadians know, and we are quite sure the Boche knows. How? we are unsure, but high command has promised the Canadian divisions that we will give them all the support we can."

The obvious solution was to bomb the dump from aircraft best suited to take the payload to its destination. Even the larger planes around were unable to deliver any significant poundage of ordnance to the target. So they looked to revert to bomber types, hoping that the use of high explosive or incendiary bomb-lets could do the job.

For several days they practised dropping bombs, first using their own favourite machines, and then by necessity, trying out more conventional bomber type crates like the Be2. Nothing came anywhere satisfactory in guaranteeing the success of the mission.

Naturally by this time the ground crew was fully engaged in the preparations, and it took the innovative thinking of Herbert Rhys-Jones who planted the idea of another approach to the problem.

Herbert sought out Adrian in the hanger where his plane was undergoing some tweaking to the tension wires. In many ways, these two men thrown together by war had little in common on the surface. Their relationship had initially blossomed early on firstly with a love of country pursuits. The onset of war made food sources unreliable even for those with considerable means. They first took to shooting together in the local area for game to supplement their meagre rations, then they moved on to cooking of all things, which added to the appreciation of their shared passion.

Adrian left his crew to work on his plane and sat down on a hay bale where Herbert was waiting. The Lieutenant knew to appreciate his friends' ideas and thoughts, which had previously opened his eyes on all sort of possibilities when working on his plane.

"I understand that the pilots are coming up short on ideas for the mission Addie?"

"'Fraid so Jonesy. "Nothing anywhere near, it's a fucking suicide run, with no chance of succeeding if you ask me." He looked inquisitively at his friend. "D'you have an idea? If so I would very much like to hear it."

Herb took a breath and starting slowly started to outlay the bare bones of his idea. Sometime later Adrian gathered all the crew in the mess twenty minutes later, with Herbert's simple plan, and it would need to get the co-operation of the artillery.

Chapter Four

Gas Attack

It was going to be another tedious evening for the Faure family. Captain Cotter was drinking quite heavily, having to be made to wait for what seemed to be an eternity for Gabrielle to arrive. He decided to arrive early having little to do, in the way of duties given to him. He spent his time belligerently scowling at all and anyone in uniform irrespective of rank. After all he was staff by God!

The sisters bore the brunt of his boorish behaviour, and all were wishing his lady would arrive soon, and leave them alone. Several officers entered the cafe, and the family recognised them as regulars from the nearby airfield. They were always welcome, and always polite. Amongst them they bought with them for the first time Dickie Watson, who joined his friends to celebrate his overdue promotion. For reasons unknown to herself Claudette found herself studying the young aviator. She knew and recognised all of the others but Dickie she had never seen. He seemed to be holding himself in somehow, in check, as if unsure he was supposed to be here, and it was his apparent vulnerability that had caught her attention.

Drinks and food were ordered in a chaotic carefree manner, like schoolboys on an outing. They were attended to with an easy familiarity and understanding, going to each table in turn. They were by far the largest contingent in the room, in which they tended to dominate entirely. The noise level natural increased, shattering the peaceful ambience of the cafe. Cotter looked on at the airmen with open contempt. He was becoming increasingly frustrated at being left alone, and feeling like a fool. He poured more wine into his cup, barely able to control his temper

The timing could not have been worse, when one of the them burst into song, quickly followed by others. "A Young aviator lay dying, at the end of a bright summers day...summers day" Gabrielle made her way through the throng towards Peregrine. Her timely arrival immediately dissipated any thought of remonstrating with these boorish oafs. The thoughts turned to the expectation of more intimate moments with his very first real girlfriend. He was of course quite experienced in the ways of sex and the releases it brought, mostly with English peasant girls, who could be dismissed with the gift of a Guinea. Gabrielle was different, the very first one he would think about on duty at headquarters, the one he would confide into his fellow officers as his first conquest. It made him feel like a real man, and he doesn't even have to pay for it.

Dickie took himself out of the cafe for a quite break. The night was clear and cold. Perfect flying weather for tomorrow. he mused. He found himself looking star-ward, and taking in the majesty of the night sky.

"Beautiful is it not?" A light voice came from his left. He peered into the night, but failed to locate the source of the voice. It was female in origin which was at least what he had managed to surmise.

"Yes, yes indeed," he replied politely.

"You are a flyer?" the voice enquired.

He thought briefly as to the how this conversation was going, and then occurred to him, the uniform was a dead giveaway. He stirred out of his musing, and turned to find the biggest, most beautiful eyes he had ever seen.

Rather than attempting an amusing reply, he smiled, nervously and turned to look back at the evening sky. Drawing in a deep breath he turned back and smiled again. "If this is your part of the world, it is indeed lovely, and I for one apologise for interrupting its tranquillity." Gathering some courage he held out his hand. "My names Dick, a pleasure to make your acquaintance". She took his proffered hand, which was surprisingly soft, and held it for a moment.

It was a full two hours of animated conversation between them where they found mutual likes of horse riding and light music. All too soon their conversation was brutally curtailed with the arrival of the transport to take them all back in good time for tomorrows operations.

*

The next few days saw the flight revert to escorting Sixteen squadron on a few missions, depending on the weather. They would usually fly above the squadrons bombers and scouts in loose formation with the Bristol, having the rear mounted Lewis guns flying slightly behind. The missions over that time were simple, to support and reinforce, protect and nurse their fellow flyers. It was a comparatively rare event to see any meaningful action before coming across the front lines. The Boche preferred to wait for the allies to come to them, which was found to be particularly astute of them.

It was mid-morning, with the wind a tolerable westerly. The flight found themselves flying over more than one fleet of allied machines, which included some reconnaissance machines being tasked to photograph a small salient in the lines. Scout planes were already strafing the forward enemy trenches with machine guns and 20lb Cooper bombs. At this time of year, at about eleven am, was the optimum time to take photographs due to high position of the sun, which meant less shadows and more definition on the resulting pictures. After just a few minutes flying over the zigzag pattern of trenches, they saw a formidable formation of EA's making an appearance. Thankfully, it wasn't 11 *Jasta*, the circus, but these machines were mostly painted in shades of green with individual markings and dark, almost black cowlings. Good visibility meant that the closing formations were quickly spotted, and very wisely the slower two seater's turned for home, and safety.

The scouts were not so lucky, as they were already flying too close to the ground to manoeuvre, and already committed for a ground attack. The first run went as expected, with the enemy troop's taken completely by surprise, and whose first instincts usually are to dive for cover rather than grab any weapons. After several minutes, and low on ammunition they rose to gain height and looked for a safe route back, and it became a choice of heading straight into the maelstrom of enemy planes lying in wait. Jenkins, a new pilot, followed his flight along the trenches, in his Nieuport, and was exhilarated at the sight of troops diving out of his path. Ammunition was exploding further ahead of him from his colleagues' efforts. He decided on impulse not to follow the others, but took a reverse course for another run.

It may have been that he expected the same scenario being played out as the first run, and he was so very wrong in that judgement. Thousands of vengeful Germans had recovered from the initial shock of the first attack, but had by now recovered their weapons and composure, as Jenkins flew back towards them. A dozen Spandau machine guns and hundreds of Mauser rifles were aimed toward the sky.

The Nieuport was engulfed in a hail of bullets, which tore through the scout plane from stem to stern. Jenkins was dead even before the machine fell from the sky and hit the ground at over one hundred miles per hour, exploding in a ball of flames. It was fortunate that Jenkins had died instantly. If he had somehow survived the impact, the recent recipients of his endeavours would invariably take out immediate retribution, and shot him out of hand.

An entire squadron of Albatrosses were already descending into a gentle dive, confident in the advantage of numbers and height they commanded. They were within half a mile of the English before the scouts' planes rose up to meet them, The Three SE's of Rogue were in line astern and came in at the port quarter out of the sun, as yet unseen. They would wait until Singer opened fire first to maximise the tactical advantage. He waited until they were almost on top of the formation, certainly within thirty-five yards, when Singer's plane shuddered with the vibration of the Vickers, and Lewis gun atop, spitting death into the back marker. This was followed seconds later with two more machines announcing the arrival of the flight with short accurate bursts into multiple targets of opportunity.

The effect was devastating and immediate. Several planes fell out of the sky in unrecoverable spins, some unfortunately aflame, others limped away smoking, seeking clear skies away from the slaughter. The survivors scattered, with each plane choosing its own route of avoiding further destruction. Immediately after the first strike came the twin's two-seater, who remorselessly poured more bullets into the wounded and disorientated flanks of a broken enemy. The rising machines of Sixteenth squadron now flew towards a disorganised and defeated foe, who had in a heartbeat lost any will to fight.

The flight leaders from the squadron sensibly turned for home, rather than further chase the fleeing Boche machines. Fuel was low, and they were still miles over hostile territory. The remaining planes made their way back to the airfield without mishap, wisely choosing to fly above cloud cover, and out of sight of Boche artillery.

It was another three days before any further flying was possible, as the volatile European summer weather decided it would be winter for a while, with cold driving rain making flying impossible. It was still pitch black, and the ground crew had worked through the night working on the four planes they called their own. The modified Wolseley Viper engines were being warmed up. A light westerly breeze was accompanied by a light drizzle, invisible in the night sky. It was an unwelcome addition to the forecast, which promised a largely cloudless day.

Dickie and Adrian were the first pilots to arrive in view. looking twice their size, with the many layers of clothing from the feet up. They tended to waddle rather than walk. Looking most un-military like, the pilots had spent up to half an hour putting on the protective layers of clothes to battle to extreme cold experienced in flying top cover. The individual choice of coats, socks, fur lined jackets, Fug boots, scarves and even underwear were meticulously donned. To finish of the routine, they smeared their faces generously with whale fat. The only way the two pilots could be distinguished from one another, even by their ground crew comrades was by the colour differences in the jackets and scarves.

The four planes rumbled along the ground to the far end of the field, and turned back deftly, into the wind. With little preamble they all engaged full power to take off. The flight matrix was one they had used on many occasions, and was proving to be their most versatile formation. The two SE's would provide top cover and support at anywhere from ten thousand feet upwards. Singer would be roughly half a mile ahead and several thousand feet below. A few hundred yards further forward was the 'twin's' Bristol Fe2b strategically placed at the optimum height for the mission.

The patrol was routine, flying over familiar ground in this sector. No enemy machines were encountered, and as they principally stayed on the allied sides, there was no Archie to be worthy of the name. The flight did have a purpose though, which was to ascertain the preferred height, formation and approach considered optimum for the next crucial mission, which was to destroy the gas cannisters. They flew in wide lazy circles, while the Bristol went about the business of scouting the immediate area around the railroad junction. The aircraft were returned to the hangers for the necessary works required for the next day.

Herbert Rhys Jones worked with the ground crew through the night on the meticulous preparation of the machines. In particular, the 'twins' crate had undergone some modifications in Jule's observer cockpit. Twin Lewis guns on a well-oiled Scarff mounting, with as many drums of extra ammunition as the limited space could provide. It was then fitted to a Morse transmitter attached the exterior of the fuselage.

Adrian and Dickie sat close to the stove and luxuriated in the warmth. Dickie nursed a mug of tepid tea, deep in thought. Adrian was skimming over a newspaper.

It was strange that these two flyers coming from such different backgrounds always tended to seek out each other's company, even in the long silences of a quiet morning. Ernie Winters and 'Nosy' Naismith were in desultory conversation concerning which of their local pubs produced the best ales, and a certain sense of rivalry ensued, with each extorting the qualities of their favourite brew.

Herbert walked in with aid of the obligatory cane, and sat by Dickie in the only chair left in the corner. It was some minutes before he chirped up with a question to Dickie.

"I was curious to know Dickie. How a chap like yourself, found himself flying for such an extraordinary amount of time." He paused, "Taking into consideration your background." He held up his hand in apology, "No offence meant dear boy, but you are in many ways unique, you know, giving your circumstances." He winced at himself for how it came out.

Dickie smiled slowly and looked up at his friend. "It's ok Herb, and it's not like the first time I've been asked that question." He took a breath, "What you mean to ask really, is how come a poor working class boy from the slums of the city, manage to get himself an expensive indulgence such as flying, usually reserved for the likes of our Addie here."

A few seconds of silence ensued giving Dickie time to collect his thoughts. "A happy accident of circumstances I call it. A wealthy factory owner asked me once what, if given the circumstances, what I would like most to have."

Adrian interjected, "Why would a chap like that give such an undertaking to a little snot from the gutter?" he teased.

Dickie playfully struck out at his friend, knowing it was said with mirth.

"Simple," Dickie responded. "I saved his little daughters life. Silly mare fell into the pond and nearly drowned, or so it appeared, I happened to be passing by, and so I jumped in to help. As it was the pond was only just over a foot deep, and she had already stood up spluttering out pond water. Yours truly was on hand to help her up and out." Dickie laughed to himself, "I was credited with saving her life. The old boy, grateful as he was, then made the offer."

"And you came up with the flying thing then?" Jones asked.

"Not at all," he replied. "I asked if I could think about it."

"After that came the flying thing?" Jones repeated.

Dickie sighed with exasperation, "Are you going to listen to the story? Good! I went back the next day, his name was Rixon, he had something to do with making bicycles I think," Dickie gazed at the stove gathering his thoughts. "I told him I didn't want something to have, but something he could take away, can you believe I was that bold?" He went on. "I said I would like him to take away something instead. My poverty, my education, my upbringing. And bless him he was good as his word. I duly went to a good school, and worked on his estate. Learnt to shoot, and he even paid for my flying lessons, right alongside the Toffs and donkey wallpapers." Dick stoked the fire to collect his thoughts. "Only I took it seriously rather than a lark like all the others. Spent all Gods hours learning everything there was to know back then in aviation. The old boy was pleased as punch as I remember. I think he came to think of me as the son he never had, bless him."

He looked around at his comrades. "Could never shake the accent though."

They laughed both at the jest, but with some incredulity and respect at his incredible story.

*

It was mid-afternoon when some of the ground crew sauntered into the mess, and announced the plane modifications were complete, and the normal pre-flight checks were also done. It was principally the fitting of a new Marconi Morse code wireless system installed in the observers' cockpit of the Bristol, that had taken so much time.

There were all sorts of issues to discuss and learn with the introduction of this new technology, including its relative reliability, and it was largely dependent on the deployment of a trailing wire behind the aircraft in flight.

Herbert made sure there was a backup system in place by means of coloured flares onboard, of which the varying course would denote the short, long, left and right fall of the shot. With the engines suitably warmed, Singer signalled for the chocks to be removed, and on that signal, all the airman turned to the men left on the ground, saluted the ground crew, who waved cheerily back. As the gaggle of planes disappeared from sight, the men left behind made for the billets, and a welcome breakfast.

On the way Eugene sidled up to Joe. "Got this idea Joe, pinched it from another crew."

Joe was unresponsive.

"We would like to give it a go on one of the SE's."

Joe still made no move to interrupt him. "The exhausts along the fuselage, can and should be shortened about this much." Eugene held out his hands as an explanation. "It'll save weight, and I reckon so increase the performance of the engine."

Joe nodded politely not really convinced of the potential performance enhancing possibilities that could transpire.

"So we shorten the exhaust pipes, and that improves the engines speed, is that what you think? and I S'pose the weight saved would help as well," he pondered

Eugene doubled down and threw his arms in a rotating style, as he did when frustrated. "That's what I thought too, but check out old 'Nosy' here." Turning his head back to Naismith walking some yards behind. "When we both came up with the idea of re-using the exhaust metal Joe then took off to the workshops to try something out."

They were nearing the mess by now, and Joe was relishing a hot breakfast and his first tea of the day and continued towards the door without comment.

Genie stopped short to let Joe through the door. "He wants to meet us all in the workshops when the boys return."

Joe stood at the frame of the door, and reluctantly nodded in acquiescence.

*

The flight was again purely reconnaissance, and it was to give the twins another good look over the ground. They were very astute at observing the ground and movements below, and conducted a reasoned assessment of troop moments, artillery deployments and supporting logistics which may herald an offensive, or redeployment in the immediate battle area. The railway junction and connecting roads that was of interest was both an important route for supplies of men and materials, and also a choke point, due to the sodden lay of the surrounding countryside. The clouds were roughly at three thousand feet and upward, interspersed with clear skies. This had the effect of providing some cover from Archie, but had the potential to hide considerable numbers of enemy EA, or even the lone scout, which is invariably harder to spot.

They reached the front lines and were duly greeted by Archie with dirty black woolly bursts bursting below them. The Bristol flew just below the cloud formations, which gave Archie a good reference point to make life considerably more uncomfortable for the airmen. Jules duly threw the bus around more than usual, and occasionally took refuge in the clouds from time to time to get some respite.

Singer was having the best of it so far, being five hundred feet higher, and largely unseen. He kept a weather eye on the two-seater, keeping station behind and above, like a protective mother. That didn't stop him from weaving and diving around the loose cloud formations, seeking out any potential threats, which he happily abused to fly with complete abandon.

At eight thousand feet the two SE's were flying clear of any cloud, and in the centre of the storm, as potential threats could come from below or as high as sixteen thousand feet in these conditions. Dickie and Adrian flew side by side in loose formation, with Adrian always on the port side. They were able cover half the sky either side, knowing their comrade was covering the other. Adrian preferred to be looking predominately left, as his neck muscles gave him some discomfort looking the other way. They could espy Singer weaving his merry way around the mountainous clouds, in a merry dance now several miles behind the lines. A waggle of the wings confirmed to Adrian his friend has seen some movement of interest, as per usual. Soon it was obvious to both of them they were hostile. Dickie turned and gained height to keep the sun behind them.

The German Staffel was tasked to give air cover to this area of the line for reasons unknown to them. They were content that they only had to patrol on their own sides of the line, and they were reassured that there would be sufficient artillery support to fend off any allied incursions. Nevertheless, the flight leader had under his command a rag tag unit thrown together, with a mixture of machines from good to almost museum pieces, and fliers who were reliable veterans to complete novices thrown into the air war to make up the numbers. As with all arms under service, the flower of German youth had already been sacrificed on the altar of defending the Fatherland. What was left was composed of idealistic youngsters, and older men thrown into a conflict they don't understand with technology beyond their understanding or comprehension. A lone two-seater was spotted at, or about where the second line of German defences were. Lt Ernst Muller led his flight to intercept, he had but six months on active duty, enough time to witness the ebb and flow of aerial supremacy between the protagonists. In that time, he was the most experienced pilot in his flight, with many friends and comrades buried in the fields of Belgium and France, whose faces were already becoming fading memories. It was an opportunity to blood his team, and perhaps gain an easy kill. He briefly scanned the skies to see if they were clear, before pushing forward on the stick to dive down on the hapless prey.

Jules had seen the EA some minutes before, and had taken the time to plan his escape route. Not too soon as to discourage the Germans to attack. He was confident that they in turn were being stalked by Singer and the two other scouts in turn. Jules made a good show of a panicked pilot turning straight for home. Mario traversed his twin Lewis guns and pulled the tags on his harness to check all was well. The 'Brisfit' had about a fifteen hundred feet to play with. Some room to dive and increase speed, but with the risk of drawing ground fire. The Boche planes were now a few hundred years behind, and Jules went to work on manoeuvring his crate with gentle touches of the stick.

Muller allowed the pilots either side of him to gainsay him, eager for the kill. He failed to notice the first of his flight roll over on its back, smoke bellowing behind. Singer was just behind the stricken foe, already looking for the next closest plane, his first victim already forgotten.

A Pfaltz fired early at over one hundred yards without effect. His wing man prompted by his colleague followed suit. Long ineffectual bursts falling well wide and behind of the target. Jules then implemented his own version of an Immelmann turn, with the startled Germans looking in bewilderment as their target was flying back towards them above, but inverted.

Jules held the Bristol in that position for a further few seconds, allowing Mario to let off short accurate bursts of deadly fire down the fuselage of the astonished Hun. Jules quickly kicked the plane back over before his engine flooded and stalled the plane. They had used this trick countless times to devastating effect, and this time they didn't even bother to witness the results of their work, with the engine engulfed in fire. It went down in an unrecoverable spin before the wings folded up, and the rest completely disintegrated.

In a heartbeat the rest of Muller's flight wisely dived away and for home, and Muller himself knew he had flown into a well-coordinated trap, with experienced pilots of which professionalism he had never previously encountered. He had enough about him to utilise all his experience, and by some good fortune found some nearby cloud cover and flew home alone. Singer managed to shoot up another two more scout planes, without any visible effect before breaking off the attack. The Boche were beaten, and following his mantra of never pushing his luck, he too turned for home. The two SE's came down either side of their leader, a little too late to inflict further damage, however Dickie in particular had read the flight patterns of the skirmish, and had rightly surmised they were now surplus to requirements.

*

A few days later Ernst was surprised by a delegation from Berlin, who seemed very interested in his recent encounter with an undesignated squadron or part of one. German intelligence had no information and they were keen to rectify that. It was an informal and gentle interview, which in many ways made Muller all the more uncomfortable.

He was quizzed as to the machine types, and the unusual, faded markings and lack of identification denoting their origins and squadron designations. The Pilots in question had come to their attention as well as the fighting prowess of the flight. German military intelligence had identified these men as a serious threat, and it was a threat that had to be dealt with.

*

The weather over the continent was gradually improving with milder winds from the west making for better flying conditions, although still intermittent with periodic bouts of low cloud and zero visibility. Members of Sixteen squadron were able to afford the men some leave, even to the extent they could get home to Blighty for a few days. This was a luxury that to date Rogue flight could not afford, and an oversight recognised by Singh-Smythe.

The obvious conclusion was the recruitment of more key personnel to take the load, and allow some rudimentary rota system to be in place. This would take time he surmised, however a partial solution was offered up by Dickie while talking to Harry over a beer in the mess. Harry was aware of Dickie's unusual background, which gave him the insight for his idea. Dickie pointed out some of the ground crew who were in the mess at the time.

"John, we have a pool of good men close to home. Men who understand intimately, the needs and wants of the pilots, and the limits of the planes they fly." Dickie leaned in closer to make his point. "Our very own ground crew. Some of them can already fly, to some extent, already, and the others would learn pretty damn fast I would think."

John pondered on his colleagues' suggestion, which from the outset already seemed to have merit.

Dickie continued. "You know that Eugene is already a good pilot, and with some more tuition, and mothering has the potential to be a fine aviator".

John countered. "He's too valuable as ground crew Dick. His knowledge of the engines set up is second to none."

Dickie got up to get refills but carried on the conversation at distance from the bar. "We recruit more talented engineers from other squadrons from the lists you have. Eugene can in turn nurture his own deputies to impart his technical know-how."

John stood up and joined Dick at the bar. "You know, it's a bloody good wheeze. We have that old RE8 sitting in the hanger not doing much, we could use that." John promised to write up a report with his recommendations to implement the plan over the next few days.

*

The cold damp air of midwinter did little to lend itself to good soldiering. Indeed, the weather had a profound impact on the PBI in the front and supporting trenches. Early evening was a time when tiredness and lethargy set in, especially after the daily dawn stand to, a daily regime on both sides of the trenches. Singer chose this time with some care to take the flight over the lines. Today was the day chosen to eliminate the threat of the gas cannisters. The visibility and lack of light would be to their advantage, and the sky still almost invisible. Rogue flight took off forlornly before dusk. It was a calm evening with a light wind, the flight flew at a thousand feet in line astern. The route chosen would take them on a circuitous route, to gently dive down from the lowering sun.

The Bristol dropped behind the others, and Jules let out the trailing wire behind early, to alert the artillery in good time.

Whether it was the line of approach or the indistinctive markings, the German artillery were late in greeting the interlopers with the 'bursting woolly bears'. Mario was concentrating on countering the concussive waves from the bursting shells below, with minimal inputs on the stick, and rudder pedals, while Jules hunkered down in his cockpit, signalling to the waiting artillery companies with his firing coordinates. Singer flew an erratic course away from the twins, to confuse and divide the enemy Archie. The two SE's flew a couple of miles inside the lines in anticipation of any EA threat, and further annoy the nearby artillery parks. Minutes late the first shells landed long and wide of the intended target. Jules saw the fall of shot and relayed his amended x-y-z calculations. It was a matter of minutes before an array of 6- and 12-inch shells were seen to fall directly on the target.

The entire area was then subject to a concentrated and relentless pounding. Secondary explosions confirmed the destruction of the considerable ammunition stored. Singer looked on with pride and satisfaction of a job well executed.

The gas cannister threat had been annulled, and with that the possibility of hundreds of Canadians suffering ghastly painful deaths, and life lasting injuries avoided. Apart from the gas was the destruction of tons of ordnance, which wouldn't not now fall on allied trenches. Any celebrations at that time were brutally cut short with the arrival of thirty plus Boche aircraft converging into the airspace, looking to avenge the raid over their own lines. They came in from above stacked five high with a formidable front of firepower to inflict the maximum damage to anything in their path.

Dickie observed the huge wave of EA diving down to the two antagonists within their line of sight, in the area they were supposed to keep clear. Dickie spotted them early, and he froze momentarily. Instinct and training screamed to fly away from such a bad position, and live to fight another day. Adrian would have felt exactly the same.

The twins knew they were in trouble. Still flying along the enemy lines they could not manoeuvre, as the trailing wire behind precluded any violent alterations to the flight path. They also had little height to dive down, gain speed and fly for home.

Singer took in the scenario with some trepidation. He could, and should have turned for home to fly from such a bad tactical position.

The problem was with his friends in the 'Brisfit' who were in a perilous situation. He had little or no options, but to stay with them, while searching for solutions to present themselves. Some of the more experienced German pilots manoeuvred port and starboard to cut off any escape route for the English planes, knowing they had sufficient numbers in place for a head on attack. Singer ignored the vulnerable plight he and the twins were in, and took his SE into a controlled vrille to lose height as soon as possible, which also gave the enemy planes no immediate target to fire at. Many German machines overshot from where Singer's plane was, and looked down at a plane in a spin, and out of reach. Singer recovered the spin and came alongside the twin's plane as if out of nothing. Looking over to his comrades he waved as to say follow me and without preamble, turned violently right and earthward. Jules released the trailing wire, allowing Mario to follow suit.

Sweat was streaming over Adrian as he observed the hopeless picture unfolding before him. He dutifully followed Dickies plane down to join the fray against impossible odds. He didn't judge his friend, or baulk in banking down to assail the massive number of targets they were closing in. Dickies tactic was simply to cause as much havoc and mayhem amongst the fleet of planes in an effort to distract them from killing their friends.

Mario latched onto Singer's tail and followed his flight path downwards. Bullets were now evident all over the plane from the vengeful Boche. Holes ripped through the fabric on the wings and fuselage, others were pinging off the engine cowling and the fuel tanks, threatening to turn them into a fireball in a second. With faith and a prayer on his lips, the 'Brisfit' followed his leader into the cloud and dust that originated from the original explosions of the ammunition stores, Singer had surmised with some reservation that they could fly through the cloud and escape the trap, and hopefully it would contain no gas, being heavy than air. The cloud from the munitions would, he prayed, be a relatively harmless sulphurous residue from the incumbent spent shells.

The chasing Hun planes thought the opposite, and convinced themselves that anyone flying into that, would suffer the worst ravages on them that the horrid weapon could unleash. The SE led the two planes through the rising smoke and dust, emerging out with enough distance to escape without further mishap.

The Germans looked on hopelessly as the English machines escaped before their eyes They were further to suffer the indignation by being bounced by two of the war's most prolific killers, who appeared unseen from behind. The two SE's flew though the formation firing in precise short two and three second bursts. They were in shock and disbelieve as to the turning of fortunes within a few short minutes.

The British planes were not that daft to turn back into a dogfight against such odds, but using the speed they commanded, and the chaos behind, they both simply flew into the same dissipating smoke screen ahead, and flew back to the safety of the allied lines.

It was completely dark when the flight returned, one by one. Flares were on hand to guide them home, and they landed safely. The pilots exited their respective planes with some effort, with the days stupendous adventures firmly imprinted on their minds. Ground crew enveloped the machines and nursed them into the hangers. In turn the planes were unveiled under the light of the hangers. They looked in wonder with every machine bearing a prolific number of bullet holes and shrapnel tears in the fabric from stem to stern.

Holes were discovered in and around the cockpits, and some embedded into engine cowling and exhaust. Blood was evident in Mario's cockpit. He never discovered he had been shot until he was in the mess. He was downing his first beer standing at the bar, when blood was seen to be dripping down his left leg. A bullet had grazed his thigh which he never registered. It was the discovery of his wound and the winding down from the day's events that allowed his body to register, he was wounded, and now in pain.

It was a night to celebrate, wounded or not, everyone of Rogue flight was in the mood. Mario sat the evening out with his wounded leg raised, with everyone else singing and drinking. Eventually he passed out, through drugs, drink and the loss of blood finally taking their toll. After a couple of hours someone in the throng suggested a trip out to Le Rouex, which was met by an enthusiastic growl of assent. All but Mario, who was fast asleep in a chair. He was quickly dispatched to his billet before they commandeered a tender, and with Joe at the wheel they trundled off in the pitch black to finish off the day.

Adrian, Herbert, and Eugene opted to stay in the mess to enjoy a more tranquil evening. Eugene was eager to know how the day played out in some detail. He was a competent pilot, and was eager to be amongst the first black men of his country to fly in combat. Adrian was quizzed remorselessly as to his recollections of the day. Everything from angle of attack, how the two guns performed and he was asked about fuel reserves, landing in virtual darkness, the list was endless.

Adrian considered he had been drained out of everything from the day. "Genie! Give it a rest, I'm pooped. Cannot we talk of anything else for God's sake... You know... Anything but the bloody war"

Eugene smiled gently at his mentor in gratitude. He went behind the bar, and mixed a potent whisky cocktail, not generally known in Europe circles, and delivered the brew in silent apology.

"Bugger me," Adrian exclaimed. "That is powerful medicine. Cheers my dear fellow. Damn me if this doesn't give the old 'bucks fizz' a run for its money"

At this juncture, the mood was rudely interrupted with Joe bursting into the mess, very animated, and completely ignorant of the relaxed nature or the gentle mood in the mess at that time. He carried a length of silver metal, around a yard in length, which had a girth to it, at around an inch or two in diameter.

He theatrically placed the artefact onto the table, spilling some drinks in the process. With due deference the audience leaned forward in puzzlement to find out what the devil has Joe been up too.

"It's an idea of mine," Joe whispered hesitantly. "It's derived from the metal that we saved from the chopping of the SE's exhaust," he explained. "The object of discussion was in fact a concertina of thin metals held together with similar slender triangular metals linking the two. Herbert picked up the sample and found it surprisingly light. He balanced it from hand to hand, giving him time as to what on earth he was supposed to make of it. Eyebrows raised he passed it along to his left, without comment. He was certain there was a point to all this, however he had too much respect for his friend to offer any opinion of worth.

Eugene had some natural affinity with engineering, and he studied the sample with intense curiosity. He looked up to Joe, "Landing springs? He ventured.

No discernible response ensued. Adrian ventured, "Anything to do with replacement runway landing plates, you know, when the grass turns to mud?" Joe hesitated for a moment.

Actually, that was a bloody good guess. I might have to give that one some thought, he mused. He pointed to the sample and then went on to place it behind his neck. "All I have here gentleman is the same amount of metal taken from the exhausts of the SE's."

With that he went on, "I reckon I can duplicate over six yards square of this material behind the pilot and replace the headrest, as some protection from flak and bullets."

With some incredulity they all looked at the sample with silent wonder. Could it be? Was it possible? Some, or any protection in the cockpit was the holy grail of all pilots, irrespective of their allegiances.

The spell was broken with Adrian standing up and throwing his hands up in frustration. "Metal that thin! Wouldn't stop an olive spat from a spit tube." He continued, "I'd rather have another coat of dope slapped on, to stop the bullets getting though." He then sat down tiredly.

With some frustration Joe flew back at this criticism. "Look at it will you. The angled diamonds in the plates will deflect incoming fire, at least some." Joe banged his fist onto the table, upsetting some drinks in the process "At least give it a go, will you not?"

*

Some of the ground crew took up the offer to practise flying, others preferring to keep their feet firmly on the ground. Not only did it empower them, to know they could actually get their wings if they wanted, but it gave them all a useful insight on the reality of flying, and how their individual contributions was of such importance to the flight. Eugene was ahead of the pack when it came to natural flying aptitude. When duties and weather allowed he repeatedly hogged the 'Harry Tate' putting in hours and hours of flying time, albeit well behind the allied lines. On John's instructions he was at first practising flying straight and level, back and forth, with gentle manoeuvres only. His instructions today was to repeatedly change the drum on the Lewis positioned over the top wing. This was achieved by holding the stick in between his knees, and pulling the gun back on the Bowden cable to replicate changing drums during combat.

When he had practised this what seemed dozens of times, he then had to gently move the stick from side to side, still only using his legs, as flying straight and level for anything more than a few seconds, could prove disastrous in battle. Despite the cold, Eugene exited the cockpit sweating with the exertion and concentration of this exercise. Eugene's ground crew surrounded the plane and helped to push it into the hanger, while checking nothing had happened to their new personal toy. Questions were asked in earnest, and they were smart questions and not just idle curiosity. "How did she fly? what was the climb rate? any stunting?"

John joined the crowd assembled around the RE8, hands in his pockets, "Well Genie, it seems you are learning the rudimentary of flight, but can you shoot? No bloody good spending all that time aloft if you can't bloody shoot."

He turned to the crew. "Give this gentleman some drums for the Lewis, load the Vickers if you will, and set up the ground targets if you please" He took few steps toward the hanger opening, and turned sideways back towards them "And gentleman, if I were you, stay well clear"

Chapter Five

Major Green

With little notice the flight was ordered to pack up and be ready to move base within forty-eight hours. General Barrington issued orders that they were to move to another sector of the line, as yet not disclosed.

Herbert Rhys-Jones heard the news, and promptly made his way to the CO's office.

"Hello Herbert," John said, whilst gesturing for him to take a seat. "Heard the good news I suppose, and no, I don't know where yet, just that it's in between Arras and Amiens."

Jones set his cane aside and gratefully sat down. "Thanks old man, a snifter would be welcome".

Two large glasses were poured. "Not the best I'm afraid, but it does the trick."

Jones took a gulp, which confirmed the whisky in question was indeed a tad on the rough side. "I know your busy John, so I'll get straight to the point.

I would ask that a number of men, pilots and ground crew could do with some leave. It has been a while for some of them, and to be candid, they could do with a break, even if for a couple of days."

Before John could intercede, he went on. "Eugene and I can oversee the transport and set up wherever it is we are going, even with a few hands light."

John nodded his approval. "Of course, old chap. Give me the names of the lucky few, and I'll get that approved. If we are fortunate, we might be able to send out a second lot for leave whilst settling in."

John raised a finger to make a point, "Only local leave mind. Blighty is off limits. I would recommend Paris, or Amiens"

Adrian, Dickie, Joe, Albert and Terry Peters were duly informed of their impromptu break, which gave rise to a flurry of packing, as every hour counted. Joe flatly refused any time off, having been given permission to install his metal 'cockpit incubator' into Dickie's crate. No one had ever seen him so animated, it being at his very own project, and he was damned if he was going to entrust anybody but himself to see to its implementation. Half an hour later the remaining four were in the Captain's own precious Talbot, 'borrowed' for the occasion. Adrian had nominated himself as driver, being somewhat familiar with the marque, or so he claimed. The journey wasn't as precarious as some had predicted, even with the roads being potholed, and congested all the way with transport, troops and artillery all competing for movement to and from the front.

Some hours later they found themselves in the centre of Amiens, which itself had not escaped the ravages of Boche artillery. With the help of Dickie's dubious navigation skill's they eventually found their intended destination. Rooms had already been reserved by the ever-efficient Rhys-Jones in the Hotel Carlton.

The first order of the day was organised by Adrian who had a wealth of experience in matters of leisure and pleasure pursuits. The others deferred to his knowledge, and purse strings, especially in the circumstances of being the middle of a war.

He organised four hot baths side by side to be made ready, which was complimented with cigars and whisky. A very pleasant hour of mundane conversation ensued. The city, despite its proximity near the front, still boasted a goodly number of restaurants, cafes and nightlife which had a ready supply of customers from many nations far and wide. The boys took to the to the streets to explore, and see what the city had to offer. Adrian led them to a restaurant in a nearby square thronging with some civilians, but mostly uniforms of all descriptions.

"Don't think we are going to get any joy here Addie, bloody place is heaving."

Adrian continued to lead the way through the crowds." Trust your uncle Wentworth Dick me lad, it's all in hand"

He led them to an opulent frontage of a French estimanet draped in hanging flowers which did a god job of deflecting the eye from the damaged masonry. Adrian marched purposefully up to the maître and whispered into his ear briefly. After some initial hesitation, he theatrically raised his hands, and beckoned the group to follow him. One table, just one table in all of the restaurant was vacant, and reserved. Not just any table, but one that was sat in a prime position at the front of the restaurant, with panoramic views of the square.

More than one set of eyes settled on the group with envy and curiosity as to the identity of these new arrivals, who were obviously feted by the establishment. Adrian was first to sit down, and was already pouring wine into the glasses set. To a man, his companions sat down in wonder and bewilderment as to their good fortune. Adrian pre-empted their questions, while still pouring out the wine pre-ordered for the table. "Preparation, execution and implementation dear boys. A lesson in combat, and in life."

Albert and Terry were in awe as to how they found themselves in such a privileged position. Dickie was more resigned to what was transpiring, knowing his old friend so well. Waiters seemingly draped themselves around the table in order to gain favour. Wine and food was ordered and delivered with due deference, which for at least three of the recipients were not at all used to. Adrian however was in his element, relaxed with the very best friends he had ever known, and now he was in a position to give something back in a life, having previously had been one used to taking. It was a long while later when they were partaking of brandy's to finish the meal, talking in low tones, and for a while forgetting the horrors of what they had witnessed, and what was to come. The food as one would expect was superb, and given the bland fayre they had been subject to in recent months, it was even more appreciated than normal. While they were relaxing and making small talk, Nosy detected that Dickie was a little distracted, and seemed to be looking at, or through the crowds for some reason.

"You appear distracted young 'un," he enquired.

"Sorry, yes, sorry. just thought I saw someone."

It was a just a matter of minutes when the source of Dick's inattention. manifested itself. He jumped up and walked into the street.

"Hello," he stammered. "I'm so glad you were able to find us."

Claudette planted a kiss on his cheek, to the applause of the table, "Silly fool you are," rubbing the lipstick off his cheek. "I'm practically a local," Claudette smiled at the ensemble demurely while a scramble to find an extra chair ensued.

"You dark horse Dickie," exclaimed Adrian. "All this time you have been courting the delightful Claudette, and we never had a clue, bloody good camouflage mind,"

Dick blushed and failed to reply with anything witty in response. Claudette however was making herself right at home, and promptly ordered more wine for the table. Terry took his leave to find where he may relieve himself. It was a labyrinth of rooms and corridors. On the way back he inadvertently crossed the path of an officer from a line regiment which he never registered or recognised. Terry resumed his seat at the table and listened with some intent as to the next phase of the nights outing. He felt a presence at his shoulder which materialised as the same officer looking particularly agitated and intent on a confrontation. He gestured angrily at Adrian, who in fairness was the smartest turned-out officer at the table.

"Given that you are not regular infantry, we still do expect your, ahem, lackeys not to swan amongst their betters."

Dickie began to rise from his seat, but was restrained by the hand of Adrian, who calmly placed his napkin on the table. Adrian looked up at what was the Captain. It was his first night near the front, and who as yet had no experience in combat. He was however upset at the brazen breakdown of military etiquette he was witnessing, RFC officers and non-commissioned officers fraternising in a notable restaurant for all the world to see. Answers was required, and he was Johnny on the spot to get them. Before Adrian could respond, he was beaten to it.

"Fuck off," It was Terry, not well known for given an opinion.

The target of this response could only stutter. "You... how dare you.. say Sir, damn your eyes," he spluttered.

"Fuck off, Sir," was Terry's reply, whilst taking another gulp of the unfamiliar wine. The table erupted with laughter, and more crude comments, ignoring the dire threats of court martial and arrest from the same officer.

Dickie leaned over to his friend who was not quite as drunk. "Are we in trouble?"

Adrian laughed to himself and sighed. "I do believe we may be, such is war," Adrian slowly raised his glass.

The Captain left without another word, returning a little later with some company. A local unit was hastily commandeered as seconded military police to arrest the perpetrators. It was an unfortunate group of infantry just happening to be passing by. They reluctantly followed the orders of the officer to arrest some 'errant flyers, disrespecting an officer'. None of them were armed, however they duly followed on behind the excitable officer into a restaurant, apparently to carry out arrests.

Wilkins, the sergeant of these unfortunate conscripts was very uneasy as to being swept along by an ineffectual officer who was clearly unhinged as to some slight he had imagined. They were lead to a table of four RFC men, who appeared to be completely unconcerned as to the seriousness of the accusations being directed to them.

"Pardon me gentleman, may I ask of your response to this here officer... charges, like." It was Dickie who rose to the occasion. He recognised the local distinctive accent of a brummie, and responded in kind with his mirrored accent. "We told him he should fuck off, he's talking to proper fighting soldiers here."

There was a pause after which Wilkins shrugged his shoulders, and casually nodded, and made to remove his men from the scene. "Thank you lads, enjoy your evening."

Rather than push his luck, Adrian decided it was time to leave the restaurant forthwith. Each one of them in turn shook the hands of the bemused company of the Worcester's who was supposed to arrest them. The anonymous Captain's night of humiliation was completed with Wilkins turning to the annoying officer.

"Do you recognise our unit sir? The poor boy was in shock, and just shook his head, "Thought so, come on lads, time we were off," It was also time for their little group to leave before they got into any more bother.

Dickie and Claudette separated themselves from the gang, to spend precious time alone.

Adrian had led them out into the night, with his intention on navigating through a myriad of backstreet alleys. Eventually he stood before an obscure door in a backstreet. Without breaking stride' he led them on, where they found themselves in a dimly lit room, They were assailed with heavy perfume, light piano music, and soft gentle arms reaching out to guide them to the waiting sofa chairs. Girls with practised ease sat beside the bemused trio. Drinks were thrust into their hands.

"Ooh, l'aviateur" Purred into the ear of poor Nosy.

Adrian sat back into his armchair satisfied his mission was complete, and listened to the unique French songbird of female company, of which they have all been starved off for so long.

*

The SE had been duly modified to Joe's specific requirements. The nacelles were wrapped behind the cockpit seat and inserted into the cone shaped headrest behind the pilots head. Once completed Singer volunteered to take it up to assess any negative impact on the handling characteristics. After an extended flight it was declared if anything, the balance of the plane was improved slightly. It remained to be seen though if Jule's brainchild was capable of stopping or deflecting bullets.

With John's blessing, all of the planes were permitted to have the protective nacelles installed. If nothing else, it would provide some psychological comfort to his men. As Eugene was in the process of expending considerable amounts of ordnance at the practise targets, it was decided to trial the framework by the placement of some panels behind. The results were mixed, some bullets were found to have been stopped or deflected, however there were a considerable number of holes attesting to the fact that the bullets went straight though. This only further encouraged Joe to adjust the thickness and angles a of his invention in an effort to achieve better results.

Singer was summoned to the Adjutant's office, to be told where the flight's new home was to be. A small airfield at Marieux. John had managed to arrange for the permanent transfer of Harry Loutham as his administration skills were invaluable. Harry was appointed as CO for appearance's sake, and adjutant, which strictly speaking was a desk job, Harry however had ambitions of flying once again, which he kept largely to himself.

There was a mixture of squadrons operating from there and it was used as a transit hub for aircraft moving closer to the front. Coming into the winter the allied casualty rates had climbed significantly, largely due to a new German machine, which seemed to outperform anything the French or British could put in the air. Notwithstanding the mismatch of machines, with the Boche currently in the ascendancy, there was a problematic squadron operating from Marieux, which had a higher level of casualties than normal, especially with new pilots.

Rogue flight was sent to bolster the numbers of experienced flyers, and if possible find out the root course of the appalling number of losses.

"The squadron in question is led by a Major H.S. Green, ex-cavalry. Definitely of the old school, and a stickler for discipline." John explained. "So your lot are going to be as welcome as a bucket of cold water, so watch yourselves."

Singer sat and read a brief report on the situation. "We are getting disturbing reports of demoralised pilots and difficult ground crew. In addition to the attrition of pilots, the problem is compounded with higher than average number of accidents, engine failures and scrubbed missions."

John threw the report onto the desk. "And what measure of authority do I have to change things if I get resistance from Green?" He queried.

Harry turned to the window, hands behind his back. "Not much," he replied. "He has friends in high places, which is why he hasn't already been recalled before now"

*

Herbert was in his element organising the move with ruthless efficiency. A line of trucks was being loaded up with all their chattels, which even for a modest sized flight was a logistical miracle in motion. None of the pilots had yet returned, which was not an issue as it would take a couple of days for the vanguard, made up mostly of the ground crew, to go ahead and set up shop at their new home. Harry took the time to seek out one of his remaining pilots who were found, as usual fussing over their machine. On this occasion they were fiddling with the intricacies of the synchronised gear. This was the mechanism which enabled the Vickers machine gun to fire through the propellers, without hitting the prop. This particular type was the first Constantinesco models that had recently become available, and was highly valued by the pilots. The ability to fire in front of the pilot had its obvious advantages in combat, although the rate of fire was lessened as a result.

He stood over the two men not wanting to break their concentration. These types of interrupter gears were notoriously fickle, and required constant maintenance to keep them working properly. It has been known for these gears to go out of synch, and shoot off the pilot's own propeller! Harry considered the hanger to be the very heart of the flight. "How go's it chaps?"

Without looking up Jules responded. "She's getting lots of love and care Harry. That way she'll never let us down."

Harry nodded, and wondered why all the planes and bits of planes were always addressed as female. Same as ships he mused.

"How would you gentlemen like a couple of days leave?"

They looked up from the ground. "Two days did you say Harry?"

They looked at each other, and Jules scratched his head, "Don't we have some cousins in an encampment around these parts?" He asked Mario.

"I do believe we do," Mario stood up wiping his hands on an oil-soaked rag. "A couple of days on the road, would do very nice, thank you sir," he said formally.

Harry Loutham was well aware of his pilot's peculiar backgrounds, as they were of Romany blood. For centuries their families have lived a travelling life wandering all over Europe according to the seasons. It was said that even the stagnant nature of the present conflict did little to impede the Romany families somehow managing to cross the lines to continue their traditional way of life. Within the hour they trundled off in an old truck southward. Not knowing precisely the location of their kin. They were of the very few people who could successfully track and locate a gypsy encampment, even without prior knowledge.

The two Romany airman found their kinsmen in remote woodland in an idyllic location by a shore of a slow-moving river. Just to be amongst their own kind was just the therapy they needed to recoup and relax. Sleeping under the stars, and catching up by the fire, and catching up with the clan's news from all over, was all they needed. The simple pleasures of riding horses, catching rabbits and birds to eat, and sleeping with a full belly of meat and mead was reinvigorating and very welcome.

*

Late the same day Adrian delivered the borrowed car and its passengers safely back to the airfield, minus young Dickie, who was making his own way back, after taking Claudette home to her family. The next couple of days was taken up with preparing the planes for the transfer. Dickie offered to plan the route and navigate the flight to the Marieux airfield, which was not very politely turned down. In truth it was only a tongue and cheek offer, which he guessed would be rebuffed.

They borrowed some ground crew from the sixteenth squadron to help them with the final preparations, but in truth there was little to do except top up with petrol and help with the start-up procedure. They were scheduled to fly just after breakfast. John wanted to brief his men about the nature of the mission, and some of the pitfalls to avoid. The ground crew were also briefed for the duration, to adapt a conventional set up with the pilots and ground crew being segregated along more familiar lines. They would mess separately, and salute and address each other according to rank. This was a preventative measure so as not to antagonise there hosts and jeopardise the mission. In fairness the ground crew thought it would be an absolute hoot, and declared they would throw themselves entirely into the pantomime. Harry was understandably concerned they would over-egg it, but he couldn't fault their enthusiasm.

A light grey blanket of sky lay at about two thousand feet, with a brisk but manageable south westerly wind. They were flying in friendly territory, but they kept a respectable height below the cloud line, as they could still come under fire from over enthusiastic artillery or small arms fire, especially as the planes were not readily identifiable as British due the stealthy nature of the paintwork.

Adrian was happy to follow his friend, and without thinking just mirrored the speed and course, His mind was still back in Amiens and relishing the memories of recent adventures. Dickie was all over the place with emotions. He had no idea when or if he would ever meet up with the lovely Claudette again. They had been inseparable for the short time they had, where they exchanged so much of themselves, he felt he had known her all his life. Then again, they were still complete strangers and it surprised him how much of himself he had given to a person he had, in total, only spent hours with.

The flight to their new home was uneventful. Eugene was happy to be part of the transfer, and by now he was very comfortable flying the old 'Harry Tate.' keeping in formation was a little tricky at first, but he soon settled in at the rear. He found himself daydreaming for a while, and forgot to keep an eye on the flight. After flying through some cloud he was astonished to find the sky empty. A brief moment of panic, was quickly replaced with self-loathing for being so unprofessional. Now he had to make amends and find the aerodrome alone.

Jules was piloting the plane for a change, and Mario was happy for him to get some flying hours in. They were both unconcerned as to where they were going, as by nature they were nomadic. They were happy in the knowledge they were in the company of elite flyers, and in turn they were recognised and appreciated as being worthy of the same unit.

They landed in turn, and were guided to the newly erected hangers by the crew. With the engines on idle they pushed the planes to the hanger entrance. Herbert smartly came alongside the Singer's bus. "Welcome to Marieux sir, hope you had a..." He got no further. A stern looking NCO stepped smartly up and saluted.

"Sir, you are to report to Major Green's office immediately," he then turned and marched away without waiting for a response.

John only then began to exit the plane. They looked at each other somewhat taken aback. "Nothing like a warm welcome, eh Herb"

"Don't you worry about that sir, me and the boys have given the Major no ammunition to use. Played it by the book as we promised." He saluted smartly. "Mind you he's a rum one. We're as welcome as the pox in a whorehouse"

They left the little band to settle in the planes, and familiarise themselves with the field's set up. Adrian was very critical of the state of the undulating landing strip which seemed worse for wear. The west side of the field was exposed, and subject to side winds which made the task of take-off and landing more problematic. The area selected by the existing curators for Rogue to set up seemed to be quite a distance from the established buildings, hangers and ancillary tents, This suited Herbert, as it would minimise any contact between the two parties.

Other than the officious NCO no one else, bothered to interact with the new arrivals. They were under strict instructions not to make any overtures with any other personnel, until they had found out the lay of the land. They kept within the vicinity of the hangers, idly walking around hands in pocket, or smoking, with little to do for now.

Just then there was the unmistakable roar of an aircraft above. The engine sounded rough as it approached, with a thin wisp of trailing smoke behind. The plane was in some trouble but still under control. It came directly in low without any pre landing circuits, and landed safely after several small hops beforehand. Dickies sharp eyes recognised it was their very own RE8 being flown in by Eugene. However, Eugene only saw the assembly of the squadron's incumbent planes, and mistook it for Rogue flight. With some deftness he taxied over to park alongside some pups. Adrian took the opportunity to walk over toward the RE8. A wry smile on his face. He would wait to see the look of the gathering ground crew waiting to assist the new arrival. Eugene cut the engine, and allowed his new friends to align the plane by pushing the wings, and placing the blocks under the wheels.

He jumped down from the cockpit, and stood beside his machine, waiting on events. An NCO approached to see what the purpose of the visit, and obviously assist in any way he could.

"Good morning sir, welcome to Marieux. Sounds like you have some engine trouble."

Eugene peeled off his heavy scarf, and pulled off his cap and goggles. He smiled back at his host. Even with the camouflage of oil over his face, it came quite a shock to see the dark genial features of Eugene.

"Why, thank you," he drawled. "Mightily neighbourly of you. I'm looking for... Ah never mind. Here they come. Must have parked in the wrong spot." He pointed over in the direction of where his comrades were approaching. Adrian was relishing the reaction of the growing ensemble surrounding the plane. He doubted any of them had seen a Black pilot before.

"Eugene, you rascal," he shouted. "What have you done to our bloody plane?" he bellowed with a broad grin on his face.

"Sorry skip... er, Sir. Engine running hot. Have it fixed in no time."

Despite orders Adrian shook his friends hand. "Down in one piece, and in the circumstances not a bad landing," he pointed back across the field. "Except we're over there."

*

John was led straight into Green's office, where he observed the countenance of his host. Major Green remained seated, with the hands clasped in front of his face. He looked to be a small waif of a man. His uniform was probably tailor made, as it cut a crisp and clean look. He had cold dark eyes, thin lips and a pencilled moustache. John snapped to a halt and saluted. "Captain Singh-Smythe reporting."

Green baulked that this newcomer didn't say sir, but he decided not to press the point "Sit down Singh," he curtly ordered. Silence ensued for a few moments. No words of welcome or offer of refreshment was expected or offered. "I was told to expect your, er flight. What I wasn't told was why."

"Orders," John replied woodenly. He had no intention of offering anything further, until he had the measure of this man.

"Orders you say orders. Well let me tell you something Captain! While you are here on my airfield you will follow *my* orders, and so will your men." He leaned forward. "Rumours of your 'flight' are about, and I do not like what I hear."

John feigned ignorance. "Sorry to hear that, Captain. You will get no trouble from my men for the duration of our stay."

Anger pulsed through Green vividly. "Your stay? you say, and pray how long would that be?"

John sighed inwardly. His diplomatic skills being tested as he had taken an immediate dislike to this man. "That is not yet determined. We will conduct ourselves appropriately, however my orders are to operate independently from this squadron, and Major, that will include supporting your squadron as I see fit."

He slammed his fist on the desk. "You will not sir," he spluttered "This is my squadron, and I will have my questions answered as to why your squalid little band has seen fit to interfere with this squadron's operation... and by what authority damn you."

John pulled out a sheath of documents, which Major Green snatched up. He didn't bother to read any of it, but simply went directly to the signatory on the last page.

"And your mission?" he barked.

"Staff have identified your squadron as having the highest attrition rate of pilots on the Western Front Major," he replied simply. "We are here to help. My squalid flight, as you put it has the most gifted veteran flyers assembled for such purposes. If we can bolster the ranks, and especially get your fledgling pilots further support and training, they may survive a little longer than they appear to have so far." John left out the bit about looking into the morale and leadership aspect.

Green looked back at John for a few moments, and stood up. "Officers dine at eight pm sharp. Best foot forward mind. Bar closes at ten. We fly tomorrow at ten sharp, weather permitting. Your NCO's and re-enlisted men will be directed to their quarters." He rang a little bell to summon his waiting adjutant. "Show these gentleman to their respective quarters"

The evening dinner was desultory affair, being formal in the extreme. Adrian stayed away for the evening, which was a surprise and disappointment to his comrades. He would normally be the first in line to stick it to the establishment. However, he stayed in his billet all evening. Some of his mates having to endure an excruciating few hours of listening to the 'donkey wallapers' promoting the virtues of the cavalry and its application to modern Aerial warfare.

Jules sat in silence listening to the boorish small talk around the table. He noticed the new pilots, identified by the relatively sharp uniforms not long worn. They offered nothing to the evening, and sat in silence heads down, concentrating on their dinner. He tried to engage with one or two of them, to no avail. They replied with bland monosyllabic replies. After some time, he took himself outside for a smoke. The evening was calm and quiet, apart from the sound of distant guns, and accompanying flashes in the far distance. Shortly he was joined by Rhys-Jones.

Herbert looked around fervently to ensure they were on their own. "Don't know about the officers, but the rest of them are in a pretty poor shape." He took the proffered cigarette from his friend, and inhaled deeply. "The chaps here are neglected, poorly trained and unappreciated, and it comes from the top, Your chap Green has no contact with his men, and from what I hear, not much interaction from the pilots either, unless that is, they are of the right class or ex-cavalry."

Herbert nodded slowly. "Same in there," he pointed at the Officers' mess. "Bloody depressing just to be around," he ground his cigarette stub into the ground "I'll let John know, and recommend he have a nose around the hangers first thing in the morning"

Dickie found himself lost while looking for his billet. As he made his way through the corridors a door on his left hand side was ajar. He could see someone leaning over a desk writing. He had his back to the door. Dickie instinctive walked in, "Am I disturbing you?" he enquired as a means of introduction.

A Young fair-haired man turned to face the door. He was just in his undershirt and braces, loose trousers and barefoot. "Oh, not at all." He blinked at Dickie "Not seen you before" he offered his hand. "Farnsworth, Peter Farnsworth. How do you do?"

Dickie responded in kind. "A pleasure, Dick Watson, just arrived."

Peter ventured into his trunk, and pulled out a bottle. "Welcome to our little part of the war Dick... something tells me you are not new to this game," he further scrutinised his visitor., "flyer of course. Must be one of the new chaps that's got the CO all in a fizz, and for that alone, you are doubly welcome".

Dickie found himself warming to his new friend, and while taking the first sip, he decided to take a punt. "Thanks Peter, and thanks for the drink. Could you tell me at all, what's going on here?"

*

Breakfast was a leisurely affair, as the flight had already been predetermined for mid-morning. Rogue flight gathered together in one of their own hangers, to collectively share what they had discovered in the short time after their arrival.

John sat in silence while he assimilated the scraps of information from the crew and aviators of his flight.

He looked over at Adrian who was sitting down, a little distance from the others. He was looking down at the floor, as if to make himself invisible. "Addie? anything from your end"

Adrian looked away pensively. "No sir, nothing."

John left it at that, and started to outline the flight plan for the morning. Dickie however was not satisfied with Adrian's response. He knew there was something very wrong with his friend.

Rogue flight was to provide top cover for Green's patrols. He didn't know it at the time, but the mission was much as the same as every mission. At the same time of day. At the same height, and on a predictive course over the German lines.

They were to fly on this occasion in two pairs, with Adrian and Dickie in the SE's having a two-seater alongside with an observer. John elected to leave his SE in the hanger, and fly the lumbering RE8. Genie was to fly as an observer, as he was very adept at firing at moving deflective targets, he would be a good choice to protect the rear of the 'Harry Tate'.

Green had a flight of bombers and scouts amounting to fifteen machines. The cloud was high and intermittent, provided good visibility. As predicted, they flew at about eight thousand feet in a formation of three, very old school Singer thought. Most allied units had dispensed with the 'Vic' mainly due to the fact a pilot spends more attention to keeping a tight formation, rather than scanning the sky for any threats. Rogue found themselves at around eleven thousand feet above and behind the main formation, and they adopted a loose 'gaggle' plan, as Adrian termed it. They crossed the lines looking for targets of opportunity. Rogue flight was keeping a very close watch on the sky above towards the sun.

The Boche would be intelligent enough to lie in wait and intercept a squadron that was so predictable. For God's sake! Singer said to himself, they aren't even bothering to zigzag. Just flying straight and level. What a buffoon! They flew over the trenches, and the flight leaders plane waggled his wings, put the throttle to the gate and began to climb.

"No Archie" he mumbled to himself. "No Archie" he repeated. As they gained height, they turned thirty degrees. Two minutes later Dick then waggled his wings, spotting menacing Black specks slightly below heading towards Green's squadron. It was as Singer had feared. No Archie over Boche airspace could only mean one thing. They had their own machines in the same area, and were prewarned by their own side. Rogue flight continued to close at an angle and await events. He had no concept of what his charges would do, and he didn't want to go straight in and make things worse. A few moments later the scouts turned towards the enemy, obviously at a severe disadvantage. The slower bombers wisely let loose with their bombs, turned westwards and dived for friendly airspace. Unusually the bombers were escorted by a single scout plane. This particular plane was flying streamers.

The Germans had become complacent. They knew where and when the English flyers would be, and were to a man, determined to add to their score of kills. They failed to follow basic principles of scanning the skies. Out of the sun came two SE's who burst in among them flying through the formation before using the speed to gain height before making another pass. At that range it took a few short bursts to dispatch what looked like Fokker's. Before they could react, they had two English two-seater's following in their wake, coming in at a shallower angle, to maximise the impact of the observers twin Lewis guns, which promptly unleashed a hail of bullets in a long devastating chatter of death.

Only a brief reply from the German Rumpler two-seater's, managed any sort of response, with the remaining Germans in complete disarray. At least three Boche planes were seen to be in spins, with one in flames. Two crashed into nearby fields, and the third came out of the vrille in complete control, and was last seen flying home eastward in clear skies. Several other machines clearly damaged, limped for home Dickie and Adrian turned tightly back into the Boche for another pass, while wisely flying in the right direction home, letting off short bursts on the way. Singer had disengaged after the first pass with a damaged rudder post and several holes in the fabric of the wings as souvenirs of their encounter. The twins followed their leader back over towards the lines. This time black bursts of Archie accompanied them all the way back to the front line.

They were assembled in their hanger. Captain Singh-Smith was incandescent with rage. "The arrogant incompetent fool," he spat at no one in particular. "Its flying lunacy. The bastard has no place in leading a squadron."

Adrian was leaning on a wing waiting for his skipper to finish his spleen. "It's bloody murder, John. His one tactic is to charge at the enemy, as if he was on a horse. No thought as to manoeuvre of any kind. They lost three today either killed or captured with two more just making it back by pancaking. Who knows what conditions the others are in."

Adrian straightened up. "What sort of a mess would have they been if we hadn't been their John?"

John nodded. "No wonder morale is at rock bottom." He sighed, "He's got to go."

Adrian blew up and took a pace towards John. "GO! GO! of course he's got to bloody go, but you ain't going to do it, or anyone else."

Dickie stepped forward in surprise at his friend's outburst. "Steady on Addie. It's not John's fault."

John shook his head. "He's right though. This bastard has friends at home, powerful friends who put him there in the first place."

Herbert had witnessed the discussions quietly, and raised his cane towards Adrian. "You sir, have been in a fearful funk ever since we've been here," he said quietly. "And don't tell me that you haven't."

Adrian nodded in resignation. "Sorry everyone, Herb's right." he took a deep breath. "It's Green, we have history," with that he walked out without another word. Dick followed a few moments later, holding up one hand as if to say leave it with me.

The ground crew were left in peace to patch up the planes, re-arm and refuel. John took a bike to get over to the opposing hangers where the squadrons ground crew were likewise servicing the remaining planes.

As he leaned the bike against the wall, what looks like an engineer, in overalls was walking by briskly and saluted. John made to intercept him. "Pardon me, may I talk to you?"

A heavy-set man turned back reluctantly to this anonymous officer. "Sorry sir, of course sir."

Ignoring the salute he extended his hand. "My name is John, people call me Singer."

The engineer looked with dismay at the extended hand. He looked down at his own greasy palms which he rubbed on his overalls, behind his back, as if to avoid physical contact.

John withdrew his hand. "I can see your busy, carry on." Despite his bulk the poor man disappeared in some haste to the safety of his assigned plane close by.

On this occasion John was unsuccessful with engaging with the man. On other occasions he was more successful, and eventually managed to get a clear picture of the rot that had set in throughout the squadron, and it all came down to one man.

As he made to mount his bike, he was confronted by the same officious NCO he had met previously. He came to a halt and saluted smartly. The CO's complements sir, and he would like to see you straight away.

*

It didn't take long for Adrian to open up to his friend, and it prompted Dickie to seek out Harry Loutham straight away. Harry in turn caught up with John on his way to his appointment with Major Green. Harry took John aside for a few moments, before addressing the impatient NCO waiting. "Compliments to Major Green, I will join him directly," and before the impatient Sergeant could protest, the two walked briskly away. John and Adrian had a brief private conversation, which finally revealed Adrian's recent behaviour.

John immediately went to find Adrian and eventually collared him in his room. "Right, Wentworth, how do you feel about confronting your nemesis. We are overdue for an argument anyway, so we might as well throw it all into the mix."

A knock on the door announced the arrival of the pair. They were met with Green and another officer who they were only on nodding terms with. The chairs had been removed, probably on purpose to force John to stand.

Green remained sitting, with a thin smile on his face. "Good of you to come at last," he hissed. He pointed his cane at Adrian. "And who is this, who has come uninvited."

Adrian remained impassive and just stared at the face he remembered from so many years ago.

"Oh him, we'll come to that in good time," John replied carefully. "You have asked to see me?"

Green continued to look at Adrian, he leaned forward, "Don't I know you?"

Adrian stared back blankly, not trusting himself to respond. Green simply turned back to John. "Heard you have been asking questions to my men. Mostly about me so it seems," he wagged a finger in John's direction. "Not very sporting old chap now, is it?"

John felt uneasy, and he didn't know why. It was the same feeling he had when flying into a bad situation during a dog fight. "I have orders Captain, to find out what is wrong with this squadron, who is responsible, and fix it."

Green didn't respond, but simply sat back and smiled. He was used to being confronted before, and he had always come out of it on top.

"Oh, I'm sure you have been very busy Smythe, very busy indeed. I'm going to make you wished you hadn't bothered."

John replied smoothly. "On our last mission together I saw a plane disengage from the scout formation, on spotting the Boche machines. That plane flew away from the fight, with the bombers, leaving his comrades alone, and leaderless. That plane had streamers Captain. That plane was yours."

For the first time, Green looked unnerved, but he composed himself, "Standing orders Captain, *my* orders. My job is to protect the bombers and escort them home. Good military practice I think they call it. I am simply too valuable to be sacrificed in a meaningless scrap, rather than preserve the integrity of the squadron"

"And send young men with no battle experience and hardly any flying hours straight to hell," John shouted. "How many have you lost under your leadership? Just how many men have needlessly been maimed, captured and killed for your *standing orders.*"

Green stood up quickly "No one of any significance old boy."

John knew he was being taunted, but before he could recover himself Green turned to Adrian, "Wentworth I do believe, Young Wentworth, Gordonstoun School." Green came round from behind his desk and stood in front of Adrian. "Didn't you think I knew you was here, skulking around, hiding," he laughed. "Of course I have known all along. Bloody Wentworth. Probably been telling tales out of school to his mates eh!"

Green looked towards John. Adrian interrupted the Major "Gordonstoun school. Green and his cronies, bullies and cowards to a man." Adrian continued. "School life blighted by scum like him. Killed my best friend as a dare during a shoot. Claimed it was an accident. His father had the whole incident covered up." Adrian's face pained in memory, and tears welled up. "My testimony was ignored, and I was beaten up for my troubles by his mates. They beat me so badly I was kept in hospital. By the time I was released our family were informed that my place in the school was cancelled."

Adrian looked over at John, "Friends in high places eh, sound familiar?"

Green took a step forward. "Yes, I shot him," he snarled. "Shot him well. Took him hours to die in agony if I remember. What was his name, the little snot, um? Atkinson wasn't it." Green leaned in towards Adrian. "No accident old boy, enjoyed every minute of it."

Adrian lashed out in a blind rage catching Green in the face and body in relentless blows, before John could grab his friend. Moments later bodies crashed in through the door and pinned the two down in seconds. It was a set up, and John knew it.

*

Rogue flight surrounded there commanding officer in growing anger. Adrian was locked up pending a court martial. Striking a superior officer was a serious offence, and a firing squad was a distinct possibility. The Major had ensured he had a witness, in the form of the officer in the room from the outset. He had also ensured there was further assistance close by, if it were needed. The trap was complete, with orders already in place with the grounding of all Rogue flight's planes who were stood down pending further enquiries. Poor John was distraught. He had let down his men, and furthermore he failed to protect them, and he was at a complete loss as to what to do. They found comfort in each other's company at least, and talked for hours, and planned together all sorts of schemes and scenarios to help their comrade. All of Rogue were in a funk, except the twins who were missing, and were not seen again that night

Jules and Mario took no time in taking a more direct approach to the problem, starting with a spot of cat burglary. With Jules as the lookout, Mario broke into the vacant sleeping quarters of one of the poor intake that was shot down the day previously. He eventually found the credentials of a Gerald Johnson in his belongings waiting for repatriation. He made a vow to Gerald in his mind that he would make a meaningful contribution to the war effort, even after death.

The next morning was taken with John's crew going over the airframes and tinkering with the filters on the engines with no meaningful purpose. They were going nowhere until further orders, which could take days even weeks, and all the time Wentworth was locked up pondering his fate. The squadron was not ready for operations until the early afternoon, due to 'technical issues' In truth Major Green and his lackeys had been celebrating long into the night.

Another of the new flyers had announced himself at the gate guard, which was slightly unusual as they normally arrived together by trucks, however he had the correct papers and was ordered to present himself before the adjutant.

Some hours later Jules found himself alongside two other new pilots, and were ordered without preamble to dump their gear, get some breakfast and prepare for an offensive patrol for mid-afternoon. Jules felt very sorry for his two new 'comrades' one of which was visibly shaking. There was little guidance in the way of introduction. Certainly, no time for orientation or training. They were going to be thrown into combat that very same day. Jules was assigned a flight and told to keep station as best he can. He was pleased to be given a Sopwith pup to fly, which in truth was a fearsome plane to fly for a 'novice' pilot.

*

The dark room matched the mood of Lt Adrian Wentworth. Gone was the youthful fearless pilot who live life with an abundance of energy and optimism, as many of that age tended to do. Here was but despondency, only amplified by the loneliness of his cell. It was a hut with no windows, which in a previous incarnation was for food storage. As such it was hastily adopted as a temporary prison. He was sat down on the hard floor with a blanket for warmth, and a bucket for ablutions.

A shaft of light came from a corner of the hut, which coincided with a board being silently moved back and forth.

"Addie?" A voice whispered "Still alive" the voice taunted.

"Mario, that you?"

"Tis but I," came the reply, "keep your chin up, and here..."

A bundle found itself into the hut. "Some trinkets to accompany your holiday, be back later"

The light went out and silence followed, Adrian cried with relief and joy at having simple contact with a fellow human being. He fumbled through the bundle and found bread, cheeses, fruit, and even a flask of whisky. He cried silently to himself with relief and joy. He was not alone!

*

They took off between two and three with the usual format of bombers and reconnaissance buses, and escorting scouts. For reasons not given to the pilots the bombers were instructed to take a dog-leg course, and periodically alter height to their objective which was some railway sidings a few miles behind the lines. The scouts were also given order to fly higher and with more freedom than at any time previously allowed. It seems that Green had woken up to the fact that he was under scrutiny, and that perhaps he should adopt some different tactics, while saving face. Jules sat in his cockpit hidden under layers of heavy clothing.

His face was completely covered with headgear and scarves, which was just as well, as his machine was behind and to the right of Lt Adam Connaught, adjutant to Major Green, who he had previously met. In fairness, Connaught was a decent chap, and by all accounts a fair flyer, having a good number of kills to his credit. There seemed to be no fixed plan or strategy in place. They were to simply over the lines of the German trenches. As expected the Boche were waiting for them above and behind their own lines. Jules saw the slower two-seater's flying in straight lines now above the German support trenches and communication lines. It was clear this was a mixed bombing and photographic mission. If the Be2's managed stayed in formation, they would prove to be a difficult and dangerous adversary. The Germans were quick to learn the lessons of their previous encounter, and were a lot more cautious in approaching this time round. It was a mixture of Halberstadt's and Fokker scout planes, of which half of them began their attack dives, with the rest staying aloft. The Be2's had just enough time to take the photos and let loose there ordnance over the designated area, before turning for home in good order. The British scouts rose up to intercept the immediate threat, with little thought but to disrupt and harass the enemy.

*

John knew something was awry, but he couldn't put his finger on it. He looked at each of his ground crew and pilots lounging in the mess, in turn. Something was amiss that he just couldn't make out what it was.

"Where is Jules?" He enquired. The silence was deafening, and what was more revealing, no one looked in his direction. "Joe, where's Jules?" he repeated.

Reynolds shrugged as if to say, 'No idea' and went back to reading 'Comic Cuts'. He found himself confused and agitated, and walked purposefully over to where his crew mate sat obliviously. "Mario, I'm going to ask you this just once. Where... is ... Jules?" Mario looked up at John with a small smile on his face. "Flying John." He didn't venture to explain any further.

"Flying? flying where? We are all grounded remember?" John was getting exasperated now. Infuriatingly, Mario looked back at his friend with the same calm demeanour. "Flying with our neighbours, so I am told, and to be fair John, the orders stated that our planes were grounded. They forgot to include the pilots."

"Oh, for fuck's sake!" Technically he was right, "To fly with them? and in what?" He scrutinised Mario for a few seconds his mind going through the gears. Mario remained impassive but resolute. The smile faded, and was replaced with a hard, cold stare. John had seen that look before. There wasn't any use in reprimanding Mario. His race held no loyalties to anyone, but his friends and family, on both sides of the conflict, and when they decided on a course of action, nothing trivial such as rank, or obedience would get in there way. John walked out of the mess without further word. He knew Jules well, he and Mario. He was going to kill Green. Of that he was certain, and there wasn't a damn thing anyone could do about it.

*

Connaught and his flight were successful in engaging the enemy, and kept them away from their escorts.

A general melee ensued with both sides engaged in a full-on dogfight. Inevitably a gap between the fighters and the escorts grew, which was the opportunity the remaining Boche planes had been hoping for.

The Be2's slowly lost height to gain speed, and to their credit were still keeping in good formation. Behind them was a single seater, with streamers showing.

Green had predictably shied away from the conflict and followed the formation to the safety of their own lines. Jules found himself detached slightly and discovered some cloud to 'get lost' in, He carefully stalked his adversary flying westward. Jules turned unseen above and behind Green and began to close in. He would get into the optimum range and firing position, and murder that bastard once and for all.

The top flight of remaining Fokker's and company were seasoned pilots. They had enough height to bounce the two slower two seater's while they were still comfortably behind their own lines. Their comrades were fully engaged elsewhere, and the Be2's were now vulnerable to attack. It was a classic scenario even with the presence of a single scout protecting the rear, All of a sudden, a lone British Sopwith emerged from the clouds and made to come to the aid of his comrade, seconds later that the same machine turned unexpectedly in a sharp roll back into the cloud and disappeared. The Boche were committed now, and continued straight on in a gentle dive. The Be2's saw the danger, and kept formation for mutual protection. They were confident they could give a good account of themselves, with the observers ready to repel any attack.

The instant that Jules had spotted the German planes diving onto the British, he abandoned his plan to assassinate Major Green, and as he turned into the cloud back towards the Boche. He quickly formulated another plan which he hoped may well work.

Green was beginning to panic. He saw the remaining Germans heading directly towards him, and his bowels turned to water.

He quickly determined that his comrades in the two seater's at least had rear firing guns, but he was a sitting duck. It was a reasonable course of action to abandon the Be's and save his own skin. Five veteran Hun pilots focused in onto the clutch of enemy targets still five hundred feet below flying a loose Vic formation. Without warning Jules emerged from the cloud close on the port quarter, less than one hundred yards distant. He aimed his bus at the last of the five Boche machines firing short accurate bursts of two to three seconds. He intention was not to destroy, but to disrupt. All three of his targets witnessed the stream of bullets striking the wings and fuselage, and before they could react Jules turned upwards and around on one wing, lining up for another pass.

The three of the Boche took violent measures of avoidance, diving and spinning in all directions. The Pup stayed above and manoeuvred to encourage his opponents to fly to safety, which they duly did. He observed the two leading planes unaffected by the skirmish and continued the attack, keeping a weather eye on the single interloper ahead. As Jules had anticipated they both focused on the single seater, which was a more attractive proposition, rather than facing five rear mounted machine guns on the Be's. Green looked back in horror and understood that he was now the target, and panic began to set in. Instinct kicked in, and he frantically turned and twisted in a vain attempt to lose them. Sweat and shivers came in equal measures, as he looked around for friendly planes, friendly skies, anything.

The Germans met each manouvre with easy graceful application of stick and rudder, and continued to expertly close on either quarter, to maximise firepower and minimise friendly fire. Tears streamed down Greens face as realisation that he was in real trouble. The plane shuddered as bullets lined up along the length of his plane. He heard the snapping of wires and felt his column shudder. Nothing he did seem to have any effect any more. The plane slowly began to roll onto its back. Still the hail of bullet impacts carried on relentlessly.

Cursing, crying and praying Green froze in absolute fear, and he began to scream. Inevitably a number of explosives bullets found the petrol tank. Which soon burst into flame. His eyes widened at this new horror, which stifled any further noises, as he fought to free himself from his harness. It took a few seconds for the wind to fan the flames into the cockpit. The plane was now aflame halfway along the fuselage. The top left wing crumpled which was the beginning of its complete disintegration. Unfortunately for Green he still had two minutes of agonising pain to endure, until the engine pulled the remains into the ground, finally ending his tortuous demise.

The two Boche planes still had the remaining English scout to tackle which remained in its advantageous position above them. Astonishingly the pilot leaned out of his cockpit, and gave a friendly wave before flying away towards the front lines. One of the Germans shook his head in disbelief. These English are madmen! How can we possibly win this war fighting madmen? he thought as he turned for home.

*

Harry and John sat patiently waiting on an explanation of Jules's exploits. They had already been briefed by Green's surviving crew of his fate. They were gushing in their praise of his taken-on odds of five to one, and saving the Be2's from serious harm. What Harry and John really wanted to know is what happened after. Jules looked back at them impassively, and took his time to light a cigarette. "I would imagine that all you really want to know, is did I kill him?" Jules paused for effect. "Of course, that was the plan, and given different circumstances I certainly would have, and without apology to you two or anyone else. We are of a people that takes responsibility for our own, which on this occasion includes your good selves. That bastard had to die, you know it, and so did we. The only difference is my civilised friends is that we think differently, that's all."

Jules didn't know if he had overstepped the mark, to who were two superior officer's. He went on anyway to explain the circumstances of the battle, and how had set up the scenario which allowed the Boche to kill him instead. Jules made his way to the door, and opened it. He turned back

"He went down in flames I'm happy to say, and hopefully suffered all the way. Bloody Plane disintegrated into tiny pieces. Your boy is Napoo! Problem solved, your welcome. Drinks anyone?"

CHAPTER SIX

'Tot Flugal'

They spent the next few days bolstering the ranks of the squadron, now commanded by the very able Adam Connaught. The turnaround in the squadron's capabilities and the improvement in morale was remarkable. Rogue flight pilots and supporting crew spent every spare hour sharing their hard won knowledge and experience with them. The pilots were taught how to fight smart, and brave but smart above all things.

They flew with them behind the lines, and spent hours going over everything from tactics, formation flying, weather watching and shooting. Above all it was the dark art of shooting, from angles and distances that are the most effective. The best pilot could be the finest pilot in the RFC, but if he couldn't shoot straight, then he's all but useless. General David Caddell put in an appearance to see how his protégés were faring. He had previously spent some time in purging all enquiries of court martial and historic dissent. Staff were, in time, content to be given reports as to the improving statistics in kill ratios and mission successes. Lt Wentworth was astute enough to appreciate the valuable assistance from Rogue squadron, and he himself was humbled by his colleagues support during his incarceration.

The ironic news that the late Major Green was posthumously awarded an MC was met with good humour, and they were even magnanimous enough to raise a toast to his memory, such was war. Orders came for the flight to relocate back to their original base shared with Sixteen. Dickie was relentlessly teased at the good news by his mates, which he took in good humour. He couldn't hide his delight at the prospect of reuniting with Claudette once more. It seemed that absence does indeed make the heart grow fonder.

It was a washout day with rain, low clouds and strong westerly winds, and it proved to be the perfect time for a farewell bash. The crew took the time to say their goodbyes and wish them all the best, in the certain knowledge that some will never make it home. David and Harry waited patiently in the office for John to arrive. He had been summoned for a meeting, before they joined in with the revelries.

John entered the room and warmly shook hands in turn. David turned back towards the office table and picked up a file. He looked intently at the document, and without opening it, he passed it to Harry, who gave it a cursory inspection.

"Do be seated John. Harry and I wanted to fill you in on the reasons why we are going back. Harry here has a directive from staff who have a particular problem they think we are adeptly suited for." Harry handed the document over to John.

The front cover read 'Most secret' Cecil continued. "Read it at your leisure please, but do not discuss or share for now. Harry, could you summarise please."

Harry nodded silently. "We are tasked to locate a flight of Boche machines, flying the new Albatross bus. They are identified principally by having black livery, and a distinctive painted Indian pattern cross. The French have crossed swords with these fine fellows in recent months.

John opened the file to gaze at the contents. "We think there are about six to eight of them, and who seem to have adopted their own particular vicious rules of engagement."

John looked up confused. "Rules? Didn't know there were any rules anymore"

The General interjected. "True, John, true. It's certainly not 1914 anymore, but these bastards have taken it to another level."

Harry followed. "We have had multiple reports that this lot have their own ruthless code, to which they shoot and kill all before them. No prisoners are ever taken, no wounded left alone to survive. French planes have landed behind the lines in various conditions, and on every occasion have been shot up and killed even after surrendering."

John lit a cigarette to assimilate the news. Harry's voice rose in anger, and stabbed at the report. "This bunch of fanatics have taken it upon themselves to introduce total war in the air."

John sucked in air. "No prisoners? you say?"

Harry replied. "Read the report. Wounded men unable to defend themselves. Men being shot up from the air while waiting to be taken prisoner. Even helpless civilian refugees trying to flee shot up for no military purpose, including, women, and children."

"Your Job John, you and Rogue flight is to find and destroy them. Target just them, and kill every single one to the exclusion of all else. We need to send the message that we know who they are, where they are, and this type of warfare will not stand"

John now understood the mission, one which was most worthy of his pilots and crew.

David pressed him further, "We need a professional execution of this John, if you'll pardon the expression. Keep your emotions in check. These bastards are also very competent fliers, and will not be easy to destroy."

The meeting was over, and John joined his team for a drink, and by god didn't he need one, he thought.

*

Rogue flight was led for the first time by Eugene in his new SE. His progress in his piloting prowess had come on at a pace. This was a perfect opportunity to test his navigation skills. It was still early in the morning and many of the pilots hadn't eaten yet, and were keen to land in time for breakfast. The ground crew had already split up, with some of the chaps already en-route, and the rest leaving after all the planes were successfully in flight. The departure was late, as Dickie's bus developed engine trouble shortly after take-off, and he had to nurse the plane back, minutes later. The skeleton crew of air mechanics quickly discovered that defective rocker arm bearing on the engine cowling was the source of the problem. There was much merriment and some side betting from the men, as to whether 'Dickie, where am I?' Watson would be able to find his old airfield on his own!

'Genie' loved the feel of his new baby from the outset. She was certainly in a different class to the old RE8. A real thoroughbred. It was Speedy, responsive, and a joy to fly. He couldn't wait to try her out with some more aggressive manoeuvres. As it was he concentrated on guiding his comrade's home. It wasn't much of an ordeal, as the ground features below were all familiar, and on a lovely day such as this, he easily found the tell-tale signs of the approaching landing area and led the flight in. Not much in the way of the set up around the fields had changed, and so they made their home where it was all those weeks ago. On arrival it was disturbing to see there weren't many pilots that they recognised, rather a unnerving number of fresh faces, who looked younger than their predecessor's. There was a choice of accommodation though, with a nearby Château being available for the pilots, in somewhat more sumptuous surroundings that they were accustomed to. It would provide a welcome respite for its officers from the crude huts previously on offer. Adrian and Eugene were comfortably sat in sofa's talking shop. Adrian was very impressed with the progress of the American, and was going through some of things he should practice on before being allowed to fly in harm's way.

Harry made his way over, drink in hand. "Welcome home boy's. Looking forward to your new billets?"

Adrian grinned. "Absolutely sir, the way a war should be fought with a little bit of luxury for our poor tortured souls."

Harry sat down and leaned forward, his forehead creased in concentration. "Look, I know you are familiar with the, um, eccentricities of the General which only he can get away with." He sighed, "Principally the unmilitary peculiarities of our little gang. Well, he has come up with another one, and I wanted to test the water so to speak before suggesting it to the others."

Adrian wasn't at all surprised. "Intriguing stuff Harry, what's on his mind now?"

Harry put his glass down. "It's the Château. You know, the one that has been offered to the pilots for accommodation and recreation."

Eugene put in. "If you are asking for an opinion, I'd like to reserve my spot in the East Wing, looking over plush green countryside, facing away from the war."

"Go on Harry," Adrian put in. "What's the barmy old fool up to this time?"

"He wants the ground crew to have the Château, and the pilots to stay on the field." He blurted and pressed on. "It makes sense too, think about it. Our crew work mostly through the nights, to get our bus's ready for the morning. You know the field is a noisy place during the day, when they most need some rest. He thinks they would makes sense, if they were to have somewhere quiet and peaceful to sleep."

"Like the Château," Adrian replied.

They fell into silence for a while as they took in this new idea. Adrian and Eugene looked at each other for a time. A grin appeared on Adrian's face. "Bloody love it. I can suggest it to the lads, but I'm sure they will agree... As long as they let us visit now and then"

*

Dickie approached the field having successfully made his way, without any further mishaps. On approach he observed the entire compliment of Rogue squadron standing in line on one side to celebrate the arrival of the latecomer. The engine noise fell silent, and was replaced with a wave of cheering and ribald remarks on his achievement. Herbert emerged from the group to shake his hands, and to inform him he had won the bet as to the nearest time of landing. He was followed by Adrian who was dangling some keys in front of him.

"Truck's all fuelled up and ready Dick. Harry gives his blessing for you to bugger off pronto. We'll take care of your crate… and tell the lovely Claudette and the girls we'll be down later."

Dickie clapped him on the shoulder. "Bloody bricks, the lot of you. See you later."

*

The office was full of smoke, coming from lit cigarettes and pipes. Three men surrounded a large map, which sat adjacent to a photographs set out in mosaic of Aerial shots taken previously behind the German lines. Harry, John and Herb were looking at the area in question.

Harry was concentrating on marking points on the map. "Here are the known points of contact that the Black Boche planes have been confirmed in dogfights and ground strafing." Harry pointed to the concentric circle already in place" This is the probable range of the Albatross., and these…" He indicated to a number of red circles, "Are the known airfields in operation in that area."

John nodded. "Herbert here is the Statistician, hopefully we can whittle the search down to a handful of airfields."

They left Herb to study the maps and photos. Harry took John into the mess, which was deserted at the time. He poured them both a whisky and looked for his favourite chair to sit in. "Before we join the others John, there is something else you ought to be made aware of, and some of it must remain between you and I."

John sat up confirming he had his attention. "I am told that we have a staff officer who frequents the same estimanet as our lot in Le Rouex. He is having some sort of sordid affair with a young local French girl. Now this girl we are told originates from the Alsace Lorraine region, which is known for its Germanic sympathies."

Harry handed over a small photograph of Peregrine Cotter. The young officer in question is said to have a loose tongue around wine and women, and Intelligence are confident that he is the source of leaked information that may be of use to the Boche."

John pondered on this latest twist. "Can't say I can remember him, Harry. Why haven't they been arrested?"

"Simple," he replied. "Our Intelligence bods have been feeding him rubbish information, mixed in with some accurate nuggets that we know the Boche are already aware of. One more thing, and Dick doesn't need to know, understand? Claudette is keeping an eye on our Boche sympathisers, and has put herself at considerable risk in doing so. Not something Dick would appreciate at this time." Harry stood up. "Come on, we are late for dinner."

As they made their way out of the mess. Harry pulled at John's arm, "One more thing John. Intelligence have suggested that German Intelligence are now aware of

Rogue flight's existence, and the Black flight we are hunting, may well have set up the scene to lure us into the same area, specifically to target us."

John was astonished by this. Harry continued. "They think that these atrocities were part of the plan to lure Rogue flight into a trap. Smart fellows these Germans eh. Let the lads know, and make sure we don't go into this mission blind."

*

A roar of welcome filled the air when Harry and John entered the cafe. Glasses of local French wine was thrust into their hands. The mood was light and full of good cheer, and so all thoughts of war were forgotten for a few hours. The next day was already a wash out as an expected downturn in the weather manifested itself from the early evening. The wind picked up and the early spring warmth was replaced by a last blast of winter weather coming in from the east. It was one of those times that you head for home and find comfort around a fire, or bed. The other option was to embrace the storm and carry on with the revelry. Rogue squadron was if nothing else but consistent, and to a man, chose the latter.

Claudette and Dickie sat apart from the large table, grasping at the little time they had to themselves. Frequent interruptions from all and sundry didn't detract the time spent together again. A magical few moments together left behind all the doubts and worries of events surrounding them. Dickie was well aware of the precarious situation of an aviator, and the cold hard facts that life expectancy was lower than any poor bugger in the PBI. They were two people thrown together in a world of chaos, and amongst all of that emerged an island of love.

It proved to be true with it being a wash out the following morning. The clouds streamed across the skies bring cold freezing rain. For the ground crew it was going to be a busy day. Harry had reasoned that if the Boche were at all aware of Rogue flights existence. They would most likely be seeking out their theatre of operations, and where they flew from. After all, it is what he would do, and the Germans were by no means fools.

*

The flight had for some time flew with their unique pale blue camouflaged paintwork, with faded roundels. Harry now ordered the planes to be transformed into the more traditional green and brown configuration with standard roundels, with the Sixteenth's insignia. To complete the ruse, temporary canvas covers to the Lewis gun on the top wing, and elevators were to be added, which hopefully would disguise the fact that they were Se5's if observed or photographed from above.

Adrian and Eugene were also in the workshops, in overalls, together with the lads, changing the lubricants as Eugene swore a thicker oil give a little more airspeed, which could take the SE's to over 140mph.

Adrian was chatting to Eugene going over some of the principles of dive airspeeds. "You know you have enough about you now to get over to Blighty and get your wings. I'm sure the CO would give permission."

He shook his head and smiled knowingly "Harry tells me I can fly operational soon anyway, so there's no need," he went on. "So, as it stands I still qualify officially as ground crew, right? "He smiled again. "So, I get to fly with you boy's in the air, and spend my downtime in that lovely Château, which you boy's don't."

Harry laughed. "You sir, are a wise man".

*

The atmosphere in the hangers amongst the ground crew was euphoric. Ernie and Albert were in loud conversation as to how opulent it was at 'Le Rogue Château' its new adopted name. Working on the adjacent bus, Terry, Joe and Herbert were loudly calling across the room extolling the many virtues of the new quarters, in comparison to the rudimentary draughty huts the pilots had to endure. The volume of this topic was solely aimed at the erstwhile fliers, who took the ribbing in good faith. They were even invited to pop over later for dinner!

Adrian was ever the one for a wheeze, and following a brief conversation with the crew, he disappeared mid-afternoon to seek out some of the other airmen. The aircraft were prepped, painted and ready for a scheduled early pre-dawn flight. By early evening, the ground crew were cycling back to their new home. Joe suggested that after scrubbing up they might repair to the lawns for a game of croquet.

Albert went further. "Followed by coffee and cigars."

They were going to enjoy this brief period of levity to the full. On arriving they were informed that unfortunately, dinner would be a little late tonight, which gave then some more time to dispense with the oil and grime the had accumulated during the day.

They were grateful to learn that they had their own mess in one of the downstairs rooms, all stocked up, courtesy of Lieutenant A.D. Wentworth. They were relaxing with a few drinks, when to their surprise the dinner gong was sounded. Somewhat bemused they sauntered into the dining room to see it had been set up for a very formal dinner. Candles, wine, cutlery and glasses, even flowers adorned the table. They all sat down excitedly, only for the gong to sound once more. One of the retained Château staff announced in French the arrival of Hors d'oeuvres, which to a man no one understood. Out from the kitchen they walked in line, napkins over the arms and food aboard for delivery, came their very own pilots. There was a roar of delight from the crew who fell about in tears of laughter at the prank. Adrian wasn't going to let them get away with just a gesture however, and the service continued throughout dinner much to everyone's amusement.

*

The weather was by no means ideal, but the abundant amount of cloud cover should give some respite from Boche Archie, and it could be used to advantage to hide from enemy planes. Rogue flight had a predetermined flight plan as per Herbert's calculations. The mission was simple to fly behind German lines around the Bourlon Wood area, where several airfields had been previously identified and documented. The SE's were tasked to follow the flight at or around its ceiling height of twenty thousand feet, as a precursor to any contact, so they could follow the Hun back to their base of operations. The rest of the flight was around ten thousand feet, in between cloud strata. If contact was made with their target, they were to retreat in good order. Contact with any other enemy planes could be engaged as normal.

Concussion from ground fire, rocked the planes, and announced their arrival over German trenches. If this was seen by enemy planes, they would have a reference point to aim for. Singer's plane clawed upward for more height, and look for privacy over the lower layer of clouds. It was rarely dangerous, considering the amount of shrapnel they threw at them, but it made for uncomfortable flying, and for newbies, it was terrifying. By coincidence, their route took them towards a nest of balloons or 'drecken' as termed by the opposition. It was a good target of opportunity en-route, however it came with its own dangers. They were inevitably protected by an unhealthy amount of artillery and machine guns. Singer hated balloon busting, but he did have a strategy in mind to deal with them, which had been drilled into all his flight from the outset. They gained height rapidly to dive almost vertically onto the target, giving some protection from ground fire. He took them in line astern for one pass only. The guns had a healthy number of incendiary bullets, which would hopefully set them ablaze. They were coming to the apex of height required before dropping one wing to dive. Dick unexpectedly broke formation and turned starboard putting distance from the rest. Adrian faithfully followed him without hesitation, which left Singer hanging, and having to recover his bus to follow. Dicks superb eyesight had caught a movement behind some clouds, which was just a speck at such a distance. At this point he couldn't identify if they were hostile or friendly, but whoever they were, they had height advantage, and were in position to cut Rogue flight off from any line of retreat. It wasn't certain even if the unidentified formation had even seen them, but Dick surmised it would be prudent to find out. Climbing at seven hundred and fifty feet per minute, they may just have enough time to meet them on equal terms. Dick was de facto the new flight leader, as his machine lay ahead of the other two, and it would be his responsibility to determine the fate of them all.

War's fate wasn't kind to them on that day. All the planning, calculations, and preparation had counted for nought, as it transpired that Black flight had found them! They had most certainly been spotted. As they closed Dick counted three machines, painted black, and all seem to be heading just for him. As they drew closer he observed that while all the Hun machines were painted mostly black, each was different from the other. A cursory glance at each one revealed that one was painted with black and white cross hatches, another with black diagonal stripes, and a third in the more conventional camouflage, with black, grey and blue.

Dick signalled the others to revert to line astern, as he headed for the Boche flying towards at a closing speed of nearly two hundred mile per hour. Before they came within firing range he yawed the plane to port for a few seconds, giving the enemy a larger target for them to aim for. The whizz of bullets could be heard buzzing around his head, and the striking of hits on the engine were unnervingly visible, 'bugger it' he thought, 'here we go'. He abruptly reversed the yaw and flew straight for the centre of the formation, in a deadly game of chicken.

All the German planes had by then then targeted the leading plane, and there aim was thrown off by the suicidal English plane heading straight for them. He headed for the smallest of gaps through the centre, and in doing so, completely forgot to use his guns! It was then the Germans broke formation, and Dick's plane shot through them with Adrian and Singer following close behind. The leading SE had smoke emitting from its engine, as it rolled into a spin. His two companions had managed to put in a good number of bursts into several planes, and with all the fire directed at Dickie, they hadn't taken any fire at all. They followed Dickie into a controlled vrille hoping that Dickie was still in control.

His plane dropped away increasing speed rapidly, which he then recovered, and flew with all speed leading them back to their own lines. The Boche were caught completely off guard and could only look on despairingly at the English planes escaping to safety. Three of their machines had been hit, with one aflame and heading for certain destruction. They approached no man's land, with Dickies engine sound becoming rougher, smoke spewing out from the side. He found some comfort from the fact that the others were okay and flew by his side. Abruptly the engine cut out completely, to which he quickly turned off the fuel taps and glided earthward from less than three thousand feet. It would be touch and go if the glide path would take him over friendly territory, His predicament was made worse by the headwind which was not helping a jot. He was at least grateful that the tank hadn't caught fire, and the smoke seemed to be dissipating, so he wasn't frying today at least, he thought!

He was now so low that his plane was receiving ground fire as he flew over the German support trenches. None of it registered with him as he looked to find a place to put the old girl down. Adrian and Singer looked down helplessly having to gain height to put them out of range of machine gun fire. Dickie skimmed low over the German front line trenches. The land ahead was an unending sea of dirty brown earth pockmarked with shell holes as far as he could see. There was no point in picking a spot to land, such was the concentration of crump hole craters hitting one was unavoidable. From fifty feet he aligned the plane to come in level as possible. At the last second, he raised the nose to meet a shallow escarpment. The crate pancaked tail first, ripping off the entire undercarriage. Despite the padding installed around the windscreen Dick face was propelled forward smashing into the windscreen rendering him unconscious. The momentum had the effect of launching what remained of the plane back into the air, and continued in flight for a short time before gravity pulled it back earthward.

He woke up groggily, and felt blood running up his face. This was due to the fact the final resting place found himself upside down, hanging by his harness. He was stuck and couldn't move. Fearing that he was in no man's land, he would be a perfect target for vengeful local enemy fire of all calibres. His eyes came back into focus, and he found himself looking into the grinning face of an infantryman. His bus had finished up upside down immediately over an allied trench, and he had the Good fortune to have friendly hands reaching up to extradite him from the cockpit.

"Welcome to Canada," a voice chirped. "We'll have you out in a jiffy. You there," he barked. "Get a corps man here. We've got a hero here needing attention."

*

The temperature must have been at minus forty degrees, as the SE stood sentinel over the converging adversaries. Jules was sorely tempted to jump the Boche planes, as his added firepower would surely tip the balance. His orders were however to observe and follow. It seemed a matter of seconds before the two units come together, and miraculously both came through the other side without mishap, with the exception of one plane in flames. As to which side the unfortunate pilot was, he couldn't tell from this far out. It finally become clear that it was a Boche plane, as three machines made their way back east, the leading one, with a smoke trail. Jules leaned back and pointed down to his cousin the gaggle of planes reforming and turning east. His job now was to follow them home undetected to that location, In his favour they had height advantage so the Boche artillery hopefully would not identify him as hostile, and in addition, the layer of cloud cover provided some protection, as long as they could still keep their eyes on Hun crates. It wasn't too long until they began to descend to a large airfield, which clearly hosted at least one *Jasta* judging by the number of visible planes stationary on the ground. It was time to turn for home. It wasn't until they were over the front lines that the Boche artillery spotted them and more as a protest fire several desultory rounds in their direction, which at this height didn't even warrant evasive manoeuvres from the two seater.

*

They were congregated in the mess waiting on any news on their missing airman. Someone suggested they go out and search themselves, as they had seen him crash land. This idea was vetoed by Harry as too risky. It was some hours later they got the call that Dick was alive, with cuts, bruises and suspected concussion. By all accounts he was in better shape than his plane that he had pranged. It was obvious from the report that that Dickie would be out of circulation for a while. it was an hour later when then the twins returned with the knowledge of Black flights whereabouts. This left the flight light handed and so Harry gathered his crew around him.

"Gentleman, it's been a good day. We know where our enemy is, we know they are a plane short," some chuckled at that. "Dickie has found a way to spend a few days with Claudette. Yes, all good news. That means our very own Genie is our new replacement."

A big cheer went up with Eugene receiving handshakes and backslapping, "Alas for Eugene, he is now officially a pilot, he is to be expelled from the Château, which is as you all know for ground crew only."

Eugene accepted this sentence with a rueful grin, but in truth he couldn't be happier. Flying with some of the finest airmen on the western front left him thrilled and nervous at the same time.

*

Joe and Albert were working late to modify the 'Brisfit' with an unwieldy camera attached adjacent to the observers' cockpit in preparation for the reconnaissance mission over the enemy airfield in the morning. They needed to pinpoint where the black flight was exactly located. This was explained by Harry to his flight crew. The airfield consisted of several concentrations of plane types, as confirmed by previously taken pictures of the field, and they wouldn't have enough on-board munitions to destroy the entire base. Secondly, they wanted a precision strike on Black flight alone to send a clear message to the enemy.

The ground crew had the engines warmed up before dawn, and all the buses were prepared meticulously as ever for the days foray. As dawn broke, four planes trundled along the grass until enough speed was gained for them to claw for height. The morning was very much as the previous day, with westerly winds and prolific cloud cover. They now knew the location of the airfield, Singer took them on a circuitous route to approach the area from the north. The twin's were flying behind and to starboard of Singer. Genie lay further back keeping station at the same height, and Adrian brought up the rear. It was felt that Adrian's experience would able him to keep station easier, and scan the skies above and behind at the same time, which only veteran pilots can master.

Several clusters of buses could be seen above and below, some hostile, some friendly. All were ignored and dismissed as of being no threat. Intermittent bursts of black Archie burst below and behind them, when they were spotted in between the grey lumbering lumps of cumulus type clouds.

By the time they crossed the Allied front trenches, they were already at six thousand feet. The angled trenches were the only visible contrasting with the brown pockmarked earth interspersed with grotesque remains of trees, and abandoned vehicles. The natural beauty of fields and farmland transformed into unimaginable horror of man-made warfare, which has already ended the lives of so many young men on both sides. Singer reflected on how dreadful conditions were for the PBI, and would understand that from the mud and carnage they endured on a daily basis, there was resentment mixed with envy aimed towards the privileged few heading westward above them.

Their course took them over the Boche lines and towards the rear, where the ground and buildings gradually returned to normality. A few miles further east it was easy to forget a war was going on at all. Singer changed course to approach the airfield. and so far they were unmolested, and seemingly unseen. At twelve thousand feet, he signalled to the others, and cut his engine. The angle of attack was trimmed so they slowly lost height through the clouds. The airfield hove into view and they could now make out clumps of planes, buildings and vehicles. On a predetermined plan the two SE's flew in wide circles leaving Mario to begin with the arduous task of filming, Genie staying with the twins to cover.

Loss of height meant that they were forced to restart the powerful Wolseley Viper engines. Judging by the number of ant like figures running in all directions, Singer had surmised they had already been spotted. They continued to descend as flak and machine gun fire opened up.

It was a safer option that staying at one height. It also distracted any of the Germans from paying any attention to the two machines circling several thousand feet above them. Several Boche machines were now moving slowly in all directions from more than one unit. Departing from his original plan, Singer pushed the stick forward to increase his angle of attack with the speed increasing steadily. He looked behind to discover Adrian on station and mimicking his manoeuvres, which gave much comfort. He checked his wings for any signs of becoming 'unglued' Experienced pilots would look for any buckling of the fabric on the wings, which was a good indicator of the maximum tolerance it could sustain. The wing's remained stable, So Singer could concentrate on his improvised attack run.

It was only going to be one pass, but it may give some insight as to the set up on the ground. Above them the two English planes circled lazily, unobserved by anyone on the ground. Some instinct in Genie prompted him to check the sun, Nothing! He hesitated, and looked again, and still, he couldn't see anything. Without further thought, he quickly turned back the crate one hundred and eighty degrees. 'I'm going get some stick for this' he thought, 'chasing ghosts'. In an instance a black smudge emerged from the glare. They were closing at an incredible rate, and more or less at the same time the two adversaries opened fire. It was just a few seconds when he flew by just feet above a Dv11 no less. The SE was flying relatively slower to the Hun, and turned quickly back as only the SE could. The Albatross flew on, ignoring Genie and using his speed to attack the hapless British reconnaissance plane. Mario waited with his twin Lewis guns trained on the approaching scout. He was somewhat relieved to see that his partner seemed to come out of the first pass unscathed. Jules started to yaw and lure the German closer. Genie had opened the throttle gate to chase after, but the Boche had a good five hundred yards on him.

Singer was now just fifty feet high and approaching the airfield at over two hundred and twenty mph. Below him and already in his sights were five German scouts, probably Pfalz's he thought, and they were starting there take off run. The poor Germans could only look back in despair as they know they were cold meat to the English. They trundled along the grass waiting for the inevitable hail of bullets that will see the end of several of them.

The English planes flew just feet over their heads. The Germans looked up to their erstwhile assassins, and to their astonishment and relief the leading English pilot was leaning from his cockpit and waving to them!

Singer laughed as he flew by in a mad furore. Ahead was his chosen target, some hundred yards ahead. A single Black machine sitting on the grass, unattended. The Vickers and Lewis guns opened up, and a line of dirt spurted up in front of the target. He raised the nose a fraction, and another long burst went straight into it, sparks flying from the engine, bullets going through the cockpit, and down the longeron running the length off the fuselage. He pulled up abruptly and made straight for friendly skies before this hornets' nest could respond. The Black plane alone sat smouldering, with the rest of airfield remaining untouched. Seconds later Adrian flew in on an identical bearing and repeated his friends' endeavours with multiple bursts of explosive and incendiary bullets adding to punishment meted out on this same plane. The petrol tanks were again holed and this time a crump of explosion as the already wrecked plane caught fire. Machine gun and rifle fire began to respond to the raid, and Adrian was the recipient of a smattering of hits, as he flew quickly out of range. The Germans emerged from the shelters shocked and bemused. Many couldn't understand how they had escaped so lightly, with only one plane destroyed. Others grimly acknowledged the clinical nature of the attack, and more than a few understood, and approved of the message that it sent.

Mario braced himself against the straps in preparation of the violent forces that were about to be impinged on his small frame. He just had time to see the flashes of enemy machine gun fire pass by before the pressures and senses impinged on his small frame, Jules threw the plane into the renversement, and Immelmann turn where Mario found himself, again dangling upside down looking for the target to show itself below. Ever the artist Jules had presented the German in line over the unsuspecting Hun, allowing Mario to align his guns to fire ruthlessly into the defenceless plane. Genie was now in range and looked up as his friends flew over him, and recover from the inverted position it previously was. The Boche plane was wounded but obviously still flyable. The twins had presented Genie with his first blooding, and he did not disappoint. As practised and instructed he flew in very close, above and behind, and put in short accurate bursts into his target. Stitches of impact ran up through the body, and into the cockpit. The pilot slumped down into the cockpit, mercifully killed immediately. His plane gently rolled onto its back, its nose pulling it downward to its final resting place some minutes later. Even before the poor pilot had lost consciousness, Jules dispassionately turned his bus for home, understanding the importance of the plates to be delivered. There would invariably be a considerable number of Boche machines now vainly in pursuit. They had enough fuel to take an indirect course home. Singer saw considerable movement of troops, horses and trucks concentrating around Vimy Ridge. They eventually arrived over friendly territory. Below, was the same ant like activity mirrored by the allied armies. The signs were a dead giveaway, there was going to be another scrap, and it was going to take place on their doorstep. Adrian landed without further mishap, but he had to complain to Ernie about a strange rattling from somewhere, which didn't seem to affect the engine's performance, He asked if he could give the Wolseley a going over, and left to make his report.

*

The frustration of being out of action was more than compensated by the attention of Claudette and her family, who fussed over him non-stop. As with all aviators a few days away from flying worked wonders, given all the inherent strain on body and mind. He spent the time sitting outside the cafe, watching the world go by, or taking his girl out for walks in the surrounding country. In the evening he waited impatiently for the chaps to visit for dinner and drinks, and catch up on the day's events.

The cafe was quiet, and Peregrine was enjoying a quiet smoke and a glass of vino, reflecting on the day's events, and anticipating another rendezvous with the lovely Gabrielle. You know, he thought to himself this isn't a bad old war. His work was fairly routine, with good billets and surrounded by staff officers who practically run this sector of operations. His interaction with anything to do with the front line was negligible.

He simply passed bits of paper from one department to another. Two things he did know for certain, one, the trenches were very dangerous places to be, especially for an officer, and two, another push was in the offing, which usually turns up with too many officer casualties. Anyway he reminded himself, keep your head down and a promotion is a certainty, without having to face a shot in anger. Dick entered the room, and as they were the only two people around, some kind of interaction was inevitable.

"Morning to you," Dick ventured.

The Captain looked at Dickie with obvious disdain. "Good morning, Sir, do you not mean! and where's your salute?" he barked. "You RFC types are all the same, slack, insolent, and a disgrace. I've a good mind to put you on a charge."

Two days of rest and recuperation disappeared in an instant, and replaced with white hot anger. He took a step towards the Captain. Damn if he was going to be talked at like that from a pompous fresh faced pen pusher. Fortuitously, Gabrielle and Claudette walked in arm in arm chatting and came in between the two.

"Dickie, here you are. You remember Gabrielle? Of course you do. Hello Captain, how lovely to see you here with us once more." She took Dicks arm firmly, "Come my dear, let us leave these good people alone."

Dick allowed himself to be led out lamely, which was preferable to be in the same room with the obnoxious Captain. Gabrielle sat opposite Peregrine and his line of sight with the upstart pilot was blocked "Hello my dear I am sorry I am a little late," she took his hand, and all thoughts of further angst was quickly forgotten. Dick was frustrated and angry, but he was grateful however avoiding a possible court martial, had he carried out the actions he had in his mind a few moments ago.

*

They were sitting outside eating a particularly delicious chicken dinner and enjoying the early spring sunshine. Sometime later a few of the ground crew joined them, including Ernie who had a wry smile on his face. He stood over Adrian shaking his hand. He turned around bemused to look at Ernie looking very smug.

"Found that little problem with your, um engine sir," he said loudly enough for all to hear. Having got everyone's attention, he elaborately rolled bits of brass cartridges onto the table. "Found these in Joe's nacelle behind you. Spent Bullets from our Boche friends that were meant for you, Sir"

Adrian gaped in incredulity.

"Seems like our Genies invention has some credibility after all. Might have just saved your life" There was an uproar in table bashing, clapping and raucous laughter that greeted this development. Joe was toasted repeatedly, to the point of unconsciousness.

Harry confirmed the rumour of an impending push, and along with a concentration of other squadrons, Rogue flight would be looking to help gain air superiority. Whether this latest stratagem would prove any more successful than previous ones remained to be seen. It was dearly hoped that the higher echelons at staff would have at least learned from previous mistakes, borne at the cost of so much spilt blood on the western front.

It was generally thought that German intelligence was comparable to the allies, and this proved to be the case some days later. The sun was low in the sky, when a lone bus flew just twenty feet above the airfield. There was little time for the ground defences to respond effectively. At almost zero feet, the dark menacing biplane darted straight towards Rogue flight's hangers. It altered its course slightly, and proceeding to pour a hail of fire directly into Adrian's beloved mess. The building seemed to shudder in agony, with the number of bullet impacts that flew on and into the building.

In an instant the plane zoomed upwards almost vertically. Out of the cockpit, a bundle with a streamer was thrown which fell quickly to the ground. The unwelcome visitor continued on, totally unscathed. It was fortunate that the mess was empty at the time, with everyone either working on the planes, or visiting at nearby Le Rouex. They gathered sometime later in the mess and inspected the damage inflicted.

Harry made his way over to where the others were gathered, "Any casualties?" he enquired to no one in particular.

Adrian ventured a response. "'Fraid so Harry. Twelve-year-old malt whisky, hundred per cent casualties. Champagne took a pasting, and considerable collateral damage to the beer supplies." Typical of Adrian, Harry thought, to bring such levity to a serious event.

The company exchanged rueful smiles, and began to inspect the room to find the full extent of the damage inflicted. Joe bought in the package left behind and handed it over to Harry. The contents were in the form of a letter, and for several minutes there was silence in the room, so Harry could scrutinise the contents.

"It's a letter," he mumbled needlessly. "Would someone kindly get some transport. We need to get to Le Rouex".

Everyone who was available was crowded in the back room of the estimanet. Some of the ground crew were left behind working on running repairs and routine maintenance of the aircraft.

Harry waited until the ensemble was settled, drinks and smokes on hand. "Gentlemen, it seems we have an invitation from our friends who call themselves 'Tot Flugal' whatever that means, and one that is specific to us. Myself, Wentworth, Watson and Smythe are all known and named in the invite." He looked for Mario and Jules "You two aren't worth a mention."

They laughed at that. "We have been formally invited to meet them in the skies in seven days' time, weather permitting. I have to say the communique is very formal and polite. No rancour, threats or bluster. More of a 'kill or be killed ' meeting, if you would be so kind!"

Dickie chirped up excitedly. "If they are fucking throwing down the gauntlet, we'll do it, and wipe these arseholes from the sky."

Harry held up one hand to demand silence from the murmur of assent. "Dickie my boy, your brain is still addled from your prang. I blame Claudette. How many times do I have to tell you. We fight smart, brave but smart. This is a stupid idea, and it's not how we fly."

From the back of the room, Adrian unfurled himself from the armchair and stood up. "Sir" he said formally. "You may be right. In fact, you are right, but the Boche know that we are gentleman, and fight like gentlemen, and speaking for all the lads," he looked out to his friends "It's a matter of honour sir, as deep down you know. As for myself, I expect myself to be there."

Jules chirped in unhelpfully "We don't do chivalry as you know sir, me and Mario I mean, but we'll be there"

Harry was remembering the Green debacle, and simply nodded. "But if we don't put in a show, the Germans will never let us forget it. The best of the English running from the superior German aces."

It was a very good point to which Mario added, "The enemy propaganda machine would have a field day with it Harry. We know it, they know it."

The evening disintegrated into small groups drinking and debating the ramifications of the Hun challenge. Harry needed time and space to evaluate all the variables and probabilities such an encounter would involve. Every avenue he considered would involve casualties on both sides, with the survivors enjoying a pyrrhic victory. Somehow, he had to think his way around the problem, keep his men alive, and come away with honour intact. He needed ideas, and someone with ideas, ideas that had nothing to do with chivalry.

*

The pounding the Germans were subjected to seemed to be the usual prelude to an impending attack. A week-long bombardment concentrated in a seven-mile-wide section on the ridge itself. A number of squadrons were put in readiness to protect the airspace, including Rogue flight. Harry knew that the proposed clash with the 'tot lot', an adopted name suggested by Herbert, would coincide with a major battle, which he considered he may be able to use to Rogue flights advantage. They were congregated in the semi-refurbished mess, and all present were encouraged to engage in the debate, They knew they were still light on numbers. Harry asked the ground crew to prepare his bus, as he was more than able to compliment the flight, although he recognised he was a little rusty. Jules and Mario offered to fly scouts, and a couple of Camels were 'borrowed' from next door. The Camels were immediately dispatched to Rogue flight hangers for a complete overhaul, with the usual upgrades to the higher standards they were accustomed to, even though the crew had less experience with the fearsome Rotary engine the Camel's had. Whisky and champagne was still in short supply in the mess, so gin became the popular drink for the evening.

As they relaxed Adrian sidled up to Harry, and topped his glass up for him. "How long has it been Harry, you know, since you've been up?"

Harry feigned injury, "You should know Addie you were up with me a few days ago on that reconnaissance patrol."

Adrian sighed in exasperation, "I meant in combat as you well know." Adrian jumped in.

"True," Harry replied. "But I've always been an athlete Addie, you know that, why I could fly rings around most of those here in the room."

Adrian decided not to push Harry any further. He understood he was a proud man, and yes, he had kept himself in pretty good shape.

From outside the mess, they could see the brilliant flashes of artillery fire lighting up the sky, accompanied by the constant noise of multiple shell impacts. It was quite a show that failed to register the misery of those who were its recipients. The next few days found the flight in full preparation for missions over the battlefield. They now had seven machines being put into a state of readiness, with three of the best pilots active, and four more that would grace any squadron in the RFC.

Back inside, Herbert was talking to the ground crew going over the final details in minute detail. The number of tracers was a topic, as it was suggested they should be reduced. Whether they should fly in formation or pairs was discussed, but it was Singer who provided the most radical proposal that made any sense.

"Chaps, we are flying over a comparatively small area of operations, right? We know that the enemy will be quite visible with their distinctive colours, OK? You will be familiar with the profile of the Albatrosses by now. At least I bloody well hope so," he goaded.

"I would imagine the airspace will be thick with machines in the vicinity, our liveries are fairly innocuous at the moment, so we won't fly anything like a formation of any kind. We'll just blend in to the myriad of buses flying all over the shop, and converge on these bastards when it suits"

It was both brilliant and audacious and met with murmurs of approval. Harry was impressed, and pleased that his little troop had come up with the folds once more.

Adrian moved over to Dick's side. "One more thing all. Our intelligence information is that the flight leader, is the most ruthless little bastard of them all, flies the plane with all Black colours, a white roundel, and red streamers, being the arrogant shit he is. Easy to spot. Take him out first, and that'll shake up the rest of 'em no end"

They now had some sort of strategy to follow, which was further discussed in earnest, Experience told them that after take-off, any and all plans can go awry. Once in the air there could be no further dialogue, and the best laid plans very rarely went well, unless they could adapt to suit.

*

The tenth of April was to be the start of the ground offensive, with a division of Canadians given the pivotal role of taking the ridge. It was part of a number of coordinated offensives on the western front. Preparation for the assault has been meticulous, with the fairly new concept of close artillery support being a key feature. The Canadians would have accurate supporting artillery fire that would be laid in front of the Canadian infantry and the creeping barrage would soften and nullify each of the enemy trench positions. The day was freezing cold with sleet and snow reducing visibility and adding to the misery of all the combatants. Rogue flight spent two days widely dispersed in the horde of supporting aircraft, bombing or staffing the Boche lines. Other scouts flew above in support and providing air cover, and it was with these machines that Rogue flight found itself hiding in plain sight.

Everyone knew in advance the combat zone so there was never an issue in seeking out the opposition. Many variants of crates were in attendance. The Germans had Fokker's, Pfalz, Albatross and AEG's. With the Flights compliment of SE's were Sopwith's, Spad's and Nieuport's. All flying over the slow-moving bomber types below. Dick was flying above a layered squadron of scouts, and his keen eyes identified a concentration of dark painted planes flying obliquely towards them. He zoomed up violently for height, and took the SE into an aileron roll, hoping the rest of the flight would see the manoeuvre, and follow suit.

Looking over his port wing he took his plane initially away from their current position to get them positioned with the sun behind them. All the time, trying to pick out any black machines. He was gratified to see several other planes rising above the rest, some using the cloud cover to good effect. In contrast the 'tot lot', if they were in the area had little or no prospect of identifying the flight. The sky was full of planes closing in on each other for what would be a mass brawl. It didn't take long before Dickie had managed to identify the numerous squadrons in attendance. In less than thirty minutes he saw the ominous dark profile of Albatross scouts. The leader was, as anticipated, at the forefront of the arrowhead formation, with an artful diamond patterned mosaic of Black, blue, red and white covering the wings. The fuselage being all black. Adrian had also spotted them, and picked out two other SE's in the corner of his eye converging stealthily, like a pack of wolves. The Boche planes could not manoeuvre very much even if they had seen the approaching planes, as they were packed in too tightly. The number of escorting planes would normally provide a lot of protection, but on this occasion the distinctive colouring of the planes negated that protection.

By this time Dick and Adrian had converged at the same spot above and behind, hidden in the sun. Singer was analysing the battlefield as usual, predetermining his flight path to cause maximum damage on the first pass. It was Singer who the Germans first spotted, and moved towards in a smoothly executed turn. Seconds later the leader found himself in the centre of a hail of bullets as Dick dived in unseen, and before he could react Dick had dived down below and pulled back up into the formation in a Russian mountain manoeuvre, firing upwards at targets of opportunity as they began to scatter. Almost without respite a second burst poured in along the length of the fuselage and into the cockpit, as Adrian flew by in the opposite direction to Dick, who was now turning to face them head on.

Singer witnessed the ruthless and deadly execution of the leading plane, and quickly broke his own rules, knowing the pilot was doomed. He pitched and rolled over, targeting one of the black machines at the rear, putting in a long deflective burst into where he knew the plane would fly into. The Boche plane staggered, rolled onto its back and lost height rapidly, with flames beginning to emerge from the front. The Boche had now recovered from the initial shock, and although shaken, they were not the types that would immediately dive for home and safety. They would want revenge, and they all believed they were quite capable of exacting it. Genie had found Harry approaching the melee and opted to fly with him. Jules was also coming onto the scene, with Mario having to fly out of harm's way due to engine trouble. Even the attentions of his ground crew could not always avoid situations like this. It may have been their relative inexperience on working on the Camel's rotary engine to blame. Mario was flying smart as had been drilled into him, and his day was over. It was now just a matter of avoiding contact with any other hostile machines, and nurse his bus home. By this time, the air was full of machines in vrilles, rolling, banking and looping all over the sky.

Machines inevitably began to fall from the sky, in flames, in bits, or even seemingly undamaged, until they smashed into the ground.

*

Harry was exuberant and having successfully shot at several Boche planes, he felt the exhilaration of having a thoroughbred killing machine in his hands. The SE was a joy to fly, and in the right hands was the match of anything the enemy could put up. He had inflicted hits on a number of planes. It was like shooting fish in a barrel, he thought. Genie matched Harry's manoeuvres and fired at targets as they came across him. In all the excitement it was the lack of recent combat hours that Harry completely forgot to prioritise the Black buses. Adrenaline was pumping through, and the exquisite thrill of air combat flooded through his frame. Singer observed one of the black planes, which was stalking a Camel, probably belonging to another flight, he thought. A quick scan of the skies confirmed no immediate threats., and he patiently stalked his prey. It was of matter of minutes before the he found himself in a favourable position to attack. From sixty yards abeam, the German finally saw the threat and threw himself into a series of sharp turns and rolls. He was good, very good. His evasive tactics would have thrown most pilots off, however Singer coolly matched his opponent, without as yet firing a shot.

Having lost some thousands of feet trying to shake off the English flyer, the German put the nose up violently prior to putting the Albatross into a controlled vrille, which would lose this persistent English flyer. The problem was, Singer had anticipated the manoeuvre, and closed range as the Boche plane approached stall speed prior to going into the spin. Singers two machine guns opened up The first bursts going through the tail and elevators. Immediately followed by a second travelling up the fuselage and into the cockpit, clearly hitting the pilot. The stricken bus was still apparently under some control, but it flew erratically straight and slow. Singer bought his plane alongside. Perhaps he could escort his victim back to an allied airfield, he thought. The Hun had flown with consummate skill, and deserved the option of survival. Slowly his opponent looked over to Singer, and smiled. At the same time, he produced a pistol and let off a few rounds in Singers direction, without any conviction of scoring a hit. Understanding the Huns wishes, Singer quickly turned around bought his plane behind the wounded pilot. He sent a long purposeful burst into him, and flew off without giving it further thought. He didn't even bother to watch the final dive of the dead airman. This episode was looked on by Harry with approval and pride. Neither he nor Mario spotted a dark shape closing in from above. Bullets pummelled Harry's right wing and seconds later into his cockpit. Both of Harry's legs were hit, as well as his right hand. He turned away to the right in a tight turn as the Fokker overshot. He still maintained control, and the engine rumbled on without any ill effect. A quick assessment of his plight, confirmed he could just still fly, and survive. He resigned himself to the fact that he would end up probably as half a man, never to fly again. It wasn't a kind of future he would want.

Adrian was in trouble, and he was in the fight of his life. He was trapped two on one, and he was losing. His bus had already received a number of hits, but as yet nowhere vital. He himself hadn't managed to get a bead on either of them. The leading Boche was expertly corralling the SE into his line of fire. It was a desperate situation he found himself, and options were coming up short He thought to himself, this may be his last few seconds on earth, which comes unexpectedly to all aviators at some point, and this may just be his time. All of a sudden a large shadow emerged from above, followed a split second later by the sickening sound of two planes colliding. It was Harry's machine, which had deliberately rammed the Hun. Both hung motionless for an instant, before falling to earth, still entangled. Adrian was sick and shocked to the core. His anger and pain manifested itself into a murderous dog fight with the remaining Hun. In a matter of a minute the German was in flames, and was doomed. Adrian changed drums, and followed his victim down to earth, still firing relentlessly until his ammunition ran dry. With tears flowing from his eyes, he made his mournful way home.

CHAPTER SEVEN

Messines

The mood in the mess was understandably sombre, Harry was dead, and Mario had gone missing. All the buses had significant damage of sorts, and the crew had their work cut out to make Rogue flight viable for tomorrow. The drinking began with purpose. It was needed to numb the shock, and assimilate the day's events, even to relive the fight over and over again. The conversations were quiet and stilted. Jules was making enquiries as to the fate of his kinsman. Eugene, John and Adrian sat quietly by the fire, warming themselves. At the moment they were two men down, and they still had a battle to fight. The fact that the 'Tot lot' had been destroyed was of little comfort.

Herbert took it upon himself to call RFC Brigade with the news. He returned sometime later, and called the flight together.

"Pardon the intrusion gentleman. As you all have had a rough day, I took it upon myself to call Brigade to find out where we stand. Murmurs of approval was the initial response. The push is going well, with the

Canadians making significant gains. They anticipate one more day of fighting before all the main objectives are met."

John Singh-Smythe," he said formally. "You are to take overall command of the flight. Congratulations." He went over and shook Singer's hand, others followed suit.

"The lads are all behind you sir, and I'm sure Harry would have approved heartily."

Singer wasn't in the mood for speeches or celebrations, but accepted the accolade with quiet dignity.

"I'm just off now to tell the lad's still in the hangers the good news." Before he left the mess Herbert whispered into John's ear, John left the group around the fire and sought out Jules, who sat morosely on his own. "Jules, we've had confirmation that Mario's bus was seen to have landed under control, but unfortunately on the Boche side of the lines."

Jules didn't immediately react to the news. "The picture is still confused and fluid, and we haven't had anything to confirm his capture, but Jules, he's alive, let's be thankful for that eh!"

Jules nodded, "Thanks John, er Sir."

John replied. "Always John to you my friend. We've been through too much to make it any different now."

Jules had already started the process of contacting his kinsmen to find out where they would have taken him.

The Romany way of life, and was not one to be inconvenienced by this war. They had ways of communicating between themselves irrespective of the stagnant lines separating the two sides,

*

The village of Le Roeux was inundated with uniforms, and the cafe was temporarily overwhelmed with customers. It was all hands-on board for the family. Claudette managed to get Gabrielle to help out. Of late Claudette had put a lot of effort into engaging with her, resulting in them becoming good friends, It was part of her thinking that it was the best way to keep an eye on matters, and befriend her. To Claudette's surprise, it was easier than first thought. As it turned out, Gabrielle was quiet a lonely, insecure girl, who welcomed genuine companionship, this time with no strings attached. As quick as the village filled up, it emptied just as fast, with the transient infantry merely passing though. It was just as well, as they had practically nothing left. Eventually they sat down to take the weight off their feet, and enjoyed some coffee and cigarettes in the quiet aftermath.

Claudette filled Gabrielle's cup. "That boy you are with Cherie, he seems to be an unpleasant type, not at all suitable for you, no?

Gabrielle shrugged her shoulders. "That English," she spat. "You must know I only see him for money. English swine he is, oh, pardon, forgive me, your man is English."

Claudette was a little taken aback at the venom coming from her friend, as the mask dropped for a moment. Gabrielle didn't stop there however, "I loathe all men like him, he is without honour. That they must pay to be with a woman."

Claudette said nothing but looked on in sympathy.

"What else must I do?" she asked no one in particular. "Our family have no money, all too old or too young. All the men, gone, just my Mama and my little sisters left," She cried a little to herself.

Claudette reflected for a moment. "You are right, my man is English, but he could have been German, and I would still love him, you see, a woman's heart has nothing to do with nations, but. I think he will die, just like all the others," she sighed. "They all do don't they?" she continued "And if he doesn't, will he stay here? Go back to his own country? No, there is no future for us I think," and Claudette found herself almost believing it. Her hands instinctively went to cover her abdomen as if to protect the spark of life she suspected was within her. What would become of them all?

*

He stood impotently by the wrecked machine. There wasn't any time to set it on fire, although in truth, there wasn't much left to be of any use to the enemy. it was one of those occasions that Mario wished he didn't understand German. The first group that approached looked non too friendly. There was some talk of shooting him outright, before any officer came. This was by no means an unusual event, especially if the said troops had been strafed recently. They were certainly a mean looking bunch, who began to roughly handle their prisoner, whilst removing any articles of value he had upon his person. He was about to lose his boots, before a large NCO appeared in the midst, and barked out threats and commands. The crowd meekly dispersed with their spoils, leaving Mario and the German Sergeant alone. He was asked a number of questions, to which Mario feigned ignorance. He understood every word the Sergeant said, and even recognised his Bavarian accent, but he thought to keep his powder dry, as it may provide an advantage at some point in the near future.

He only knew his captors name as Braun, but he turned out to be a genial host, and offered his charge foul tasting cigarettes and harsh ersatz coffee. They remained close to the wreck for a considerable time, and the reason for that eventually became clear. Mario looked on as a large car approached them slowly and came to a halt a few yards away. Mario stood up knowing the new arrival was for his benefit. A smart looking German aviator saluted formally introduced himself in his native language. He returned the salute casually, but remained silent.

The lieutenant held up a hand in apology and reverted to English. "My name is Lieutenant Paul Toelke. I am here to escort you to our squadron as a welcome. Have you been treated well?" He held out his hand.

Mario took the German's hand firmly. "Thank you, yes, your Sergeant here has been most accommodating. May

I compliment you on your English. Sergeant Mario Wallenburg at your service," Paul beamed at the compliment, "Thank you Sergeant, may I address you as Mario. We are to be friends I hope."

In the car Paul explained he was to be taken to the nearby aerodrome for dinner as guest of honour. Mario found Paul to be quite endearing, which was a common thread for most pilots either side of the war. He chattered on about his family, his comrades but mostly about flying. There wasn't any mention of conflict or boorish boasting, Paul was impeccably polite, and seemed genuinely delighted to make his acquaintance.

In time they were waved through the gate entrance of an aerodrome, where Mario readily identified the traditional layout of front-line airfield. Hangers, fuel bowsers, and a tower, very similar to his own, as well an assortment of ancillary buildings, mostly of a temporary nature. Paul took him to his billet to freshen up before dinner. The room was sparsely decorated with a bed, a stool and a bucket. On the far side was a small window for light, not big enough to climb through, he reflected. Mario quietly followed, and engage his guide in trivial conversation, and at the same time his eyes were registering everything of note that may be of use in any attempt to escape.

*

Orders were given to move Rogue to yet to another location, this time at La Lovie. Herbert considered the constant upheaval disruptive and rather tedious. At his suggestion they made arrangements to operate a two-base system. They would leave everything behind except for most of the machines, and set up duplicate facilities at their new home. If they had to move again, they could use all the gear left behind from where they are now.

John was advised to set up out of sight of the Château, which was stuffed full of senior red tabbed Staff officers, who would not appreciate way the flight operated.

After landing John found an area of rough grassland and hedgerows in some dead ground, which couldn't be seen from the Château. Herbert was impressed. "Worthy of Wellington himself," he concluded. The arrival of the SE's didn't go entirely noticed however, and it wasn't long before he was summoned for a briefing. He was relieved to see General Barrington was present in the meeting, which comprised of officers from other squadrons based there. The usual array of maps were laid out on a table. The General began with an overview of the mission the RFC was to undertake.

"Gentlemen we are to prepare the ground for a push on a ridge near Ypres, here." A cane tapped on a one of the larger maps. "Messines," He state flatly. "This operation in support of an infantry attack at a date yet to be determined. The General stood to one side. "This is an officer from the Royal engineers who will fill you in."

The Captain gave some further insights as to the methodology off the attack, which involved the use of a creeping barrage, and the use of tanks again. The RFC would be expected to support the assault with ground continuous patrols of ground strafing and bombing. Before that momentous day however, they had a task for the RFC that had never tried before.

It transpired that the engineers were digging a series of tunnels towards the Boche trenches on the ridge. It was planned to plant explosives underneath which were to be detonated just prior to the attack. The Boche of course were digging their own tunnels, to locate and disrupt the tunnels. The problem was that tunnelling was noisy, and the enemy could listen in and simply dig in that direction. The RFC were given the task to fly over the area continuously on daytime low-level patrols, as a nuisance, but more importantly to provide noise, and lots of it. At night, the artillery would provide a relatively small but continuous barrage for the same purpose. The briefing was over, and the assembly dispersed. John was uncertain as to why Rogue flight was invited, as surely, they're few machines wouldn't make much difference.

General Barrington led him into an ante room, where he was met by two RFC types. "Captain Singh-Smythe I would like you to meet Lieutenant's Peter Cauldwell and Aubrey Haviland.

They shook hands formally. "These fine chaps were sent on to me by dear Billy Bishop." The General explained. "I did ask Billy if he would join us, but he sent his apologies, citing the fact he likes to fly alone, but did recommend these fine chaps here to bolster the ranks"

Cauldwell was a tall fair haired New Zealander, who had previously served with 56 squadron. A confident, independent individual who made friends easily. The other was another Brummie, however Haviland, was from a far more privileged background than their very own Dickie Watson.

Aubrey was a lot smaller, and carried a manicured moustache. Both had the air of capable aviators. "Persuaded them to transfer using your name of course John."

He studied them both silently. "Do they know our modus operandi David? No kills, no medals, no recognition."

Barrington nodded. "All explained John, including Addie's free bar. I've also got you a couple of fine chaps to add to the ground crew, both cracking fellows."

The General took them back all back into the briefing room, which was now deserted. They went over the photographs around Messines ridge, Rogue flight's role would be to provide protection to the low flying squadrons below, a job well suited to them. It was also a good opportunity to get the new arrivals blooded in terms of how the flight operates. John led them from the Chateau back to the mess. He ventured. "How did you chaps find your way into our neck of the woods?"

Peter looked knowingly at Aubrey. "Aubrey here was stuck in training squadron's sir. I was with 56 squadron. Heard some whispers about you fella's, and here I am. The General thought it would be amusing if he just put a couple of SE's in front of us as bait. Aubrey here was furnished with a map with this 'drome circled, and that was it."

John laughed at that. Peter continued. "Think it might have been some sort of test. We spent bloody days getting here, only for the ground crew here to take 'em away as soon as we landed.".

John stopped suddenly. "First lesson... Peter, isn't it? Those crew as you call them are now your best friends. The work they are doing now on your machines will keep you alive, if you've your wits about you, My guess is they would have been working through tonight to modify your buses, to fly quicker, turn tighter, and not fall apart in your first bust up with the Boche. Take my advice, buy 'em all a drink when you meet them next"

*

Claudette was taking a chance she knew, but she had seen a vulnerable side to Gabrielle. She offered her a place to work in the cafe, so she may give up her other work. She didn't elaborate that she knew of her previous clandestine incarnation. In turn Gabrielle promised to apply herself to her new work. She was relieved and grateful to have a new opportunity at a normal life, which her friend had given her. Claudette informed the authorities of her arbitrary decision, and was dismissive of any concerns raised or other consequences. She would of course keep a close eye on things, and report anything untoward. It was a few days into her new life, when Captain Peregrine Cotter arrived looking to perpetuate his tryst with the lovely Gabrielle. He was intercepted by Claudette who told him in no uncertain terms he was no longer welcome.

Cotter flew into a fit of rage. "You will tell me where she is," he demanded. "Do not presume to interfere Madam, I could have this place shut down, just like that." He clicked his fingers and took a step closer at the same time, Claudette stood her ground" You must leave. Gabrielle will not see you now, or ever." Cotter muttered some threats and left frustrated and angry, with thoughts of revenge and consequences swirling in his head.

She decided to call her contact who she hadn't heard from since her decision to remove Gabrielle from danger. This set off a series of events which had probably been in place regardless.

The visitor that Gabrielle had her clandestine meetings with was picked up. Cotter was transferred to a front-line Regiment with immediate dispatch. Claudette was allowed to keep Gabrielle under her wing but under close supervision.

Captain Cotter obnoxious ways did not go down well on the front line. He was extremely vexed to have been rudely yanked from his comfortable posting to a company of volunteer country 'oiks', and he spared no time in taking it out all and sundry. In return no one cared to show him any field craft or the necessary ways of the trenches. Cotter was forever cursing the mud, the food and his men, as he trudged through the narrow trenches. His uniform was splattered with mud, and his feet were wet and freezing. He made his way to the little bunker that was little more than an improvised wooden dug out that was now his home.

One of the primary rules he never learnt in the trenches, is to keep your bloody head down. A Hun sniper shot him through the head within a week of being posted. He was irreverently tossed over the side by his own men, not even worth a burial. His final remains lay in no man's land, until a whizz bang left no trace he had ever existed.

*

Mario did his best to make himself presentable, He was to represent the RFC in the company of his enemy. Paul came to escort him over. "Do not worry my friend, our people are here to meet you as the guest of honour. They are like excitable children tonight, and very proud to have you in their midst" Mario was touched by his friends concern, He was a little nervous, as he had only ever seen such men behind the sights of his Aldis.

They were greeted by a roar of noise as they entered the dining room. One by one they came to shake his and slap him on the back. He recognised common German phrases for comrade and welcome, with a few references as to his squadron, and the plane he was found with. He could just as well have been in his own mess on the other side of the lines, such was the similarities.

Even before he had the chance to sit down. he was given a stein of beer, Many of them had obviously been drinking some time before his arrival,

Fervent questions assailed Mario from all sides, with Paul there to interpret. Paul had some difficulty in keeping order, such was the volume of noise, and poor Paul was being verbally assailed from all sides. Mario let himself enjoy the moment and began to relax amongst his fellow aviators. They sat down to dinner, which was impressive in its presentation and substance, Mario confined himself to complimenting the food, the quality of their flying and the machines they had, which seemed to go down very well, They had now moved on to the wine, which was freely flowing,

He was caught out on one occasion where a young pilot made references to a colleague about the Se5a and a name which came out in English ' Sewing machine' which was the name of Singer's crate.

Paul leaned over to him. "He is asking if you fly with Captain Smythe. He thinks your planes markings, were the ones who destroyed our black planes."

This was awkward, there was no denying the evidence of his SE, which was there for all to see. He went to pick up his glass of wine to forestall an answer, and noticed a palpable silence had descended in the room. His game was up he knew. Fate was in his own hands once more he decided, so let it be. He turned to Paul. "So you say they were destroyed then?" he smiled malevolently.

"Yes, that was our mission," he said flatly. Paul dutifully relayed his response word for word. An ominous silence followed by reference's to the black flight. The man who had originally asked him the question made his way towards Mario and stood before him. He looked at Paul and made a statement, which Mario understood anyway.

Paul said quietly. "We apologise to you and to your Captain. We are soldiers and fight for our Fatherland, but we fight with honour. This is not our way," he shook Mario's and smiled. "Tot Flugal is Kaput."

The spell was broken with an enormous cheer from all within the room. Mario breathed a sigh of relief at this unexpected turn of events, The crisis was over, and the drinking continued with abandon. Paul led the toasts from then on, which seemed never ending. He showed some pictures of his family, and his girlfriend, followed by his address which he had already written down. "May we meet again Mario, after the war I mean, you must come and visit, yes?"

Once again Mario was touched by his companions sincerity. It was clear that he was supposed to get blinding drunk, as a parting gesture, before being taken back to Germany to sit out the war. The whisky and brandy followed with champagne. Mario duly drank steadily, but remained sober. They wouldn't know that his Romany heritage came with a legacy of extreme tolerance to alcohol, as many of his colleagues back at the mess could attest. At some point Mario decided to declare himself ready to retire, which satisfied his hosts, that their work was done. They soon began to disperse slowly. Paul was asked by one of the more astute pilots as to where Mario was to sleep, and advised he put a guard on his door. Paul reluctantly agreed, although he doubted if it was at all necessary given the circumstances.

"I will take you back now my friend to sleep. In the morning there will be someone to take you back to Germany. Is there anything else I can do for you?"

Mario pulled himself up unsteadily. "That bottle of brandy on the table would be nice Paul. keep me warm through the night."

They made their way out, where Mario availed himself of a large heavy greatcoat hanging from the wall, and carried on without pause to follow Paul to his billet. Farewells were brief but meaningful. Paul left him with his guard outside his room, and promised to see him off in the morning.

It was the same room he had been in previously before dinner. the guard was stationed outside in the cold, and he didn't look to happy about it. Mario gave him the bottle of brandy, which was gratefully received as some sort of compensation. He had formulated a tenuous plan to escape, which would depend on the guard drinking himself into insensibility, and slipping by him sometime during the night. The lock would not be a problem, as he had learned the art of picking locks in the encampments when he was a child. The equipment for which remained untouched inside his boot. Patience was part of the strategy, and so Mario used the time to revisit the window. It was tiny, but he was curious to see if he could prise the frame away to enlarge the opening. With some effort and little noise he managed to take the frame out, which left a bigger gap, unfortunately what was left had several sharp edges. He decided to get a couple of hours sleep before deciding what to do. In the early hours he revised his plan and decided to try the window. He was a small man with some knowledge and experience with contortionist techniques in the circus. He threw most of his clothes out of the window, including the coat he had borrowed, leaving just his shirt and underwear to give some protection against chafing against the jagged wall opening. He was committed now, and so, carefully he led with his legs and slowly pushed himself through the aperture. He was cut to ribbons from head to toe, but he finally squeezed himself through an impossibly small space. After squeezing through he dressed himself and made his way toward where the guard was. He was found to be sat propped up against the building, sound asleep. He could have walked through the front door after all! Mario wrapped the large greatcoat around himself and made for the guard gate at the front of the aerodrome. This now was not the time for subterfuge, he thought. This phase of the escape now required boldness. He confidently strode over the open ground, and for some reason even he couldn't reason, he stopped to ask one of the guards for a cigarette, and engaged in trivial conversation, before making his farewell's and strolling nonchalantly through the gates to disappear into the night.

*

The patrols were organised so that Rogue flight could keep a presence over the trenches in pairs. Singer would take Eugene, Adrian would have Peter with Jules, switching to an SE, having Aubrey. Dick was given extended leave to recover from his injuries, and was packed off to England with a lift from a friendly two-seater. It was Rogue flights job to protect the planes flying low over and around the ridge. They were there just to make a nuisance of themselves and of course noise. it would be a matter of judgement to fly low enough to be heard, and high enough to escape the lethal small arms fire from below. If they got it right they could stay in the air for a couple of hours in relative comfort, if they were left alone, that is from hostile enemy scouts.

Historically the German Imperial Airforce were reluctant to cross over to the allied side of the lines, being content to fight the war preferably over friendly territory. It was Singer who was first to encounter a flight of brightly coloured Fokker's who ventured over to contest supremacy over the ridge. Singer signalled Eugene to come alongside before taking them both down through light clouds to attack. The leader was identified easily as being the leading plane, with the obligatory streamers. They were still some half a mile from the slow-moving, low-level targets ahead. They were bounced by the pair coming down at over one hundred and thirty miles per hour from the port side and above. Singer concentrated on the lead plane, which took multiple hits to the cockpit and engine, before they knew they were there. Eugene carefully latched onto one at the rear, and fired one long burst, before his Vickers jammed. The formation immediately broke apart and fled to the east. Singer's bullets had a devastating effect on the Fokker's engine, which stopped, as did the propeller. The wounded pilot remained immobile, and was unable to do anything but keep his bus from going into a spin. At this low height he just managed to stay under some control. The plane hit the ground with enough force to flip over onto its back, breaking the unfortunate pilots neck, killing him instantly. Eugene's victim fared no better, with his machine bursting into flame. He was fortunate to hit the ground, before the flames could reach the cockpit. The German was found alive, and was taken to hospital, where he died of his injuries just two days later. The other two Fokker's escaped without incident without firing a shot.

He looked over towards Eugene flying alongside, with approval. He was going to become a fine pilot, if he could stay alive!

*

The train sat idly for over an hour, in which time Dick had fallen asleep alone in the carriage. There was the noise of new arrivals vying for seats in the near empty carriages. Dick stirred into a sort of consciousness, disturbing the quiet that he had enjoyed. Men's harsh voices mixed with the trample of boots, doors opening and arguments between different groups. The door to Dick's carriage was roughly slid open, and a group of infantry stood at the threshold looking in at the empty seats. Dick had his feet up on the opposite seat. A large coat was being used as a blanket with his cap keeping out the light. The men were from the Warwickshire infantry, on their way home to Birmingham. There was five empty seats going begging, with what looked like an officer hogging it to himself. Out of habit, they hesitated to intrude, and began speculating on their next course of action.

From underneath his RFC cap a voice rasped out. "You lads coming in or what, you're letting the bloody cold in?" Dick sat up and motioned them to avail themselves of the seats. In a few moments, the sets were filled with words of appreciation. They stared at his uniform.

"Thank you sir," one of them ventured. "You, look like and officer, but you sound like one of us."

Dick was now sat up straight and fully awake. "Dick Watson from Hockley Brook, nice to meet you," he announced.

*

It was all familiar, but he had changed, and he found himself looking at the place he had called home from a completely new perspective. He thought he would despise the grime, dirt, and poverty. Folk walking with their heads down, walking in every direction. Then there was the noise and smells that were strangely comforting, The myriad of small local shops, and pubs on every corner, the trams, and horse carriages going in every direction, He was home, and he embraced its vibrant feel, which he had been deprived off for so long. He stood before the tiny two up two down terraced house where his family still lived, For no reason he could fathom he chose to knock on the door. rather than just going in, as he had always had previously. The reunion was predictably emotional, and plans were made on the spot to celebrate Dick's return. He found himself sat in front of the kitchen fire in his dad's favourite chair. He soon fell into a deep sleep, from which he didn't emerge for the rest of the day.

*

The cafe looked delightful at this time of year. The flowers and fauna around the square together with the little tables and chairs was an oasis of tranquillity. The little water pump and fountain complimented its distinctive charm. In the little while that Gabrielle had joined the family, she proved to be a revelation, as she seamlessly fitting in with the busy schedules. In a short space of time, she had several innovative ideas showing a degree of untapped acumen, and began to implement improvements to increase its profitability. So much so that Mama Faure could take things a lot easier now. It was perhaps inevitable that she and Claudette were fast becoming close friends.

They were sat outside the cafe watching the files of infantry marching through. Column after column filed though. Gabrielle ventured. "Such a shame, what a shame. Those poor boys"

Chloe smiled in sympathy. "It is this terrible war."

It was all Chloe could think to say in sympathy. "No, no Chloe, you do not understand. All those men, hungry men, with no time to stop to eat."

Chloe was distracted by the handsome men looking back at her appreciatively. "Mmmm," was all she managed in response.

She sought out Claudette later that day, and laid out here idea to expand the business. With some reservations Gabrielle was allowed to try it out. She persuaded a couple of women at a loose end from the village to help, with the promise of extra provisions for their families in lieu of pay. A few signs were put up a mile either side of the hamlet. Within a week marching soldiers could pick up prepared packages of food, without stopping but for a few seconds. The initiative was so successful, they ran out of provisions very quickly, and had to barter for more foodstuffs from neighbouring boroughs. Claudette was so impressed with its success, she persuaded Mama to promote Gabrielle to a full partner in the business.

Claudette was reading Dick's letter for the third time, before putting pen to paper. She wrote lovingly to him, and as ever told him how much he was missed. She didn't have the courage to tell him she thought she was with child, but stayed on safer topics. She wrote at length of Gabrielle's success, and what a tower of strength she had been. He wouldn't receive her letter until he returned from leave, but it gave her comfort to know he would be thinking of her.

*

It had been a long day of patrols, and both the pilots and ground crew were feeling the strain. The long summer day's meant longer hours in the air, and when they returned, it was down to the ground crew to repair, replenish and service. Herbert now had the able help of Bill Mellor to rotate the shifts, so the men would remain in good shape, as well as the buses they were responsible for. Adrian was looking forward to his first drink, and some dinner. In truth it was the drink he looked forward to more. His nerves were on edge, and the strain was starting to show. Contact with the enemy had been intermittent, but they were all aware now of certain symptoms of fatigue that has rendered many pilots unfit to fly, often permanently. He received a message to report to the Château. That was it, no name, nothing. It was the last thing he needed right now.

"Jules, I'm needed at the Château, God knows why? See you at dinner."

Jules thrust out his hand which magically had a glass of whisky. "Here, take your medicine before you go. By and by, I've had word from the family about Mario." He left Adrian dangling for further details, but Jules just put his finger to his lips, and walked away.

Adrian was ushered into one of the many rooms towards the rear of the Château, and came face to face with his father.

"Hello Adrian," he said simply. Adrian was at a loss for words. He hardly knew the man that was his father. The scowl was apparent on his face, as he took in this unexpected turn of events. He didn't hate the man, in many ways he had been very good to him. He just didn't know who he was.

"Hello, er sorry. I've had a long day, why are you here? I mean, no disrespect, but this is a military establishment"

Lord Willerby Townsend motioned his son to take a seat, and proceeded to pour two glasses of whisky from the decanter. "My fault my boy. There's a lot you don't know about me. That does not mean I have not followed your life career with great interest."

Adrian scowled at that. "I wouldn't know, why would I? You have never been there for me. Interest, what interest?"

Willerby let his son vent his anger. he leaned over to refill his glass. "To the extent son that I have been made aware of the strain you are under, and the fact you are drinking too much." Adrian was appalled and impressed at the same time at the extent of his knowledge.

Lord Willerby chatted on for some time, much of which was about his mother, which was his first love. The family made sure that nothing came of the romance, as being deemed unsuitable, and so he dutifully married within the aristocracy. The marriage bore two sons, one of whom sadly was killed in 1916.

Adrian appreciated the generous allowance he had been the beneficiary of all his life. He had even been allowed to use the family's name, which was certainly due to the influence of his mother. He wasn't aware however of his father's influence in ensuring his mother's haberdashery shop, she had built up in the past few years, which had flourished under her management.

"You would know of course my wife died a few years since. I recently, by chance, came across your mother and we have kept in touch." Adrian thought he saw his father looking vulnerable for the first time ever, He was not sure where this conversation was going, but he knew for sure that the coming together of the pair would not have been by chance as he described, He was a wily old fox, and obviously well connected.

"Thing is m'boy as odd as it may seem, I would like permission to court your mother" Adrian had to stop himself laughing in his father's face at the absurdity of it, but he caught the look of sincerity in his eyes, which stopped him short.

"Your serious aren't you?" It was all he could think of to say, Willerby just nodded absently, "How is your good friend Dick by the way. I understand he pranged his bus."

Adrian was confused as to why he would change the topic of conversation. "Er, yes. He's back any day now, All fit and well thank you." Willerby took a sip and leaned back in the chair. "He has a girlfriend I believe, French. Claudette that's it, and a friend, let me see Gabrielle."

Adrian understood this was no idle gossip, but was impressed by the depth of knowledge he had in his possession. "I do believe that our Gabrielle was a naughty girl, got herself in some trouble. Some staff wallah with a loose tongue, and an undesirable guest from the other side?"

Adrians scowl disappeared, and couldn't help but smile, He now understood. It was his father who had a hand in getting Captain Cotter transferred to the front, disposed of the agent, and kept it all under wraps. It made sense now, that's why he has free access to places like this, and there was surely more to this man than meets the eye. Adrian stood up, and offered his glass in a toast, "Permission granted," he said simply.

*

Dick's return to the cause gave everyone a big lift, and was the catalyst for celebrations. As much as he enjoyed some time with his family, he had been itching be back. Adrian uncharacteristically gave his young friend a big bear hug. John was glad of the timely addition of a further machine to help with the workload, but as they were working in pairs, they had no one for Dick to fly with.

Later in the evening Jules had returned from one of his trips beyond the airfield, Adrian grabbed a beer for him and went over to see how he was. Jules took the drink, and drained the glass in one go.

"Thirsty work Addie"

He ignored Adrian's protestations and went to get a refill.

"C'mon Jules give it up, you have that look on your face when you are up to something."

Jules looked offended.

"We know that Mario landed safety. We know he was taken prisoner." Adrian waited for more, but Jules remained silent. Jules grabbed his arm and pulled him closer.

"We heard he made to escape, so they tell me, the family I mean."

Adrian knew he was now being teased, and decided to play along.

"He escaped as it happens."

By now a few others had gathered around to hear the tale. "He went to look for his kinsfolk, who were in fact looking for him, and as it happens, they met."

Jules took another long slow pull on his beer. looking back at his captive audience. One or two were asking questions which Jules studiously ignored.

John and Dick were also listening in to the unfolding tale. "They made an attempt to bring him back through the lines just last night, you know, the way we do," he decided to put them out of their misery. "Mario made safe passage two hours ago, and as we speak is enjoying an overdue shower courtesy of King George."

The mess erupted into a cacophony of cheers and congratulations. It would be some time before they would learn the entire detail of this episode, but for now it was enough to know that one of their lost souls had returned. John nudged Dick in the arm. "Think we might have found you someone to fly with"

*

It became necessary to put up two flights of two machines, as the Hun were becoming more aggressive, and put more of their scouts in the air to contest the skies. Both sides knew an attack was pending, and air supremacy was a priority for both antagonists. Rogue flight needed to double the numbers to prevent being overwhelmed in numbers.

Dick and Adrian were up with Aubrey and Peter. They were at three thousand feet watching over a dozen assortment of slow-moving reconnaissance and light bombers, mixed in with scout planes to complete the picture. Rogue were flying a pattern similar to the Lufbery circle, but in this case over a wide circle of sky covering nearly three miles. It was a suggestion by Aubrey, which was readily adopted, where the pilots could collectively keep eyes on all points in the sky. Eugene eyes landed on some specks in the sky unusually coming from behind their own side of the lines. He hesitated for a moment as they were too far away to be identified. He chastised himself for his naivety They must be hostile, as they had the white fluffy puffs around them, confirmed they were being shot at by our own artillery, Dickie's SE flew back over the top of Eugene, with Adrian in tow. His keen eyes had also locked on, and he had reversed his course to attack. The difference was that he was a veteran flyer, with the quicker reflex actions that come with it. Eugene and Peter had to respond quickly to get back on station. Dickie looked astern briefly and appreciated the fact they both had responded with laudable swiftness. The Boche planes were stacked two deep as they approached, and were in a relatively tight formation. The SE's had a slight height advantage as the two sides met. They were up against some brightly coloured scouts, several of which were triplanes. The four SE's had a speed advantage which they used to dive down from a quarter angle and put in a burst without fear of the enemy guns being able to reply. Adrian focused on the lead plane and witnessed the effect of his attack as bullets impacted on the rear end, and rudder. He never noticed that one of the triplanes had followed his line of flight. The Boche turned flatly on its axis, putting the twin Spandau's slightly ahead. Adrian felt rather than saw the bullet impacts on his engine, through his cockpit and down the port side behind him. The SE's engine screamed in protest, and the cockpit was holed multiple times, with several of the instruments taking hits inside. Mercifully, he was not hurt, but the stick in his hand told him he was in a world of trouble.

Peter and Dick harried the Boche relentlessly, by diving down and through, zooming back above the pack ready to repeat the manoeuvre. Many of the enemy planes had been on the receiving end of at least one burst from the elusive SE's. Of the few that did manage to engage the lower formations, found they were welcomed by more scouts and two-seater's, who were in sufficient numbers to ward off any meaningful attack. Eugene watched with some concern at the precarious situation poor Adrian was in. His machine was intent on going into a spin, and using the rudder and stick he could just manage to recover, only for his stricken bus to do the same. Every time he came out of the spin, he had lost hundreds of feet in height. He was sweating profusely in the effort of keeping the plane viable, otherwise, it would go into an unrecoverable dive from which he wouldn't recover. Eugene watched in horror at this pantomime of death being played out. To make things worse, the triplane that had wounded the SE was following his victim down, and waiting for an opportunity to finish off his kill.

Eugene in turn stalked the Boche patiently above and behind. He dived down to get the SE pointing upwards just twenty yards behind. Three short bursts from the two machine guns, ripped through man and machine in seconds. The triplane fell away with its dead pilot to crash just behind the reserve trenches, much to the delight of the resting infantry nearby. Adrian saw the ground loom up towards him. He was grateful that the wings hadn't been pulled off with the repeated strain of stall and recover. He judged the moment he would have to recover and feather the recovery long enough to land. He misjudged the height slightly as the bus hung some feet aloft. It fell vertical with almost no forward speed. The landing rattled his teeth and sent spasms up his back, but he was down. Adrian sat in the cockpit dazed and confused, somehow he was still in one piece. He finally decided that he and the plane had to part company, and he was grateful for the arrival of the hands from willing infantry helping him out. He looked back with fondness at the wreck, he was sorry to see it in such a state, but it had kept him alive and delivered him safely down.

*

Orders came through for the flights to desist. John had rightly surmised that the tunnels had been completed, and the mines would be now in place. It gave the pilots some time to recuperate and relax, even so, most of them were to be found to be working alongside the ground crew. Some of the crates needed new engines, replacement barrels and magnetos, the list was endless. Adrian in particular fussed over his newly delivered SE, fresh from the factory. He was particular adamant that his joystick was one from the old Pup's and the throttle assembly of choice was actually French. Even then he wouldn't leave Ollie Peters alone until he had further had the stick altered with rounded wooden handles with leather strapping, all of which had to be hand-made, by Ollie's skilled hands.

Despite the respite from flying, the tension was mounting within the flight as the day of the offensive came closer.

The briefing for that day was one that would suit Rogue's unique talents. The general staff were very pleased with the ruse utilised in masking the digging of the tunnels. They surmised that this distraction could be used on the day of the attack.

The use of new technologies, including the introduction of the tank, had so far had produced mixed results.

The first tanks were slow, and only had thin armour which was vulnerable to artillery, and even the heavier calibre small arms fire. They were also unreliable, with all too frequent breakdowns. To help even the odds, the RFC would use its range of machines available to mask the noise of the tanks during an assault to further confuse the enemy. They would then be used in ground support, especially in locating and destroying concealed artillery positions. With this in mind, John ordered the SE's to be fitted with six cooper bombs each. The twins were back in there beloved Bristol, which was also capable of carrying some ordnance,

*

The men stood outside, sitting or standing, waiting for the mines to be detonated. Some of the others preferred to stay inside. Herbert and Bill were completely focused on a brutal chess match, in which Herbert was coming decidedly second best. The clock came closer to three in the morning, and the numbers outside looking east were growing. Conversations were short and stilted.

In an instant, the night sky lit up across their frontage as if in slow motion. Adrian looked on dispassionately not really understanding what to he was witnessing. A brighter flash of light appeared on the skyline, with the visual display of a dark shadow ascending, throwing thousands of tons of earth rising up skyward. No one had ever seen anything like it. The largest explosion event in human history was being displayed before them, and the astonished assembly looked on with horror and fascination. The bright flash morphed into a blood red colour. Seconds later with was followed by a massive rumbling which gradually grew louder. This was followed by the shock wave, which threw several men standing onto the ground. Others sitting on chairs were thrown backwards at the same time. It took a few seconds for the impact of what they saw to register, followed by much excitement, and even slight hysteria from some, at seeing what man was now capable of.

*

An hour later the seven scouts of Rogue were over the battlefield. They had to remain at some height to begin with, as there was a sophisticated rolling barrage laid down by the artillery a few hundred yards ahead of the advancing infantry. An hour into the patrol, Dick spotted a few tanks on the far right flank that were subject to enemy shellfire that was spouting lumps of earth close by. He took his bus down, and flew over the top and onward to where he thought they would be heading. A flash from behind a church wall revealed a hidden battery of mobile artillery. He took the SE down at a shallow angle and let loose his bombs directly on top of them. Looking back he was disappointed to see he had only caused superficial damage, as the low wall had taken the brunt of the resulting explosions. He flew once more over their position this time at a higher level, knowing they would be ready this time with a considerable arsenal of small arms fire including machine guns. Dick contented himself with firing flares over their position. He repeated the action until he had almost used them all up, but was gratified to see that someone in the tank crew understood, and subsequently the three tanks rained fire directly onto the artillery pieces. As Dick made is final pass, he saw with delight dozens of Hun infantry with hands raised walking towards the tanks.

His wave to the tank crew was returned with much enthusiasm by those of the tank crews. With petrol running low, he made to home to refuel and rearm.

Chapter Eight

Encounter with Voss

Bill Mellor was standing in front of John in the office. He was fast becoming an essential element of the inner working of the ground crew. Herbert was forever speaking his praises, and he had developed a well-deserved reputation as a thinker, a scholar and very intelligent. It was his first foray into the CO's office on a problem within the ranks.

"Make yourself comfortable Bill, how is the chess coming along? Found anyone you haven't beaten yet?"

Bill shrugged neutrally. "Don't think that will happen anytime soon John, Addie has come the closest, but he's impatient. Always goes for the quick kill."

John laughed, "He'll never change, is there something I can do for you?"

Bill was a bit nervous at broaching the subject, as he was but a Corporal, and only transferred over recently. "It's nothing really sir, not for a busy man such as yourself, well it's to do with leave."

Bill went on to explain that he had learnt that three of the flight were due some leave, Peter, Herbert and Ernie. Peter really wasn't bothered about going on leave. Coming from New Zealand, he didn't know anyone outside the flight, and had nowhere really to go. Herbert was different, he too refused to go on leave, and had done so before on several occasions. Ernie was all packed up and ready to go, but in reality, he would spend most of his leave time travelling to and back from his home in London.

"Herbert comes from Cornwall, so it's impossible for him to get there and back, which is why he has never taken up his dues, and believe me sir, he of all of us, needs some time with his family."

John took out his pipe and absently toyed with it, while thinking. Bill's analysis and conclusions were very astute. He was certainly right about poor Herbert, who has recently become morose, and difficult to deal with, even with himself.

Bill interrupted his thoughts. "I do have a solution of sorts, well, the bare bones of a solution but it will take a man of some influence to make it viable." He went on to explain that air traffic between France and England had become routine. Delivery of replacement machines going one way, and flights the other way for supplies, intelligence and many other demands in support of the war effort going the other. If it could be arranged to get Herbert a lift over the pond, the it would be a simple case of organising a connecting train straight to Plymouth. Herbert's family live just the other side of the

Tamar river, just a few miles further west. If that could work for Herb, then it would be even better for Ernie. with family in London. John saw the sense in Bill's thinking. He may be able to persuade General Caddell to endorse the plan.

"Nice work, Bill. Not going to help our Kiwi friend though is it?"

Bill had anticipated this issue. "Correct sir however a few days in the fresh air and delightful company of the Faure family in Le Roeux, just a quick drive down there would do the job. Perhaps Dick would oblige with the driving."

John couldn't help clapping his hands together. "By all that's holy Bill, you are a sly one, remind me to never play you at cards. Leave it with me, I'll see what can be done"

*

The constant patrols made it difficult to arrange to get all the aviators in the briefing room all together. Plans and photographs were already on display. John had a staff officer with him from the Château next door. John made a brief introduction to the stranger but pointedly omitted his name.

"This gentleman will outline a mission Rogue flight has been given. Before we start, we have a new pilot arriving today. Name is, let me see, George Child. Good pilot by all accounts. Addie? where are you?"

Adrian's hand shot up through the cigarette smoke from the back. "Find someone to take him through his paces will you! and get Bill to assemble a team to go over his bus as well?"

A disconnected voice responded, "Consider it done Sir."

With little preamble the staff Major gave an outline of the mission. It was to be in two parts. They would deliver two people to a designated spot far behind the lines near Hamburg. They would then pick up two more operatives at the same time, and bring them back to la Lovie. The rest of the flight would at the same time assault a nearby aerodrome to distract, and mask the noise of landing the two Brisfits, and ensuing take off, which will be less than a mile away. The flight would then reunite and escort the passengers back. The Hun would almost certainly be on the alert by then, and not too happy with such an incursion. The journey back would be very likely to be more hazardous as a result. The Major held up one of the photographs. "The field selected for delivery is reasonably small and difficult to locate. For the men selected to land, they need to study this particular and the surrounding area well. You will arrive over there at dawn. We have given strict orders, that no flares or markers will be allowed to help identify the ground. You will have four days to learn the route, the layout of the 'drome, and prepare your planes accordingly. Good luck to you all" With that he left, leaving any questions to John to answer.

*

Despite Herbert's protestations, he was packed off in a two-seater on a flight back across the channel, as was Ernie Winters. The General had come up trumps, and found passage for the pair with little difficulty. He further suggested they use this as a blueprint to get others home as and when their leave was due.

Herbert found himself warming up nicely on a train, after the arduous flight. He had to admit it to himself he was in need of some rest, and to find himself going home, had lifted his spirits enormously. He hadn't laid eyes on his children now for two years. Would they recognise him? he found himself becoming quite emotional at the thought of seeing them all, and he could not stop a few tears escaping at the thought of their reunion.

Ernie too was looking forward to a reunion with Nancy, his wife. They had only had a few months of marriage before the war broke out. Letters between them had been intermittent, and some of the content from her had lacked the warmth and detail he would have hoped for. He told himself, she was never one for writing, and she did work long shifts in one of the back street pubs, with its unsocial hours. Ernie decided to walk the final half mile through the patch that he had grown up in. He was greeted by one of two people he knew locally. The familiar streets were comforting, and he tried to take it all in. As he drew nearer to his own street, he found himself by his local, the Crown and Anchor, a traditional London corner pub just two minutes away from home. On impulse he decided to go in for a quick drink. He was greeted in muted tones by some regulars sat or stood at the bar. Several men shouted over to the landlord to put one in for Ernie, which he thanked in turn. "Hello Ernie, nice to see you," the landlord said. "Your usual? brown and mild isn't it?" He was flattered the landlord had remembered. As he waited for his drink, an old acquaintance stood next to him, putting his near empty pint pot on the bar. Ernie recognised him from school, a man called Joseph, although he had always been known as 'Napper'. He remembered that Joe had been gassed some years previously.

"Hello Napper, what are you up to these days?" he ventured.

The man coughed for a while, something he now had to live with. "Ernie, good to see you. Me? found a little job on the market, not much to sell though these days. Back on leave?"

Ernie took a draught, "Just on the way home now. Having just this one, and go and drop my gear,"

Napper dropped his voice to a whisper. "Nancy knows your coming home?

"A look of confusion came across Ernie's face. "No time, it was a last-minute thing, why?"

"Joe shook his head negatively "Sorry Ernie, not my business. You just take care y'hear." With that he sloped off without another word. Something in the back of his mind told him something was awry. Without another word he left the pub, not bothering with finishing the pint, which remained half finished on the bar.

His keys were in his hand as he stood outside the front door. He hesitated in going inside, fearful of what waited for him inside.

*

The car's gears screamed in protest under the brutal treatment from Dick's driving. Peter just sat in petrified silence as it took corners at ridiculous speeds, which the squealing tires confirmed. Now Peter loved the adrenaline rush of speed as most young men did, more so being pilots, but Dick was taking some liberties with Peter's nervous system, as they navigated the narrow French lanes. They stopped briefly to refuel, where Peter's offer to take over the wheel was rudely rebuffed. In no time at all they found themselves on the outskirts of the village. Dick pointed out a battery of artillery stationed by the edge of some woodland.

"What the bloody hell are those doing here?" he growled. The car came to a standstill in the square. Claudette was first to see them, and she quickly crossed over and flung herself into Dick's arms. They embraced for a while before separating. Dick, he noticed that she had put on weight, but she looked good for it he thought.

"Just an overnight stay I'm afraid darling, just delivering the cargo. Here, I'd like you to meet Peter, all the way from New Zealand. Claudette pouted at the thought of such a brief time they had, but quickly decided to make the one night special. As they shook hands formally they were met by Chloe and Gabrielle, who looked at their handsome visitor with appreciative eyes. Peter bowed, and smiled at the two beauties before him. A different campaign had just presented itself to him, he thought. They both took an arm and led him inside to the estimanet, with the happy couple following on behind. Claudette skipped at Dick's side. "We will have at least one night together, no?"

She went on to describe the food being prepared in detail, as well as the wines they had bought up from the cellar. "Perhaps now we will find you a brandy first, as you my love, are to be a father." She stopped and looked at him sympathetically. "You have gone a little pale dear."

*

Herbert's knees buckled underneath him as he neared the village of Cawsand. It was one of two fishing villages overlooking Plymouth on the other side of the Tamar river. He could now see the sister village of Kingsand which was the closer of the two. Cawsand lay behind, where his wife and children lived in a small, terraced cottage. Dozens of small fishing boats were lined up on the beach with people milling around in a hive of activity. The fishing there varied in accordance with time of year, with crabs being fished in wintertime, before pilchards and herring later as the year progressed, as it had done for generations.

He found himself tearful again, with emotions welling up from within. What was wrong with himself, he thought. His hands started shaking, and he had an overwhelming compulsion to just turn around, and head back to France. He fought the absurdity of it all. Perhaps he was going insane? Herbert found himself looking up at the lane where he lived, fighting with himself as he drew nearer to home. He couldn't possibly present himself in this state. From nowhere came a squeal of delight, "Daddy's here, Mum, Daniel, its Daddy."

Before he knew it he was crouched with his beloved daughter in his arms. It was then he understood, he was going to be alright.

*

He never did go through the door. Something was amiss and he knew it. Ernie stood on the corner and waited on events. He was down to his last two woodbines when the front door opened. A man emerged from the inside and turned back towards his house. A figure leaned out and gave the man a kiss. He recognised the outline of his wife Nancy. 'So that's the rub of it' he thought. He fought down a cold rage rising from within. The man wrapped a cape around himself, and walked towards him. Ernie stood frozen in the shadows, and watched the interloper walk by. His entire frame was cold with pain and anger. It was a fucking copper! A copper doing this to him, when he was away fighting the war. A fucking copper. He decided to follow him, not really sure of what to do next. The policeman took the route on a path alongside the canal. The policeman's instincts were honed, and he turned to find a shadowy figure behind him. "You there, what's your business?" he barked.

Ernie continued to approach. He recognised him now, Stanley Blake, PC Stanley Blake of all people.

"Hello Stanley, recognise me?"

Stanley's face looked back in shock into the face of his lovers' husband. "Now you behave yourself Winter's or I'll have you arrested."

Ernie was now but a few yards away, "For what! You fucking shit, for fucking my wife!"

Stanley spluttered incoherently and made the mistake of reaching for his truncheon.

Ernie was on him in a flash with a flurry of punches to the head and torso. He went down, and tried to cover up from the relentless blows. His head came up briefly only to be further assailed by repeated kicks to the prone body. Blind with rage, Ernie continued to rain down blows even after Blake had stopped moving. Ernie looked down impassively, and then scoured the area for any signs of activity. "You fucker" he said quietly. One push forward from his foot sent the unconscious man into the water. He stood there for several minutes breathing heavily, undecided on his next course of action. He briefly looked back towards where his house lay before picking up his bag to return home, to France.

*

Peter found Dick in the mess.

"Here he is," said Peter. "Papa Watson, how does it feel?"

Dick panicked and went to shush him before anyone overheard. "Shut up you fool, nobody knows, yet, and that's how it's going to stay for a while."

Peter threw up his hands in apology. "Sorry young fella, mum's the word."

Dick sat back down, and decided to change the subject. "You are just in time, we are finally leaving for Hamburg the day after tomorrow. Anyway, so how was your leave?"

Peter's face lit up "Marvellous Dick, simply marvellous. Its Gabrielle you see..."

Dick switched off from listening, as he could pretty much predict how the rest of this conversation was going to be.

*

John asked for Jules and Mario to meet him in his office regarding the impending mission, or at least that's what they assumed. They both stood over the photo's for the umpteenth time. It was always known that they would be flying the two-seater planes to deliver and extract the passengers. The additional Bristol delivered had been sent on to the ground crew, for its obligatory modifications. They spent some time going over the plans in minute detail. John presented them with their own plans to take with them.

The two passengers were safety ensconced in their billets waiting for transport. They kept to themselves, and made no fuss or demands, but kept a professional low profile. The twins thought the meeting over, but were detained by John unexpectedly. "Is it the case that your people can readily move in between the lines at will?"

Jules was cautious in his response. "Not exactly sir but it can be done, as Mario is testament to. You have something in mind sir?" Jules was never one for wasting words.

"This is strictly off the record chaps. Nothing to do with the flight. Call it a favour, that is, if you can deliver."

Jules became impatient with John. "We are not a conventional people as you know sir, and we really don't give a toss about conventions. Perhaps you would like to come to the point."

John nodded "I need you to take someone across the lines tonight. He will need to be further given safe passage on to a neutral country until this thing blows over" The twins looked at each other amused and turned back to John. "Course we can, do we know who and why?"

John explained that he had had Ernie tucked away at the other side of the aerodrome, and he needed him gone before the authorities put two and two together, and come looking for him. "Killed a copper that was fucking his wife. Spur of the moment thing. Thing is, we need him gone before the mission. Adrian has offered to fund his passage, and to keep him going for a while"

The twins conferred quietly for a while. Mario was first to chirp up. "We can do it, where is he? Policeman you say! Bugger it, we'll do it for free."

The farewells were brief and frenetic. Not everyone had the chance to say goodbye. John made sure Ernie knew that he had the entire flight's best wishes, and hoped to see him sometime in the future. In minutes he had disappeared from their lives, perhaps forever.

*

A quiet summer's night was broken with the sound of planes being trundled over grass, and the mute conversations of dozens of men. It was pitch black as low thick cloud blanketed the skies. The flight now comprised of two Bristol two seater's complete with their passengers and six SE's. Adrian walked over to John and tapped him on the shoulder. Without a word he pointed out two men, who were presumably there charges, making their way to the Bristol's.

John exploded with anger, as he stood in front of them. "What on earth do you think you are wearing?"

The two men looked at each other in confusion. They had on their normal clothes, which were nondescript jacket and trousers.

"Am I expected to go to all this trouble just to deliver two frozen corpses eh?"

Adrian tactfully took them both by the arm. "Leave it with me sir, I'll have them kitted out in a jiffy."

John heaved a sigh of frustration, but let the matter drop. On John's instructions they were to fly in three sections of loose pairs, with the two 'Brisfit's' bringing up the rear. Most of the pilots turned off their instrument lights, opting to rely on their night vision to see better. A roar of engines starting up sounded even more intense as it ripped apart the tranquillity of the night. Eugene thought they could probably be heard from the German lines. Ten minutes later they had emerged through the blanket of cloud into a clear moonlit sky.

It was a surreal sight as the gaggle of planes flew above the clouds reflected by the moonlight. It was as if they could actually land on the stuff. Singer lit up the compass to check the bearings, as the planes fell into formation. Something was wrong, John turned his head around several times before he understood the anomaly, Some of the others had also identified the problem. There were too many machines! How it had come to be John couldn't guess, but there was seven SE's in the sky not six. It must be Child in the seventh plane. He wasn't supposed to be operational yet, but somehow in the confusion of the nights activities he was there, like a spare part. John assessed the situation, and decided quickly to carry on, and take the errant flyer with them. George had either wilfully disobeyed orders or it was just miscommunications, either way it will have to wait. George settled himself behind the two seater's which John observed with satisfaction. He at least had a good tactical head on him.

With the flight there and back, they only had enough fuel for a few minutes maximum over the target, even with a favourable wind.

Twenty minutes into the flight, Adrian took his machine down below the cloud cover to check for any ground references that could confirm they were on course. Twice he emerged shaking his head negatively, and continued on the same course further east. On the third run he confirmed their position, and by hand signals successfully conveyed a slight adjustment to port.

The early morning light was now making life a little more comfortable, and the cloud had breaks opening up which made navigation easier. They could now see the large airfield below in silhouette. The twins took themselves out of formation and headed some way starboard towards the landing zone. John cut back the throttle and led the flight down in a gentle dive. It was predetermined that the fight would attack in the same formation the simplicity of this in the half-light would hopefully lessen the danger of mid-air collisions. Singer was incredulous that the Boche had made no attempt to protect the planes by disbursement or camouflage. They were lined up in long lines in the open, as if on parade. It was probably the illusion of being so far behind the lines, which lay behind this obvious blunder. John took one last look around, and lined up his machine to attack.

*

Jules by nature was a calm resolute creature. He had been raised to believe in fate, and a natural order that defined events that befell him. A courageous man, where not much would ever surprise or test his faith. That same resolution was now being severely tested, as he flew in a wide circle unsuccessfully trying to locate the specific field that they had to land on. He was becoming increasingly frustrated, as the whole operation depended on him. To make matters worse, there was a low mist hugging the ground which masked any of its features that could guide them in.

From the ground, a flare flew upwards from his starboard side. He put the plane on its wing and descended towards the flare's origin. It was completely against standing orders, and completely necessary he thought. Someone down there knew what they were doing. The field thankfully hove into view, and Jules lined up to land, with Mario in tow. They managed to land without mishap, and only came to a halt after he turned the bus back around and was in position to quickly take off again. He felt an appreciative slap on the shoulder, where his cargo jumped clear and walked briskly towards the hedge line. Very soon afterwards he saw his replacement approaching, and was amused to see it was a female. He could only see her eyes behind the swathe of clothing. She nodded to him before she lithely mounted the plane and strapped herself in. Jules understood from that that, she was no stranger to the observers' cockpit. Mario's passenger was busy doing the same, and Jules waited on the signal for when they would be ready to leave.

*

Singer's bullets ripped into the first of a line of Boche Halberstadt's and large Gotha bombers. Adrian too was seeing the effect of his bursts, with plane after plane twitching under the multiple impacts. Many began to smoke, and others caught fire. Several building hove into view behind the planes which were probably the men's billets. Singer stopped firing, as he had no interest in murdering men in their beds, although he didn't care if they were rudely awakened in the meantime!

Dick decided to take his plane obliquely towards another line of Fokker D.VII's and what looked like Aviatik's. which had so far remained unscathed. He was content just to drop the cooper bombs on them for the first run, opting only to use the machine guns on the second pass. By the time George was making his run at the rear of the formation, there was a distinct lack of targets, as yet not destroyed of damaged

*

The explosive and incendiary bullets caused multiple explosions and fires, which spread from plane to plane. Dick took his machine out of the other side of his run, still careful to keep clear of Singer's flight. Men were seen to be running in confusion, in all and every direction. Singer replaced the drum on the Lewis for a final run. He had already ordained there was to be just two runs maximum. They were to leave before the ground defences organised themselves, and also to save ammunition, which they would almost certainly need to get themselves home. The final pass was less dramatic than the first, even with the unloading of the bombs. The plumes of smoke were now obscuring any remaining targets. Singer turned away and upwards from the carnage, with the SE's falling back into formation behind him. Above the clouds, they could see the two Bristol's above a mile or so away. The two seaters duly turned to fall in behind the SE's for the homeward journey, Peter and Aubrey now brought up the rear as added protection for the Bristol's.

It was now daylight and the protection that the night afforded them had gone. There were brief periods of ground artillery behind the lines that sent up an ineffectual barrage. It was never going to be the case, that it posed any threat, except for the fact that it identified their location to the enemy, which was unnerving being so far from safe skies. Singer steered a variable course to avoid contact, however his fuel status meant those options were limited to minor changes. Dick kept a keen eye all around by scanning the sky in sections. He was grateful for the silk scarf which reduced friction on his neck, as he continuously turned looking for threats. The skies now appeared to be busier than ever, but the ones spotted so far were far away as to be of no immediate concern. They were half an hour into the return leg of the journey, when before them loomed large cluster of Boche planes, as if in wait for them. It was inevitable that they would have at least one encounter. Singer reduced power and waited on events. He had at least the comfort of superior speed in the SE, which he was gambling the Boche would still be unaware of. It was one advantage he wanted to keep in his pocket, at least for now. He knew the Bristol's were slower, but at least they were faster than the factory-built models, thanks to the efforts of the ground crew. He was happy with the formation as it was, as it was his intention to punch through the trap, and continue west. The Germans were more widely dispersed, knowing they could use the superior numbers to outflank their counterparts. Singer led the flight away from the enemy scouts, as if to avoid contact. This quickly prompted the leading planes to fire from some distance, thinking their outnumbered prey was attempting to avoid a fight. Judging the right moment, Singer pushed the throttle forward, and reversed course. Some of the less inexperienced pilots, were caught out and struggled to regain formation. Dickie, Adrian and the two Bristol's were more familiar with Singers habits, and mirrored the violent manoeuvre, staying close behind. The Boche were certainly not prepared, and were taking fire from the English scouts before they managed to fire a round. The enemy had to scatter, and quickly lost all cohesion in seconds. By the time Peter and Aubrey caught up, One of the Fokker bi-planes managed to quickly turn to find himself behind Peter's bus. He managed a few bursts, before Aubrey fell in behind, and raked it, rendering it a flying wreck which fell away out of the fight. George was the only member of the flight not to have a supporting wingman, and soon found himself alone, and fighting for his life. Singer was hopeful that they could quickly fly through the pack, and seek safety by diving away at speed, avoiding a dog fight against such odds. The Boche pilots were very capable, and reacted with commendable courage in pressing home their attack. Jules had to change tactics, not having Mario protecting his rear, or at least that was what his assumption was. He was focused on turning as tightly as he could to keep one particular scout from getting in behind. He then found he was the nearest spectator to this same plane being hit, and subsequently catching fire. The guns responsible he saw were his own! His erstwhile helpless passenger behind him had seen off the threat with some aplomb. Jules shook his head in admiration, whoever she was, she was no stranger to working a Lewis gun, in the air at that!

Dickie found that George was in all sorts of trouble. His machine was smoking badly, and two Boche planes were harrying him from behind. Adrian now found himself supporting Singer, and flew behind him, while he was chasing off a couple of Fokker's who were diving away from the fray. There wouldn't be a better time to break away than now, so he put his bus into a vrille and headed west into clear skies. Adrian mirrored the tactic and at over one hundred and forty miles an hour, they soon put distance from the remaining EA. Mario and Jules were already several miles ahead, as they managed to head homeward in the confused fighting. They couldn't see any signs of Dick or George, but the fuel situation was now critical, and they had no option but to head for the front lines. Behind them they left three Boche planes in smouldering ruins on the ground, with several others damaged. They still had some way to go, and as soon as Singer caught up with the Bristol's he led them above the sporadic cloud cover, to put off the attentions of Archie that had resumed to harry them all the way.

Dickie found himself coming out of cloud into empty skies. He was surprised to find that that one minute you are fighting for your life, and the next you are all alone in the world. He had no idea what the ultimate fate of George was, but he was hopeful that his intervention was enough to help him survive the encounter. He looked around and knew he was completely lost. Dickie had always suffered from his inherent weakness in navigating, and it as always his fear to end up lost miles from home. Obviously, he could tell generally which way was west, an so he forlornly followed his compass, and watched for the sun.

*

The flight managed to land at a friendly British aerodrome not far behind the lines. Singer thought it prudent to refuel, and rest. He was exhausted, and it would be the same for his pilots, and passengers. It had been a long gruelling flight, but there was enough light left in the day to get back to La Lovie. The two passengers took the opportunity to find some transportation from there, with a blushing Jules having a kiss on the cheek as a reward. They availed themselves of tea and sandwiches, as they waited on the bowsers to refuel the machines. It was in the mess that Eugene explained how he had witnessed George's final moments. His plane was in flames, as it hit the ground and disintegrated, and there was no chance he would had survived. John couldn't help but feel guilty at his death. He failed to protect and nurture him. He had always prided himself on keeping a close eye on incoming pilots, until they could find their feet. George was left to fight alone on his first outing.

"It's not your fault John." It was Adrian who sat down beside him. "He wasn't supposed to be flying today. It's just one of those things."

John looked away in embarrassment. "I still should have done more. I could have sent him back, or got someone to fly with him, and what about poor Dick? I may have lost him too."

*

Dick took the SE down to five hundred feet, and out of the corner of his eyes he saw the wings of a plane obscured by a copse of trees, bordering a meandering river, He thought that it may be George's machine. There was also a house and outbuilding nearby, the inhabitants of which may be able to provide some assistance.

The last thing he would have wanted was to damage the undercarriage here in the middle of nowhere over enemy ground, so his concentration was such that he failed to notice the type of machine sat at the far end. Dick throttled up to taxi back to facilitate a quick exit. It came as something of a surprise to see that it was a Boche plane. Dick alighted from his SE and walked tentatively towards this disturbing apparition. In his state of shock he didn't appreciate the distinctive colour scheme. It had silver grey wings with the cross on the lower wings. The fuselage was yellow with a heart, a crooked cross and laurel leaves. The tail was white with green wheel disc's to complete its individuality. It was obviously intact, and bore no signs of damage, so it must have landed deliberately. From the direction of the farmhouse a portly whiskered gentleman made his way toward him. There was some confusion in communicating with him. Dick wanted to find out if he could get any petrol or food, and tried by the age-old method of talking slowly, with elaborate hand gestures but his main concern was the location of the owner of the plane. The old man pointed vaguely in the direction of the river, and made his way back to the farmhouse. Not knowing if he understood anything, Dick wandered down in the direction of the river. As he approached there was some dead ground which uncovered a figure lying on his back. The figure turned out to be a German aviator who was fast asleep! Not knowing quite what to do he just stood for a few moments. The stranger opened his eyes and took in the figure stood before him.

He smiled and stood up. "My secret is out," Dick understood the German who seemed unconcerned at his appearance. He held out his hand, and they shook hands, he turned and bent down to retrieve a wine bottle, refilled his glass and handed it to Dick.

"English?" he asked. Dick nodded his head and took a mouthful. The Hun gestured for Dick to sit next to him. "My name is Voss, Verner Voss. This is my favourite little place to get away. Here there's no war for me, here you are my friend, Prost!"

"Cheers! "Dick replied.

Verner went on to explain that he often stopped by here to relax for a few hours. The farmer nearby furnished him with little treats on his visits, such as food and wine, to which he was paid, supplementing his meagre income. The two aviators sat comfortably by the river and chatted amiably mostly about flying, and nothing of the war.

Voss was incredulous when he heard that Dick, and all of his friends, never bothered to keep score of the machines they individually downed. It was an approach he had difficulty in understanding. Nor did they appear to be interested in gongs, with not a one of them having or wanted the attention that came with it. Voss found this young Englishman to be completely endearing, and he decided on the spot, that he wanted him to remember him on their first meeting. Brushing aside all arguments, Voss adorned Dick with a medal of his own, in recognition of the English flight. It was one of his own that he took with him in combat. They talked of pilots they knew or recognised. French, German or British, some that were still active, and many that were now dead. Voss had not previously heard of Dick, which was not surprising. He had however heard of Singer, and his 'sewing machine' though, and he laughed at the mention of his name. His good friend Richthofen has crossed paths with Singer before. Dick knew of this encounter, where he remembered Singer describing the fight. Richthofen had managed at one point to latch onto Singer's tail. Luckily for him, his guns jammed, and he just flew alongside him, waved and flew away.

Verner listened to Dick's version of that day. He playfully slapped Dick on the back, "Not quite the case, my friend. Manfred told me himself, that he fought one of the best men he had ever met in the air, and it was an even match in many ways. He was fortunate to find himself behind your Singer, and on the one occasion in his career, he just decided not to fire, such was his admiration."

He told Dick he was now worried for his friend Manfred. He had not been the same since receiving a serious head wound back in July. His flying was more erratic, but he has refused repeated appeals, even from Werner, to stop.

The conversation was interrupted by the farmer, who had with him, a can of petrol, and some cold chicken pieces to eat. Dick was embarrassed as he had no money with him. Werner generously paid on his behalf. Voss walked Dick back to his bus. "Dick my friend, this place is my little secret, and now it is yours too, I hope we may met here again." Dick agreed but deep down doubted that he would ever find this place again, but promised to keep his secret safe. Werner handed him a piece of paper with his address in Germany.

"Please do not get yourself killed Dick, and we will meet again my friend, when this war is over, yes?"

Before he made for the cockpit, Voss put one arm around his shoulder, and chopped down with his other arm extended, in the direction he should fly for home, and pointed out some landmarks that may help him to return here, if ever he had the chance. It was the first of several visits to the field, many of which he found his friend sat quietly by the river.

*

The mood in the mess was subdued, among the few that were actually there. The loss of George and Dick weighed heavily on the men. The ground crew had been kept busy well into the evening, with many of the pilots opting to work alongside their colleagues to keep themselves busy. It was Aubrey who was given the job of going from the mess to the hangers, and on to the individual billets, a message had reached them that Dick was alive and well. He was Bruay-la-Buissiere, and will be back first thing in the morning. Relief swept through the flight, which prompted a quiet celebration, as the mess began to fill up. Aubrey didn't have any information as to what or where Dick had been in all those hours, but the general consensus was, it would have something to do with him getting lost.

CHAPTER NINE

Genie goes home

They waited in the late summer sun, for the prodigal one to arrive, including most of the ground crew who were currently not needed elsewhere. Herbert was particularly pleased that the boy was okay. He was a brilliant aviator, with a bright future ahead of him, and he liked to think he had something to do with this emerging talent. The Se5a looked a pretty sight as it came into view. The machine taxied close to the hanger, and Dick climbed gingerly out, accompanied by a howl of insults and jokes at poor Dickies expense. With as much dignity he could muster, he made his way to the mess to get a decent cup of tea, ignoring all questions regarding his whereabouts the last eighteen hours.

Once inside he removed the layers of protective clothing down to his RFC tunic. The removal of the scarf around his neck, revealed a ribbon, from which hung the Pour le Merite. Dick looked back at his comrades who stood in stunned silence for a few seconds.

"Gentlemen I am honoured to inform you all that Rogue flight has been awarded The Blue Max by the

German Imperial Airforce. If you will excuse me, I have a report to make." He left the mess in uproar, enjoying immensity his moment of notoriety.

He duly made a brief report to John, omitting any reference as to where he came face to face with Voss, it was only then he found out the fate of George Child. John was satisfied with the report's brevity, although he was curious of his bizarre encounter.

"You can tell me more about it later. Come on son, let's get you some breakfast" That evening the pilot's and crew was in very high spirits, in stark contrast to the previous evening, such was the way of men in war. A cake was produced at dinner with a delicately made iced replica of the medal.

Some days late Ollie Peters produced beautiful wooden plaque with the distinctive blue cross adorned, which duly took pride of place, amongst the many souvenirs of which was mostly, bits of downed Boche plane parts on the mess walls.

It was later in the evening that John announced the promotion of Eugene to lieutenant, which was loudly applauded by everyone assembled there. Herbert was concerned when he heard the news. He later asked John quietly why he had favoured Genie, as there were several men senior to him, who would expect promotion first. John acknowledged his friends' comments. "Your right Herb, I have managed to convince the General it was particularly deserved. The men you speak of were all consulted and readily agreed, most of them told me they would have refused promotion anyway. Good chaps the lot of them. No, Eugene needs that rank so he gets the respect he deserves as a commissioned officer in His majesty's Flying Corp." Herbert now understood, he had seen some of the negative reactions from others, especially on leave. The worst offenders were often those from his native country. Eugene was flattered and delighted with his new status. for the first time since enlisting, he felt he had found himself at home.

*

The flight was due to go on patrol in the middle of the morning. There was a part squadron of bombers, and scouts who were to target a battery of heavy artillery. The scouts in turn were to destroy a nearby nest of observation balloons, just a mile or so behind the Boche reserve trenches. John had received a deferential request for the SE's of the flight to provide additional cover, to which he readily agreed to.

He was in the little office going through the ritual of gathering his assortment of jacket, gloves, scarfs and headgear, at the same time just pouring over a map of where they were to go. A knock on the door was followed by Adrian wading in, similarly attired. "Someone to see you Sir, redcap I reckon."

Before he could protest at the timing, another man strode into the office, without waiting for introductions. "Captain Singh-Smythe. Chivers, Military Police. We are here to arrest air mechanic Corporal E. Winters, on suspicion of murder."

John looked at a small balding man, with a thin moustache wearing an immaculately pressed uniform, complete with a swagger stick. John looked at the officious looking man with open contempt.

Adrian put in sardonically, "There's another one of them snooping around the hangers Sir."

Adrian's scowl matching that of his Captain. John towered over the MP. "Ernie Winters is listed as missing presumed dead, and the courtesy of some notice of you visit would have not come amiss eh!"

The policeman was not used to having people speak to him in such a manner. He was the type who enjoyed intimidating people in the pursuit of his suspects, and a mere RFC officer would not be one to hamper his investigations. "Captain er Smythe, we are talking about the murder of a police officer, and I would remind you of the consequences that come for obstructing my investigations, may have severe penalties, do I make myself clear. I wish to see the listing, and it is the case is it not, his family have not been informed of your man being missing?"

John took a deliberate step closer. "Your first time at the front, is it? he spat. "I reported him missing myself," he lied. "And what would I possibly have to say to his wife? Murder of a policeman eh. I'm told he accidently drowned, poor sod. My guess he had never been anywhere near the front either. Too busy visiting Winters home I hear."

John pushed passed him and spoke to Adrian, "Inform the ground crew that these 'gentlemen' may be asking them questions while we are away," he turned back to Chivers. "My patrol takes precedence over your investigations, you may of course protest through the provost Marshall's office. I don't suppose we'll meet again Captain. Come on Addie, we'll leave bantam jack here to have a look around."

On the walk to the waiting SE's Adrian sidled up to his friend. "Think you've made an enemy there John."

*

They caught up with the bombers a mile behind the lines, and they continued to climb up to eight thousand feet. Dick and Adrian were leading the flight, with Kiwi and Eugene behind. Singer took Aubrey up to ten thousand feet, with the twins as usual bringing up the rear. They were ignored by Archie this time, as the guns concentrated on the larger formation below them. Most of the squadron's Pup's and Dh2's peeled off in the direction of the balloons leaving the ageing Farman's to continue on. Singer considered the attack on the balloons was far too obvious, giving the Hun time to winch them down before the scouts could arrive. Whoever was leading the squadron had obviously come to the same conclusion, and abandoned the attack to re-join the bombers. Luck was with them however, as the bombers began to lose height on the approach to the artillery park. The formation was quite formidable again by the time they came under attack by a number of largely Pfaltz scouts. climbing from a lower height from the north.

The squadron appeared to be holding their own, with the Farman's steepening their dive to release the ordnance as quickly as they could. The pups engaged the EA before they could get it among the bombers, and a general melee ensued. Singer kept his flight out of the contested airspace intending to follow the bombers instead. Ahead of Singer, Dick waggled his wings, and turned towards a new threat coming from the direction of the sun. Singer still couldn't see them yet, but they must be above, as Dick took his bus higher. For once they were evenly matched in numbers, although the Boche for the moment had a distinctive tactical advantage in height. Singer saw the German machines approaching in fairly tight group of two flight of three, in a Vic formation. Singer signalled Eugene to take off further to port. Seconds later He took himself and Aubrey to starboard, leaving Dick and Adrian to engage head on and alone. Dick's SE was first to open up, firing one quick burst, and yawing very slightly, and repeating the tactic on another machine. He wasn't hopeful of doing any real damage from that range, but it would hopefully disrupt the accuracy of the returning fire, and make sure the Hun was focused on just him and Adrian. One of the Pfaltz machines however was hit luckily, with smoke emerging from his stricken engine. Adrian felt the impact on bullets striking his cowling, and propeller. Sparks emerged in front of his windscreen. He had only managed a two second snapshot before they flew either side. Singers four machines came in from both flanks, and poured devastating fire in to the sides of the German's. Two fell away in quick succession, out of control, with one having one of the top wings collapsing, with its supporting struts having been shot away. The Bristol came on to the stricken plane that Dick had damaged with his first salvo. Mario applied the coup de grace with his opening shots. It too fell away with flames beginning to lick down the sides. Two of the surviving EA found themselves thus far unmolested. Both dived away to safety, shocked and appalled at the mauling they had received. Singer waited for the flight to regroup, before turning for home. He could see the large formation of Farman's in the distance also heading west. He wouldn't know if the patrol had been successful or not. For now, he was content to lead his band home, with nothing more than a few holes and splinters to show they had been in a scrap.

*

A surprise was waiting for them when they landed, as there was only a skeleton ground crew available. The rest had left on orders to transfer to Bailleul. The mess was still intact though, where they all eventually gravitated to. The patrol had been one of their most successful to date, and the contribution from newest of them, namely Kiwi and Aubrey had not gone unnoticed.

The two aviators from Brum were conversing idly over a beer. Dick had never been anywhere near Acocks Green. Apart from the odd jaunt to the Lickey hills, he grew up and generally stayed within just a couple of miles from where he was born. Although they both grew up in the same city, there life experience were very different. Dick was surprised to learn that Aubrey was training to become a doctor before war broke out.

"I'm also a Christian," he announced grandly.

"Nonsense," Dick retorted. "I've watched some of your antics. You're as bad as the rest of us."

Aubrey looked skyward as if offended. "I am I tell you. My particular kind of faith does away with the need for a church, and we have taken out the guilt thing, cheers."

Dick couldn't tell in all honesty if he was jesting, but he appreciated his unique outlook on life. John went into the mess looking for Eugene. He found him with Adrian who was attempting to teach him the art of darts.

"Eugene, I've had a communique from General Caddell, and it concerns you."

Adrian made to leave, but John pulled at his sleeve. "Addie I may need your help with this one, here read this."

Eugene was a little agitated at coming to the attention of Cadell.

He nervously lit a cigarette and waited. Adrian mumbled several unconnected phrases "Mmm. our friends from the Colonies... Heard of us it seems... very flattering... ah, here we go. They are requesting that Sergeant Carpenter. Bit behind, aren't they? They want Sergeant Carpenter to transfer to the America Airforce, in recognition of his unique skills in both engine maintenance, and help in training of new pilots. They want him to join a team to improve things for their lot. Cheeky buggers, tell them to sod off Sir."

John took back the letter, "It's up to Genie of course, I think the Yanks are a bit desperate though. They are losing too may airmen, both with unreliable machines and combat losses."

Eugene stubbed out his cigarette angrily. "Tell 'em no," he said simply.

Adrian patted his leg. "Quite right Genie. Just tell them our Eugene here is actually a commissioned RFC officer and is far too valuable to be released, end of."

Eugene was grateful for the endorsements from his friends, but in the back of his mind was a feeling of guilt in turning his back on his mother country. John duly wrote back a more considered reply, with some misinformation for good measure informing them that 'Captain' Eugene Carpenter thanked them for their kind consideration, but has declined. He qualified that by stating in his opinion, Genie was one of the finest aviators on the western front. John finished off by suggesting that the Captain may be persuaded with a promotion, and perhaps to consider be put in charge of his own squadron. That'll give them pause for thought he concluded.

The move to Bailleul was a fortuitous one for Dick and Peter, being considerably closer geographically to

Le Rouex. They were given leave to visit overnight, which was duly taken full advantage of. The airfield was a large affair which accommodated a number of squadrons including a mixed French unit. Dick asked Herbert if he could look at the prop. It was vibrating noticeably which may have been the result of bullet impacts in his previous fight. With that matter taken care of, they managed to acquire a dilapidated tender, and left with indecent haste.

*

It was the turn of Ollie Peters for some leave, and he opted to take up Herbert's offer of a few days in his home village in Cornwall. He had no immediate family to go back to, and the thought of mooning around his tiny mining village in North Wales, didn't really appeal to him. The good people of Cawsand had arranged for accommodation for anyone of Rogue to use. They would also provide everything for the visitors needs for them to rest and relax. It was now Herbert's little project, which was heartily endorsed by the villagers, and so, the Herbert 'express' was born. John used Bill Mellor's considerable organisational skills to set up the transport via air and train down to the West Country, which enabled Herbert to occasionally enjoy his visits at home. Ollie found himself sat on one of the tiny beaches just watching the coming and going of the fishing fleet. He loved this little part of the world. The sound of quiet waves lapping the shore, and the feeling of the warm sea breeze on his face. He was looking forward to indulging in a few pints in one of the tiny pubs. Ollie enjoyed conversations in the hostelry, anything to do with the weather, the fishing hot spots and other mundane issues of the day. From time to time the war would rear its ugly head in some fashion, and Ollie would find himself switching off.

Ollie's particular skills in the hangers was with wood. He was a gifted carpenter, and loved to engage with any developments of the airframe that may come to light. In recent weeks he had been fascinated by the usage of V struts in some downed Boche machines, which he thought could be adopted to the SE's. Today he was equally intrigued by the graceful lines of the various fishing boats that fished the inland waters of the coastline. He drew some critical looks from more than one, when he ran his hands down a keel, or peered up at the masts. He did try to engage in conversation with some lingering boat crew, but the mixture of seafaring terminology and the Cornish accent proved to be a formidable barrier. It was then he decided he knew where his future lay, not necessarily here in Cornwall, but in boat building. He had only ever known working on machines built for destruction. The concept of using his skills in the future, to build something for a living did not escape him.

*

They had to wait for an age before Gabrielle and Claudette found time to sit with two very impatient pilots. At the first opportunity Claudette closed the cafe. With impressive authority she shooed the remaining customers to the outside tables outside, citing her man was here for a brief visit. They obliged good naturedly, wishing her the best for the future. She was by now clearly showing, even though she now took to wear loose fitting clothes.

The two pilots hardly saw anything of each other, spending the few hours they had catching up with their respective companions. Dick was worried that she was working too hard and should be taking it easy. Claudette bristled at this perceived criticism. She loved being busy as it made the days go quicker. The idea of lying in bed or sitting idle was something she wasn't looking forward to, even though it would soon be inevitable. "Will you stop fussing Cherie, the doctor thinks it's good for the baby to keep moving. Dear Chloe is ready now to help more, and Gabrielle has more than enough staff now," She decided to change the subject. "The guns have gone, did you notice? You wrote to me worrying about that too."

Dick felt a twinge of guilt. He promised himself to be less tetchy, and more supportive. "That's very good news. You look so well my love. Tell me how this venture of Gabrielle's is going"

*

Peter and Gabrielle were outside sitting by a small table, sharing a bottle of chilled wine in silence. Gabrielle was very adept at small talk, avoiding more sensitive issues regarding their future, and their place in it. She understood Peter's reluctance to talk about his time in the air. She had heard of the loss of George, although she had never met him, and it saddened her because it hurt him.

"The old women of the village have agreed it is to be a boy. They are never wrong," Peter wasn't convinced, but deferred to their wisdom.

"He'll like that," Peter said. "Just need a name now. perhaps they will call her Gabrielle?" he teased.

She shook her head from side to side. "No, no. It is a troublesome name."

Peter reached out to rest a hand on hers. "It's a beautiful name, and you my lovely are a beautiful person."

They were making preparations to leave, when Gabrielle dashed indoors to her room. "Wait, I have something for you," she returned with a letter, and handed it to Peter. "It came a few days ago, it is only addressed to the café Le Roeux, for your Mario Wallenburg."

Peter examined the letter. Curious he thought, it seems to have come from a field hospital.

*

They returned to Bailleul, and Dick decided to go straight over to the hanger to check up on his SE. He found out from Ollie that he had replaced the propeller. Dick made the mistake of asking Ollie how his leave went. Ollie then launched an extensive report into his revelation of discovering boat building. Dick was very pleased for him, but he wasn't expecting a lengthy rendition of Ollie's life plans. Adrian was also in receipt of a letter recently. It was from his mother, Abigail.

He found some time later to read it lying on his bed. Much of it was mundane family and business news. One paragraph stood out regarding his father. Lord Wentworth was back in France, and was intending to meet up with him. It was obvious they were still in contact with each other, but his mother was too shrewd a lady to disclose anything more. She asked Adrian to receive him with kindness, as he had suffered some bad news of late. Adrian caught up with Dick in the mess and was pleased to see his friend in high spirits.

"There you are Addie, 'bout time. Here get Addie a drink. It's going to be a boy. The women in the village have said so."

As good a reason to celebrate as any Adrian thought. Peter was the last to arrive and he found Mario and Jules sitting with Aubrey and Eugene telling long exotic tales of life as a gypsy, which they listened to with fascination. Peter gave Mario his letter. "This came for you mate, posted to the cafe in Le Rouex."

Mario looked at the letter laid before him on the table. He was confused. Neither he nor Jules ever get letters, not their kind. "who's that from?" he said absently. Jules just huffed at that and looked down to the table, as if to say 'Open it' Mario read its contents twice before whispering to his cousin. "C'mon, let's find John, were going to need a twenty-four-hour pass."

The letter was from his friend Paul Toelke, the German pilot who looked after him so well when he was captured. Mario laughed as he read some of the contents to Jules.

"He's written in English as the letter would have a better chance of reaching him, although he now ruefully understands that Mario is fluent in German."

He explained his subterfuge on escaping from the aerodrome at the time.

Mario read the letter twice before remarking. "Poor bugger got himself shot down, and is in a field hospital. He's asking to see me."

Mario put the letter into his pocket. "Fancy a ride, Jules?"

Jules replied, "Okay, but I'm driving."

By the time they found the hospital where Paul was, he had been transferred. It took several hours work to track him down. Mario finally found where Paul was, it was as he searched the cots in one of the tents that he heard a weak voice call to him.

"Here Mario, over here."

He looked over to a man swathed in bandages around his torso. He hardly recognised him, he looked so pale and emaciated. Mario held his hand. "Sorry to see you so Paul, but I'm glad you're alive" They chatted for a while.

Paul squeezed his hand. "I have to ask something of you." He looked up at Mario imploringly. "My fighting days are over, as you see. I want to go home. To live or perhaps to die, but I want to see home. I thought perhaps as you know the way. You may get me through the lines?"

Mario was stunned at the audacious request and was unresponsive. Jules pulled him aside. Mario thought he was going to chastise him for even contemplating such a foolish, and illegal enterprise. Jules however had no such qualms.

"If he goes through the system in captivity Mario, he will die. Look at him! If we try to smuggle him through the lines, he will also die," Mario smiled at his cousin. "So what do you suggest?"

They left the hospital promising to return. Jules bribed an orderly to take care of him, and make sure he isn't moved.

They drove back to the aerodrome to confer with John. He agreed to the plan they had devised, and left them to it. He had learnt from past experience not to delve too deeply into a world with different rules to the rest of them. He took them off flying duties for a couple of days, as the patrols were fairly routine of late.

They returned the next day with a suitable tender, and took themselves off to where Paul still lay. They found him in much the same condition. It was early evening, and the hospital tents were quiet at that time. The two of them donned a couple of aprons, and took an available cot. The twins lifted Paul from the bed, and stole him away from the hospital. They drove back gingerly, finally getting him settled in Mario's billet back at Bailleul. Mario dragged along Aubrey for his medical skills to see that Paul was suitably cared for. Apart from changing the bandages there was nothing else he could do for him.

"Paul, can hear me?"

The young German looked up at Mario. "What's the name of your aerodrome? Can you point it out on this map?"

*

At six the following morning Mario was over Marckebeke. He flew low over the airfield in one pass, and dropped a note wrapped around a rock with a bright streamer that fell onto the ground. He didn't want to hang about after that. He opened up the throttle to speed away as quickly as he could. The message was to propose his intention return tomorrow and leave Paul in their good care.

The next morning at the same time he was again over the same airspace. This time he was in the Bristol with Paul sat in the observers' seat, covered in layers of clothing. With a sigh of relief he observed a flare rise up from the ground. It was the signal suggested in the message dropped twenty-four hours previously, to confirm it was safe to land. Mario fell down towards the field and gently landed on the enemy field. It took no time at all for hands to be reaching into the back seat and lift Paul out, and quickly lay him on a waiting stretcher. Hands reached into Mario's cockpit and shook his hand with an occasional *'danke'*. Paul was then placed into an ambulance, and he was gratified to see him wave. Mario saluted his friend, and then opened up the throttle to fly home.

*

Adrian had flown three patrols over the Cambrai area, principally to get the lie of the land. They had no contact with any EA and even the ever present Archie was feeble in comparison to previous bombardments. He was climbing out of the cockpit stiff with cold, when Bill informed him that Lord Wentworth was in John's office, waiting for him.

Willerby was sat in John's chair nursing a whisky when Adrian opened the door He was mindful of his mother's words of warning, regarding a recent misfortune.

"Father," he said awkwardly. "It's very good to see you."

He noticed for the first time his father was in uniform. It was in the form of a Colonel of the Sherwood Foresters. He went to shake his hand, and noticed that he looked demonstrably older, and his face was creased in sadness.

"Hello son" He looked back at Adrian who still had his face covered in grease, from his last patrol. He looked ever the warrior his father thought.

"Here, let me get you a drink, how was your patrol? I suppose the uniform comes a little unexpected eh." he offered. "Think of it as a prop son, I use it to throw my weight around sometimes, when the need arises." Adrian was beginning to see his father from a new perspective.

Willerby put his empty glass on the table. "James is dead." He said quietly. "His cruiser HMS Cressy, sunk. Submarine they think. That's both my sons now, gone." It came out as a stifled cry. So that was the news his mother was referring to.

"I'm so sorry father," Adrian went to refill his glass. His father stood and faced a landscape picture on the wall.

"Thank you son," He paused. "I'm sorry I've not been a father to you all these years. Never mind, that's not why I'm here." He took the proffered glass. "I've spoken at length with your mother, about the future that is." He turned to look back at his son. "I want to name you as my son, and rightful heir to the estate, and be a father to as I should have done years ago. That is if you will allow it"

*

Eugene was found to be in the hanger complete with his arms covered in oil. He was helping Joe on a spare Wolseley engine recently arrived from the factory. John had to shout over the volume of noise.

"Genie, get yourself cleaned up will you." He waved a thin wisp of paper in his hand. "We are to expect a visit from some American Colonel this afternoon. Those Yanks don't give up very easy, do they?"

Colonel T. Butcher and his aide arrived by car some hours later. They were ushered in to John's office. John introduced them to Adrian who was there at John's request. The Colonel brought with him a Captain Hulthen, a Lafayette Escadrille trained pilot, and one of their best aviators. He shook John's hand enthusiastically, "A pleasure to meet the famous Singer Smythe Sir," he drawled

The Colonel had been dispatched to convince Eugene to reconsider the request. He pulled out John's letter of response, for reference. "It mentions here in your letter Captain that we may be able to avail ourselves of Captain Carpenters service, if we were prepared to promote him, and have him lead up his own team."

John looked at Adrian struggling to keep a straight face. The Colonel put the letter back in his pocket, "Captain, we appreciate how you guys feel, about losing a good pilot, but I'm here to ask you to consider the bigger picture. He would help turn around the air war for us. I'm authorised to offer both promotion, and he would lead a team of his choosing, as you suggested in your letter."

John turned to Adrian. "Would you ask Eugene to join us if you please."

Eugene duly followed Adrian into the office. For reasons only known to himself, he still had his overalls on, and his hands were oily and covered in grease. He was casually wiping his hands on a rag, as their eyes met. He smiled at the pair sat before him. "Guess I ain't what you were expecting Sir," he said flatly.

The Colonel was obviously well versed in diplomacy, which is why he had sent her in the first place. "Pleased to meet you, er Captain. You are the Genie? the guy who can fly?

Adrian put in, "A genius with engines too."

John let the uncomfortable silence linger deliberately. "Well, if you've changed your minds, we'll not keep you Colonel."

It was Adrian who stepped in again, and casually pointed at the aide. "Forgive me Captain, I'm told you are one of America's finest."

Hulthen simply nodded to acknowledge the compliment. "How about we send you up against our Genie here, see how you both get on. You okay with flying an SE?"

Hulthen looked to the Colonel for guidance, who shrugged. "Up to you Captain."

Hulthen stood up. "Fine, just give me a tour of the cockpit first?" Adrian slapped him on the back "Good man, let's get you kitted out." Twenty minutes later they were both airborne circling the aerodrome. Colonel Butcher and John were both furnished with a seat. The hangers were quickly emptied as all the personnel came out to watch.

Hulthen was impressed with the SE and quickly found it was not dissimilar to fly than his own aircraft. He decided to take the initiative and simulate an attack hoping to catch him off guard. Genie flipped his bus around almost into a stall and turned on his axis. Hulthen was astonished to find himself now the prey, with the SE almost on his tail. He spent the next five minutes trying to shake the man, even going into a viscous vrille. Every manoeuvre he used, it appeared that Genie was getting even closer. Eventually he raised his hands to indicate his surrender. Eugene took the machine down almost to ground level and flew just a few feet directly over the astonished seated audience. He wasn't finished however, and he regained height and attacked the Captain again. It was more of an even match this time. the Captain was good, very good, but the end result was the same. Hulthen had to admit to himself he had witness a master at work. When he was done, Genie paid the two seated officers another visit this time roaring directly over the pair, this time inverted.

The Colonel stood up to face Eugene, and warmly shook his filthy hands. They were joined by Captain Hulthen who also shook his hand. "It would be an honour to work with you Captain." He graciously said.

The Colonel's head dropped as if in thought. "My apologies Eugene for my rudeness. I can promise you I make this work, if you would still reconsider, and come with us."

As Eugene struggled to respond, Adrian pulled him aside gently, and whispered in his ear. "I understand how you feel Genie. trust me I do, but think of the difference you could make, and help your people," he pushed a finger into Eugene's chest. "And there's the other war, the one of your race. You have the chance to break down barriers, and carve a path for others to follow."

Adrian stopped short. "Sorry mate, starting to preach now."

Genie smiled that smile of his. "It's okay Addie, it was actually a pretty good one"

It took an hour for Eugene to collect his belongings and say his farewells. He was whisked away in the Colonels car, and left the flight for good. John and Adrian made their way to the mess, to toast their comrade. Adrian commented. "Another one for the books John. We've seen one of our own go from mechanic to Major in a matter of months."

Later that evening Adrian was quite drunk, and he was musing over the startling change in his circumstances with Dick. "Don't know how it all works really, Me, part of the aristocracy, and am now invited to go up to the estate. Which is somewhere in Derbyshire. You'll have to come too Dickie."

John was seen to enter the mess from his office with Herbert in tow. Herbert managed to get everyone's attention for John, and went to get a beer. "Another push chaps I'm afraid. Meet in my office tomorrow nine o'clock sharp. Your Lordship, Dick," he quipped. "Could you pop into my office."

Adrian stood up to a chorus of irreverent catcalls, wishing he hadn't told anyone now.

He walked in and Adrian's eyes were drawn immediately to the maps laid out "Cambrai?" John was pulling out his pipe from his pocket. "Yes, not much for us to do though, or so they tell me. I intend to put up just two pairs with the twins in tow. With Eugene gone, that leaves us short, so I'm rotating the spare pilot for leave." He started to pull on the pipe. "That's not what I've asked to see you about though"

He left the office with a solemn expression on his face, ignoring the inevitable jokes regarding his new status. He sat down next to Dick, and stared at his drink silently. "What's wrong with you, John upset you again." Adrian patted his friend's arm "I'm very sorry to tell you Dick. It's to do with your German friend, Werner Voss, he's dead."

*

The flight was briefed in the morning of the push on Cambrai. This time there was to be no preliminary artillery barrage. The battle would rely on the combined usage of tanks, artillery and infantry. Squadron of scouts and bombers would be in support, gaining local air superiority. Others were to be used for ground strafing the trenches. Rogue flight would as usual would stand sentinel from above.

For the first few days they enjoyed the luxury of spectacular gains, which saw considerable successes against formidable German defences. Over the course of time however the advance ground to a halt. The Boche launched a furious counter attack on the flank of the salient. With them came large number of Boche planes hell bent on clearing the skies of the English machines

In the early days, they flew in three pairs, with John electing to accompany the twins. He had hoped he would be able to issue leave passes for one pilot in rotation, and some of the ground crew, who sorely needed a rest.

They found themselves flying almost continuous patrols in an effort to stem the tide. Singer reinforced the message to dive and fly, avoiding dog fights at all costs. They didn't need Dick's keen eyes to seek the enemy out, as the skies seemed to be full of machines. Singer took the flight down to intercept over twenty Boche planes of assorted types. He managed to get in position to come out of the sun from above. The initial clash saw two Boche scouts drop from the sky, never to recover. There were so many targets, that it took little manoeuvring to have a machine in the sights. The Bristol quickly had two scouts behind, putting in ranging bursts. Jules damaged the closest machine with his first shots. it was enough to discourage further hostility with the Hun who prudently elected to fly for home. The other Hun however, pressed home his attack. It was time for their party piece, Mario concluded. He turned the machine quickly over, and reversed course. Jules braced himself for the straps to dig in. The Bristol was inverted, and flying back toward the unsuspecting pilot. The Lewis guns chattered raking the plane below along the length of the fuselage. It quickly fell away with its pilot riddled. He never felt the flames which rapidly took hold.

Singer took the flight up and out of the fight, as he surmised most would need to replace the ammunition drums. Peter was out of the battle trailing smoke and he headed for home. He never made it to the aerodrome, and pancaked his bus short of the runway.

By the end of the third day. half of the flight was down to three machines, with the other having taken damage that would take days to repair. Peter was concussed from his crash, and unable to fly. The Bristol lost its undercarriage after the fifth sortie of the day. His pilots were soon totally exhausted, and the ground crew had worked themselves to exhaustion. Herbert saw that Adrian was showing clear signs of nervous exhaustion, and he was quickly dispatched to the care of the doctor, before it got worse.

John now finally found that he could only put up two SE's in the air. He and Dick took to the skies, now with now just the two of them to do what they could. Singer chose his ground carefully, often opting out of a fight, until they had a clear advantage. The machines had done so many hours, they were becoming unreliable.

On the last patrol of the day, Singer picked out a two-seater that had fallen behind his formation. He fell on the Hun, and fired from only forty yard behind. The guns jammed, and he found himself staring at the observers Spandau's which opened fire. he only had time to lift the nose slightly to put his engine in front of the incoming fire. The engine began to scream in protest, with the damage. The firing ceased abruptly. Dick had taken his SE above Singers, giving him a clear line of sight, and then attacked nose down from the rear and underneath, which crippled the Boche machine. It too began to emit smoke, and he turned to limp for home. Dick watched the Fokker dispassionately, and was of the opinion they would never make it. He flew alongside Singer would was thankfully unhurt. The stricken bus however was making an awful noise, and would probably seize up shortly. Singer signalled to Dick that they were bound for home. He knew that for the first time ever, Rogue flight was non-operational, and out of the war.

CHAPTER TEN

The Shell

General Cadell undertook to use all of his persuasive powers to find replacement scouts for the flight. The problem was made worse, as the Se5a was in great demand from squadrons from all over the Western front. He was offered some very capable Sopwith Camel's or French Nieuports instead. John wasn't having any of it. It could have been argued that the ground crew were specifically trained to service the SE. The truth of it was, his pilots had fought and in some cases died in the SE5a, and it was more of a superstitious attachment to the type. Herbert and the crew worked wonders, to get three of the existing machines in the air and battle worthy. The fighting in this sector had died down, and this gave the flight some time to recover.

Adrian was packed off to Blighty on extended leave. Lord Willerby persuaded him to travel up to his estate in the country to recuperate. He even managed to arrange for Abigail to join them. Peter had recovered from his concussion, and seemed to be no worse for wear. He and Dick flew a few patrols, but for now the crisis was over. John made no demands of his men while they collectively regrouped. They flew voluntarily citing the need to keep their flying skills up to par. The patrols were often interrupted by the vagaries of the autumn weather, which for once was welcome.

*

Dick had received a letter from Claudette informing him he was now the father of a baby boy. The birth was not without its problems however, and without going into any details, she was bed bound and weak, but on the mend. He read those few sentences over and over again, not really believing the reality of his new station in life. He and Claudette were bound together for ever, and a new living being was dependent on him. She went on to make some vague reference on moving to Amiens, should the need arise which was a puzzling remark to make. Her final words to ask what would he want to call him. It never occurred to him until that moment, that he would be given that responsibility.

Peter had also received a letter in the same batch from Gabrielle. In it she was more forthcoming with the latest news. They were preparing to move to Amiens as a precautionary measure. A battery of artillery guns had returned to the edge of the hamlet, but this time they were firing from there onto unseen German targets. This had provoked counter battery fire with resulting explosions in the nearby fields. She asked him not to tell Dick, as he would worry. He's not the only one he thought.

An animated Dickie Watson announced his good news, and his request of a name for the baby provoked much debate. Bill Mellor started a book for people to make a wager on. He first task was to let his family know, and he also wrote to Adrian nagging him to return to the fold to help wet the baby's head.

*

Out of a west wing window Adrian looked over the formal gardens of the house. There wasn't much colour in the gardens at this time of year. The ground was covered in a thin layer of frost, and the water surrounding the fountain was frozen. The room was cold, with the fire being unlit, which he hardly noticed. In fact he enjoyed the cold air. He also enjoyed walking the dogs, or taking a horse out on a hack. The last few days did much to revive his spirits, and he was feeling much like his old self again.

He met his mother at breakfast as usual, and discussed the plans he had for the day.

"I think I would like to spend the day with you, if that's okay. I'm taking the train to London tomorrow."

Abigail looked up to protest, but thought better of it. "Only if you are sure," she replied. "As we have so little time left, I should tell you that Willerby has asked me to marry him."

Adrian wasn't really surprised at this development. "What have you told him?" he asked.

"I said I would have to discuss it with you."

Adrian smiled at his mother, she was he reflected still a very attractive women. "Does he make you happy?" he asked. "Abigail just nodded, embarrassed at the question." Then you should marry." He kissed her tenderly on the forehead. "Now, what do you want to do today"

*

The telephone call from the General brought some welcome news. Rogue flight would be taking delivery of no less than six SE's. John was delighted at the news. "Thank you Sir, how on earth did you manage it."

Caddell laughed down the line, "Oh just a slight of hand m'boy. Misdirected paperwork and that. They were bound for the far east. Much good they would do out there. Good luck to you"

John found Bill and Herbert bent over a board playing chess again. He gave them the good news. "The General has purloined some spare engines too."

Herbert didn't trust himself to take his eyes off the board. "Give the lads a week to work on 'em John, and we'll have them all up to scratch for you."

Bill moved a pawn which Herbert eyed suspiciously. he looked over to where Dick was, reading a paper. "What about Reggie?" he ventured.

Dick dropped his paper to his lap. "Reggie? Reggie Watson? Not a bloody chance." He went back to his paper.

"Dick! "He called out across the room. Herbert here thinks he'll have the new buses ready in a week."

He got no reply. "I Thought you and Peter might like a few days leave, you know, meet your son?"

In a flash Dick was on his feet smiling, "Thanks John, Where's Peter?" As he dashed for the door John called out to him, "In his room I'd imagine. Use my car! How about calling him John?"

Dick didn't take in anything except for the 'use my car' bit.

"Oh no you don't," Peter growled. "You're not driving the bloody car, not after the last time". Dick was not going to argue, and threw him the keys.

*

It was a beautiful sight to see as six brand new Se5a's come in to land. As yet they had no paintwork, apart from a basic coatings of dope. Within hours of landing, the first three selected were taken into the hangers, to be practically stripped down and rebuilt. The engines would be modified, as well as the many alterations and tweaks, which from their own experience will give their pilots an edge. There would be individual adjustments demanded from the pilots to accommodate their own peculiarities, usually parts they preferred from other types. The other three would have the bland indistinctive colours of greys and blues adorned to match the season, while they wait for their turn for the overhaul. Adrian was told of the replacement machines and decided to visit the hanger out of curiosity. Hands in pockets he went from one bus to the other, and rightly concluded that none of the first three were meant for him.

Bill noticed the familiar scowl on his face, and went over to talk to him. "Didn't think you'd be back so soon. Your bus is next door being painted."

Adrian saw the logic of the pecking order. "Not to worry Bill. look I'll see you all in the mess later. Seen Dick or John around? better check in I suppose."

Bill went to walk back to his bus. "Dick's buggered off to see his boy. John has taken Aubrey out on patrol"

*

They weren't looking to find any trouble with just the two of them. The strong westerly winds today could easily push them too far into Hun territory, which Singer was keen to avoid. A lone French reconnaissance plane was being harried by two Boche scouts. The situation before them at first sight was certainly one that the two SE's would normally intervene in. The problem was the other two Boche scouts sat in waiting another thousand feet above to ambush them. One thing in their favour was they were just inside of their own lines, where the enemy were reluctant to venture. Singer decided to take them on one after another. They flew directly towards the French two-seater. He was valiantly twisting and turning his machine to put off the aim of his attacker's. His rear gunner was still firing, trying to keep them both at bay. The two SE's went either side of Frenchmen and opened fire on the Germans. They immediately veered off in opposite directions. By the time they had regrouped the Frenchmen were behind the lines, which was enough for them to turn back eastward deprived of their kill. Singer simply flew on after the initial burst and left them behind, hoping they had done enough. He was now fixed on the other two that were diving down, now just at five hundred feet above. He was grateful that Aubrey was still at his side, and undamaged. Without so much as a degree of course alteration they went straight for the enemy. The Germans saw their colleagues flying away, and the English flying directly on to them. This led to indecision, and that indecision caused them too to refuse battle. They turned away, not really understanding what had just happened

*

They were only a mile or so from Le Rouex where the car had to slow down to circumvent a shell hole in the road. Peter steered it round gingerly. Dick was asleep, or at least half asleep, and didn't notice the pockmarked fields on either side. Peter did however, and as they drew nearer he noticed with alarm at the visible damage to some of the outlying houses on the edge of the village.

Peter felt a twinge of fear deep from within him. He shook Dick's arm vigorously. "Dick, wake up. look! Wake up" Dick roused himself as they reached the village perimeter. He couldn't understand what he was seeing. There was rubble everywhere, and a lot of damaged houses, some of the buildings looked to be untouched, but the signs were ominous. They had to walk the final few hundred yards into the square, as the road was now impassable. In deathly silence they turned the corner on the opposite side from where they cafe stood, or where it used to stand. Nothing was recognisable of the quaint cafe they thought of as home.

"They must be in Amiens," Peter suggested.

"Gabrielle said that's where they were going. She told me in her letter. We should go there."

Dick didn't trust himself to reply. He was finding it hard to keep himself in check. They both turned to see an old man standing silently behind them. They knew him as a retired soldier who lived in the village and frequented the cafe.

Ten minutes later they were stood in the churchyard staring down in disbelief, at four anonymous, freshly dug graves. Such was the devastation the folk that buried them couldn't identify with certainty who was who. Peter knelt before one of the mounds and began to sob inconsolably. Dickie stood frozen, staring down at his whole world, his future, his dreams lying underneath a few feet of disturbed soil.

Some hours passed before they could muster the energy to leave.

They both finally walked forlornly to the car. A man stood there waiting for them. it was the Pastor who they had met previously. He was a warm genial man, who had shared his favourite wine with them many times before. They had spent long hours in his company over the last few months, as he related exotic tales of his former life in the army.

He made to give them some comfort, it was a Boche shell, a direct hit. They wouldn't have suffered. His words were obviously having little affect, as he saw the tortured face of the two airmen before him. The Pastors demeanour changed suddenly. He grabbed Dick arms firmly and shook him with surprising strength. "You must not mourn my friend. Not yet. Your son needs you now. Do you hear me?"

Dick appeared to see the pastor for the first time. "What did you say. He's alive?"

"Yes, yes, your son, he lives."

Peter drove them back in silence. The boy was alive and well. He had been taken into care by the nuns from the local catholic school, and moved to Paris. That was all the Pastor knew. He alone would have to find him, a long way from home, and in the middle of a war.

*

The flight was once again viable John had at his disposal new machines and fresh pilots. John gave no comfort or respite to either Kiwi or Dick. He wanted them at their best, and if it took extra hours of shooting practice, then so be it. Dick was also given practise flights to improve his navigation. Both Adrian and Herbert were appalled with John's relentless pursuit in getting the flight operational, and even more so of his attitude towards Dick. John was well aware of the disapproval of the treatment meted out to Dickie and Peter. Adrian tried to broach the subject over breakfast, as diplomatically as he was able.

John looked back at him blankly. "We have just come back from virtual annihilation gentlemen. We've laboured hard to get the machines and pilots operational again," John heaved a sigh. "Of course it's hard on the boys Addie, very hard, but your life and mine, and all the rest of us, depends on them being back with us."

Adrian could understand his thinking, but he still had concerns, "You are right of course John, and I'm sorry if I sound critical, but his child in his eyes is lost, somewhere in Paris. Y'know he may just go off anyway, that's all that I'm worried about."

John had not considered that possibility. "If he does Addie that is desertion, and if caught he'll be shot."

He found Dickie by his SE talking to Herbert. He had just finished a solo flight, to brush up on his navigation. Adrian waited until they had finished. Dick looked up and walked towards him. He looked drawn and pale. "Still with us then?" he said lightly, but Dick understood the underlying message.

"It was just talk Addie, just desperate talk. I'm not going anywhere, but I'll find a way, somehow"

Adrian put an arm round his shoulder. "Worry you not my love. Your friend Addie here is taking care of it." Adrian had already decided to write to his father, when he heard the awful news. He was the one person he thought may be able to help, and for once he reached out to him as a son to a father.

*

Abigail stood by the clock at Paddington station, clutching a small bag. She had received a confusing message from her fiancé to meet him their post haste. No explanation was offered, but she did as he had asked, and patiently waited on developments, ignoring the questioning stares from passers-by. Willerby appeared from nowhere, and embraced her briefly, before taking her bag, and guiding her to a platform. She allowed herself to be taken to a train with just two carriages, which was sat there in front of them.

"Willerby, would you mind telling me what's going on, where are we going?" They entered the rear carriage which had a man and a woman already inside who greeted her by name. Willerby spoke to the man, a smartly dressed individual.

"We can push off now," he said curtly. Abigail took a seat at random.

"Willerby, I demand you tell me what this is all about, and how on earth did you get a train from. and who is that?"

Satisfied that he could do no more, he sat down opposite.

"No names I'm afraid, procedures you know! but thank you for your leap of faith m' dear. You and I are going on an adventure. Thought you would like to see Paris" He explained. "Your… our son contacted me asking for help y' see. So, you and I are going to Paris under some pretext of being a diplomatic delegation. These two good people here are assigned to facilitate that. Hence the private train, and a commandeered boat."

He looked over to the aides. "We do have a boat, don't we?" he asked.

They both nodded and carried on going through paperwork.

"That's all very impressive dear, but you haven't told me why?"

Willerby told her of the shelling of Le Rouex, with Claudette and her family being killed, and Dick's predicament. They were now on their way to recover the child, and bring him home. "It's Adrian's best friend, and he's reached out to me, to us, so here we are."

Abigail reached over and put her hand on his cheek. "We'll find him dear, we'll get him home"

The aides had managed to path the way with some efficiency. On reaching Plymouth, a car was waiting to transfer them to the docks. They were then ushered onto a Frigate no less, being the only vessel to hand. It was Willerby's considerable influence in London that had made all this happen. He only asked for a boat for transport, but even he was surprised at the loan of a large ship of war seconded into service. Two days later they were safely embedded within the British Embassy in Paris.

They were ensconced in a large office on the ground floor of the embassy. The two aides were supported by additional staff as demanded by his Lordship, with the task of locating the English child bought back via Amiens. They were only a day into the search, where they discovered where the baby had been initially placed. Enquiries were made which had the effect of immediately making the church authorities suspicious, The child was quickly relocated to another unknown address, as a result.

Abigail was incensed "Why would they hide him from us?" she demanded of the aide.

He pushed over the communique he had received. "It's all couched in polite language madam, but in simple terms the Catholic church are not prepared to hand over a baby, born out of wedlock to a foreigner, and one that is not of the faith at that."

Abigail was horrified at this turn of events.

Willerby interrupted them. "Don't be disheartened my love. Our very smart friend here anticipated this, knowing how they operate, and has had eyes on the convent for a while"

The aide acknowledged the compliment. A map was produced. "He is currently in an anonymous house in the suburbs, here, in Levallois. We of course cannot help further, officially that is"

Willerby looked at the unfamiliar map. "Which means Abby, it's up to us."

*

Low grey clouds skidded across the skies. Nothing would be flying above the cloud ceiling, which had the effect of compressing the airspace available. Singer had the flight escorting nine twin engine French Cauldron's that operated from the same airfield that Rogue used. Flying alongside was Dick, which was at his insistence. Whether it was a vote of confidence in him, or to keep a close eye, Dick wouldn't know, and frankly he didn't really care. They were over German held airspace for the first time since Cambrai, and that was all that mattered. The French had a separate ground strafing mission, and could only muster a few Spad's for support of their own.

There were supply dumps and railway sidings that were the target sited at a strategic location where several connecting roads met. It wasn't long before they drew the attention of a larger Boche formation who were patrolling less than two miles away. Singer could see them as they approached, calculating they would be able to intercept before they could reach the slower two seaters. The French took their machines lower a little earlier than planned, to put more distance from the Boche. As they started their strafing runs, they were met with substantial ground fire from machine guns and artillery. One of the bombers was hit almost immediately. He dropped his ordnance, and turned for home, trailing smoke from one of the engines. Nothing they could do could prevent the threat from below, but Singer was confident that they could break up this attack coming in from above.

They were but half a mile away, closing in just below the cloud base. As usual Singer had his machines in loose pairs. When they were just coming into range, Singer dipped his nose to fly below the enemy. Dick followed suit, as did Aubrey and Kiwi behind. Adrian however decided on impulse to confuse the issue, and took his SE up into the cloud. It was a risky manoeuvre he knew, but they were flying a loose formation. The main problem with this, he knew, was disorientation, so he decided to turn fifteen degrees to port, and count out the seconds. Mario looked up, thinking Addie had gone bonkers. He saw that all the SE's in from had dipped their noses which gave him a clear run to meet the Boche planes head on. The Germans were a dangerous mixture of modern scout types, Flying with two layers one above the other. The opening salvo from the leading four all went harmlessly over the SE's, now below. Singer reversed the dive, and poured fire into the Boche, before they could adjust their aim in time.

Singer took his flight down once more and quickly reversed course to attack from behind. The Bristol flew unerringly at the scout nearest to him on their left flank. The scout flew into a stream of incendiary and explosive bullets, and caught fire almost immediately. Jules had no targets as yet, and was content to look upon the skirmish as an onlooker. Out of the cloud Adrian's machine emerged from above, with the undercarriage being the first part to become visible. He had miscalculated slightly, as his wheels came within a hair's breath of an enemy Scout located at the rear of the top tier of machines. He winced at the near miss, and was too shook up to turn back straight away. It did however have the positive effect of putting the wind up the poor man he almost hit, who dived for less crowded skies, and never turned back.

Singer followed the scattered formation for a minute or so, until he was satisfied they had enough. He saw that the French machines had turned for home leaving clouds of black smoke rising from the ground behind him. As he turned into a lazy circle, he noticed one of his flight had failed to regroup, and was losing height rapidly. At first he thought the machine was in trouble, but seconds later a second plane, also an SE followed him down. He kept station to observe the first SE in a steep dive, He could see that it was deliberately firing downward at an artillery battery. Dick! the bloody fool, and that must be Adrian following in his wake. He too opened fire at the guns. Dick climbed again out of range, obviously out of ammunition, and he was relieved to see Adrian apparently unscathed. Singer was beside himself with rage at his stupidity. Dick came alongside, and realised he had taken some damage. It didn't feel right. Singer saw that some of his undercarriage was missing, with parts also hanging off.

They arrived back at the aerodrome, where Singer let off a flare to warn the ground crew. He then signalled Dick to land first, and led the rest to take a circuit around. Dick landed heavily, with the undercarriage failing beneath him, his machines belly skirted along the grass, and finally coming to a halt, facing the way he had come from. A few minutes later the resulting war of words between the two erupted in front of the others. Dick remained hard faced as his commanding officer who took him to task in no uncertain terms.

Dick's response was equally brutal. "So now you want to court martial me for fighting the fucking enemy! Go ahead, see how far that gets you. Few days ago, you were thought I was a going to walk away. You want to make your bloody mind up!"

Adrian pulled Dick away before he got himself into more trouble. Herbert did the same with John, before he could say anything more"

*

Abigail sat impatiently looking out of a window of the embassy. Willerby had taken himself off some hours earlier, accompanied by a rum looking type. The stranger was in fact an old military acquaintance, with particular set of skills useful for these occasions. He was unshaven and roughly dressed, which was to render him invisible to any casual observer. They had left to do a 'reconnaissance' of the house where Dick's son was being secreted. The house was found to be in a quiet cul de sac. Willerby's acquaintance was dropped to monitor and observe, and if possible, have a closer look in and around.

Suitably demure clothes had to be found for Abigail, suitable for the operation, and she was surprised to find an outfit was delivered the next morning, and she found to her relief they were perfect for her size.

"It has to be today," Willerby announced. "We now have access to the house, thanks to our friend leaving the back door unlocked." On the table was a crude drawing showing the probable location of the baby, and the two occupants. from conversations overheard from inside. "We know there are at least two females inside, and we know he is being moved again shortly." He looked intently at Abigail. "I know you imagine this as an adventure my love, but this is dangerous ground we are treading on. If caught, we can expect serious repercussions."

She ignored his warnings, and picked up the clothes for the job. "Nonsense my dear. We have come this far for the boys, now what's your plan?"

The same scruffy acquaintance that went with Willerby yesterday, was now a smartly groomed gentleman, who was there to drive them to the location. On arrival Willerby strode towards the front door announcing his arrival by loudly hammering on the door. The commotion he caused drew two Nuns to confront him, as was hoped. Abigail went around the side of the house and gained entrance through the kitchen door. She carried on into the back room, and was confronted with not one but two cots. A young girl, possibly a trainee was sat in attendance. It was Abigail who recovered her composure first, "Le enfant Anglais" she demanded.

The girl's eyes went to the cot by the window. She strode over and picked up the baby, this caused the young girl to stir menacingly.

On the front porch of the house Willerby was causing havoc by citing multiple breaches of fictional city ordinances. His French carried as much authority as his native English, and the unsuspecting Nuns were coming off worse in the exchange. The noise was enough to set off the poor infant in the other cot under the young girls charge. Abigail cut short the girls protests, by instructing her to attend to the distressed child. Within the next few minutes, the child was safety in the waiting car. Willerby exited the house still threatening retribution and fines for undefined misdemeanours. They eventually made their way to the Embassy without further incident.

Three days later the child was found to be the latest resident of the Willerby estate's nursery.

*

To make matters worse for the flight, Dick and Adrian's maniacal attack on the artillery was lauded by the watching French aviators who considered it heroic. They responded in typical French fashion, as somehow they were well aware of the single German gong the flight had in its possession.

A delegation made its way across the aerodrome to present the *legion d'honneur* to add to its battle honours. In turn, the guests were treated to an evening in the mess, further strengthening the bond between them. John was sat quietly in the corner with Bill and Herbert. He knew the flight was now fractured, and he was at a loss on what to do next. Discipline had to be maintained, but had to be tempered with leadership. Dick wasn't in attendance at the mess for the party, choosing to stay in his billet and write letters home instead.

The weather was problematical for airborne activity, and under normal circumstances John would have likely postponed the patrol. He was hoping that it may the start of the healing process, but it only exposed the glaring chasm within them.

John was sat alone having breakfast, not bothering to take off all of his kit. Bill sat down with a mug of tea, and looked at his commander in silence. "Bill you're putting me off my breakfast, what can I do for you."

Bill ignored the terse tone of his Captain. "Would you listen to an idea of ours, without prejudice that is." Before John could respond, Herbert joined them, which was obviously premeditated. John continued to eat, but looked at Herbert suspiciously.

"If I knew what that meant Bill, I could help. Something I can do for you Mr Rhys-Jones?" Herbert looked back at Bill.

"It's an idea that Bill wants to propose, which I'm here to endorse John. It's a proposal dreamed up by your ground crew, and think it's a worth a listen"

The two led John into his own office, where some maps were laid out. Adrian was already inside waiting for them.

"You too?" John huffed.

Adrian shrugged his shoulders. "Not my show John, this comes straight from the hanger, and they've put a lot of work into this."

Bill confidentially outlined the mission, which was simply that Rogue would find and destroy a dangerous artillery battery. Bill point on the map where the battery was.

John was annoyed and confused. "We are a scout unit. We have no business attacking artillery. That's for bombers, or our own guns, and why here?"

Adrian put in "It's the battery that destroyed Le Rouex John, the one that killed the girls."

John now understood, and chose not to dismiss it out of hand. "Gentlemen," he said softly. "I appreciate your sentiments, but we cannot operate our missions out of revenge. You don't know its location, and you don't have the machines to do the job."

Bill had anticipated John's response, and handed John a brief report. Bill had gone to considerable lengths to ensure the mission would be sanctioned and approved.

It was further confirmed by General Caddell as being a legitimate target! The battery had been found, by the simple expediency of asking the British battery still stationed at Le Rouex, who in fact did know its location. The final part of the jigsaw was obtaining a squadron of bombers to agree to undertake the mission, with Rogue as escorts. John knew he had lost the argument and reluctantly agreed.

"Who are the damn fools that are flying with us?" he sighed.

Adrian's face lit up. "It's an American squadron of Handley's courtesy of our old friend Eugene"

*

Later that day, Adrian sought out Dick, who was working by himself on his SE. he was still morose and withdrawn, not at all himself. John told him the news about the bombing raid, which John could see had an immediate impact.

Adrian had some better news to impart, however. "Had a letter from my mother today, Dick, here look. They found your son, see here! They found him, took him, and brought him back to England."

Dick was visibly stunned at the news. "He's home Dick, and waiting for his Dad."

Tears began to stream down his oil smeared face. "Here's a picture they sent with the letter, I've got one too, see."

With hands shaking he held the small photograph. "Don't know what to say Addie, how can I ever thank you?"

Adrian folded the letter away. "Go see John, and make it right. Weather permitting, we are on patrol tomorrow, hunting guns."

*

Abigail had opted to stay up in Derbyshire for the time being to take care of the child. It was surprising to her how quickly both she and Willerby had become attached to the child. The idea of being responsible was at the beginning a terrifying proposition for his Lordship. He went to great lengths to convince her to remain at the estate. In truth she took little persuading, especially after the extreme measures they had undertaken to rescue him.

"It's from Dickie Watson dear," she opened the letter with a paper knife, and read the contents to herself. Willerby walked into the library to join her.

"How's the boy doing?" he asked. "Adrian's last letter told me he was not at all himself."

She carried on reading all the way through. "Oh bless the dear boy. He speaks of his immense gratitude and affection. Asking after his son of course. Listen dear, he has asked if we would consider being his godparents, bless. What do you think? oh, and he has a name for him."

She handed the letter over to him. "When you have finished reading that, I shall write to his parents in Birmingham, and invite them to visit, so they can see the child. If that meets your approval dear?"

Willerby mumbled absently. "Of course, Abby, that's a fine sentiment. So the child's name is to be Claude. I think his mother would have approved"

*

The pre-flight briefing was predictably short, but incisive. John appeared to be more like his old self, and was chatting amiably with Aubrey. He didn't even seem to mind when Adrian stumbled in late, as usual.

"Chaps, as you know today, we are escorting Eugene's 'fat boys'. We will rendezvous and escort them to the target. Our job is to keep them safe there and back."

He checked with the map. "About four miles behind the lines. Flying in pairs as usual, but in a wide dispersal, front and back, left and right of the formation. Use your flares if you spot trouble, but don't assume help. There may be more than one threat,"

John turned deliberately to Dickie, "Dick, your job will be to lay down the flares over the target for the bombers. You are not to engage, clear!" It was John's assertion of authority for all to witness.

Dick was impassive. "Very clear Sir" The briefing was over, and for the first time in a while, John knew he had his flight back.

*

The American's were found in good time at two thousand feet. Although they had detailed maps of the course and target, Singer aligned himself, and Dick above and ahead of the bombers for protection, and to confirm the course for the Americans. The twins in the Bristol would fly above and behind, Aubrey and Peter would fly above.

Singer found there was one too many SE's in the air. The plus one had bright distinctive colours of the American air force. It was Eugene who waved at his former comrades as he flew by. He finally settled below the bombers, and began to weave and swerve his machine to frustrate the gunners below. Dick knew they were close, but as yet couldn't see the battery which would be partially hidden by large hedgerows, and trees. He took the SE down at full throttle at a shallow angle to lay down his flares. His task was made easier with the spectacle of machine gun fire rising up from the ground. He could now see the barrels of the guns all at about a forty-five-degree angle. The SE was now only a few hundred feet above the guns, when the first of the flares arced upwards. Singer could now see the guns and guided the bombers to their target. Despite the noise of bullet impacts, Dick continued to let off more flares, this time downward.

Adrian was watching with horror. "Get out of there you mad bugger,' he growled.

The Americans arrived over the target, and one by one unloaded their large payload. The ground around the guns erupted, sending earth skywards. Singer circled above and watched in fascination as direct hits announced themselves on the battery itself. Ammunition and shells servicing the guns exploded adding to the carnage.

Dick took station besides his commander, and stared down without emotion at the destroyed guns. He thought he would have been elated at exacting revenge for Claudette, instead he felt empty and slightly ashamed. They lost one two-seater on the way home, from Archie. They encountered some threats from small numbers of nearby EA, but none were able to press home an effective attack. Singer skilfully marshalled his few machines to shoo them off. They finally separated to return to their respective aerodromes, with Eugene opting to stay with the other SE's.

*

Major Eugene Carpenter chose to spend a night with his old comrades He was greeted as a returning hero. Much of the night was spent in catching up with his friends from the hangers, as well as his fellow aviators. John was a little hesitant in celebrating the success of the mission. He was mindful of the cost of two young aviators who died in the bomber, so very far from home. Eugene had just finished congratulating Dick on his contribution to the day's action.

John was sober in his manner. "Eugene, I'm sorry you had to lose those men. It wasn't their fight after all".

Eugene considered his friend for a while. "John, don't you go all morbid on me. They were good men, yes, and they'll will be missed. We've both lost men, and there'll be more for sure" Eugene smiled at his old friend and offered his drink to toast. "Let's celebrate them tonight, in a fine old style."

Chapter Eleven

Get Richthofen

General Caddell paid a visit to Bailleul, and came bearing gifts. His visit was expected, but although everyone kept a keen eye out for his arrival, they were wrong footed when the General unexpectedly appeared out of the passenger side of a large tender. John wasn't too surprised at this, knowing the General's eccentric ways. He stood by the door of the lorry, anonymous in an oversized greatcoat, stamping his feet into the snow-covered grass. Joe Naismith walked across his path with his head down, blowing into his clenched fists to keep them warm. He neither recognised the General nor acknowledged him, as he continued his overdue journey to the latrines. Another person stepped out from the inside of the vehicle. This one was much younger, and of medium build and height. His features were covered over by a thick scarf, and he too was buried under heavy winter clothes. His hat and boots visible marked him out as an aviator. Caddell made his way to the mess with the young pilot following in his wake. As they approached the sanctuary of the mess, Herbert caught up with him, from the direction of the hangers.

"Morning General, was expecting your usual car Sir."

Caddell looked briefly to one side. "Herbert, ah yes the lorry. Bought some gifts of winter cheer. You might like to round up some of your chaps to unload." Caddell stopped to look back at the field. "Chaps are up I would imagine. Must be bloody freezing up there."

Adrian was the first into the mess, still in the act of removing his flying gear. He was quickly followed by the others, who all made their way to the warming fire. Caddell sat quietly with the youngster watching them come in one by one. He was immensely proud of this little group, as he got to know them. Boys hardly out of school, who were performing extraordinary feats of heroism daily in the cold unforgiving winter skies. Aubrey declined to hog the warming fire with the others, as he knew it would give him chilblains, and he was the first to note the pair sat to one side.

"Morning Sir, good to see you." he said louder than necessary. The others turned around, and further greetings followed. John took off his pairs of gauntlets and sat down, eyeing up the stranger.

"Morning John," he said lightly. "I come bearing gifts."

They shook hands warmly. "General, always good to see you. Who's this rascal?"

Caddell ignored the question. "Never mind him, as I have said I come bearing gifts, and I wish you to note the sacrifice of a long bumpy ride in that old crate".

He waved airily in the direction of the tender. "In order of merit, I have for you a crate of malt. Warm flying clothes for the men, and a new engine for the Bristol. Where are they?"

Jules and Mario were still by the fire.

"Mario! where are you?" He shouted across the room.

Mario replied, "Here General, did you get an engine for us?"

Caddell raised his hand. "I did m'boy and a sore backside in the delivery. A Falcon no less, Rolls Royce, it's in the back of the truck."

Above the laughter Mario and Jules thanked him, and left to see their new acquisition.

Caddell put the newcomer out of his misery. "Ah, almost forgot, this is Sergeant Leslie Ballard RFC, dragged him out of training school. Don't let the dim-witted look in his eyes fool you, he's a fine aviator."

John felt sorry for the lad as he shook his hand. "Welcome to Rogue, Leslie," John looked around the room. "Aubrey, over here. This is Ballard, find him somewhere to sleep, and then take him up with you, and show him the ropes for a few days. Give him one of the old SE's"

In the office sat John, Adrian, and Herbert. Caddell sat in John's chair exchanging pleasantries with them for a while. John was wary, as he guessed that the gift bearing officer must come with a price.

"Couple of updates for you chaps. You will have witnessed the skies are getting busier by the day. We are putting more buses in the air, as well as the French and Americans. Grant you the quality of airmen is problematical, but the powers that be think we are winning the numbers game, and that's all that counts."

Adrian wasn't impressed, "Sir, some of those boys are just fodder for the Boche, with only a handful of hours, they don't stand a chance."

John agreed with him. "They need at least double the hours in the air before they can be of any use Sir."

Caddell held up a hand "Not for us to debate here chaps," he countered. "The numbers though are making your lives more difficult to cope, and the thinking is we need a change of tactic to keep Rogue viable, but we will talk of that later. We have been given an assignment deemed perfect to suit your talents"

The General went over to the large map on the wall of the entire western front, and pointed to the Somme area, already well known to everyone assembled.

"Reports from intelligence sources are predicting a German offensive, come springtime. They are massing men and materials. Expect a rise in the number of our reconnaissance boys, who will need protection." The General paused. "Secondly, somewhere near Doual we think is where Jasta 11 operates from. Your task is to find its leader, you will know his name gentleman, one Manfred Von Richthofen. Your job is to find him, and kill him."

A silence fell over the room.

"Can't be done sir," Adrian sad flatly. "He's has the flying circus all around him. Dozens of Germanys best airmen." He folded his arms petulantly and scowled. "Anyway, we are fliers, not assassins."

The General's face hardened. "Don't give me that knights of the air nonsense!" he exploded "You are a soldier Lieutenant, and you will obey the bloody orders."

In this mood, John knew the General meant business. "May I ask why Sir, he's just one pilot. He's downed a lot of planes, but then so have we."

The General handed a thick file to John. "The Baron is more than that. He is a symbol, a flag to rally round. He poses more of a threat than the numbers of kills, and bloody cups he collects. Read the file, you will find it useful."

After the General had said his farewells, and had just enough time to grab some sandwiches before going out on another patrol. Singer decide to take them for a jaunt over where it was thought Jasta 11 were likely to be, without letting his flight know beforehand. They were at only at five hundred feet when he saw two SE's going through some exercises. It was Aubrey and the new chap. He flew in an extended arc, so he could continue to observe them briefly. From his practised eye, he thought the new chap, damn it, what was his name! He thought he handled his machine with some authority, at least the General still has the knack of finding exceptional young talent.

A large formation was seen some miles away, which John went to investigate. He kept above as best he could, however they had been seen themselves. and the large intimidating formation came straight for them. It was John's turn to take to his heels. In a few seconds he had reversed course and took the flight home toward friendlier skies.

*

In the office the men stood round a map discussing different methods of firstly locating the whereabouts of *Jasta* 11 and then when they did, how could they complete the mission?

John had invited his usual favourites for this intercourse, being Adrian, Herbert and Mario. In turn Herbert brought along Bill Mellor, and Adrian had invited Dickie. "This will be the proverbial needle in a haystack chaps, any and all suggestions please.

Several days later, they had gone through and had exhausted their repertoire of plans, all of which were discarded as unworkable. It was Herbert that came up with an inspirational idea, or at least he was presented with one.

"Give it to Bill, the mission I mean. He'll root out your man for you."

Everyone there was surprised at Herbert's statement to put it mildly. He was already known as a bit of a boffin, and so John allowed him the floor. From nowhere Bill produced a stack of papers, and laid them out covering the map. "It's all down to mathematics, here. First, we have to find *Jasta* 11, and then the devil himself. we, or should I say I will coordinate with every other squadron in the area, to log each and every contact."

He looked at John unabashed. "I'll need the use of your, telephone and office for a while Sir."

John was slightly stunned but nodded in agreement. "I can then lay out a pattern of behaviour, with all the variables, you know, weather and so forth. From there we will build a picture of predictive flight possibilities, for you chaps to intercept."

He paused for any objections. "Bill, we know there is more than one circus, how do we find Richthofen's?"

Bill rustled through some papers. "Here are some observations we know of logging the markings and colours on the *Jasta's* 11 machines. Someone with good eyesight like our Dickie here should be able to identify them." He went on. "First task is to find where they operate from. I suggest an initial wide pattern and high-altitude observation patrols. Find the planes, and follow them home."

John duly gave his approval, and set about organising the SE's into patrols of two to begin the search. The meeting dispersed and most of them left for dinner.

Adrian and Dick hung back, having not said a word in the meeting. It was with a sense of foreboding that John let them have the floor.

"Dickie here knows something of the man, after his previous trysts in no man's land with Voss," John looked over to Dick intrigued.

"Voss told me that Manfred isn't the flyer he was, after his head wound last year. He also told me about when you two met, and he spared your life." Dick finished abruptly.

John was a little annoyed now. "So, what are you telling me Dick. That he'll be easier to shoot down? and what if he did let me live that day? How is that relevant to our mission?"

Adrian jumped up. "Have we looked at the possibility of capture, not kill? If we could devise a way to get him down, without compromising the lives of our chaps, would you consider it?"

When they left John's office Dick whispered. "Well that's the first hurdle, anyway. If we do succeed in taking him alive, are we doing him any favours?"

The question remained in the air, unanswered. "And how do we achieve this little miracle in the first place?"

Adrian scowled in thought. "Not a bloody clue old fruit, we'll need some help on that one."

Leslie Ballard was spending his first evening in the mess. He felt awkward and out of place. He had only ever been in training schools, with no front-line experience at all. Ballard was the son of a rural banker, and had a protective middle-class upbringing, He would not have looked out of place in a school choir, having a clear complexion, and light curly hair. He sorely wished he was back in flight training, at least there he was at home, and even liked. Ballard carried the stigma of being a disappointment to his family, and in particular his father. His expensive schooling had only proven to his family he had little aptitude for anything. It was with flying that he found he had a talent. It was a natural environment in which he excelled, and in the months he was in training he had outclassed his peers, and impressed his instructors. It was General Caddell was astute, and devious enough whisk him away, before he was allocated elsewhere. On the wall he stared in fascination at the two plaques representing medals, both foreign. The French Croix de Guerre he understood, but the German gong was confusing. The door burst open with a small group of men entered together. Some were obviously aviators, others were in grease covered overalls. As one they picked out the young vulnerable man sat alone. He was quickly surrounded and assailed with questions and friendly greetings. It was half an hour later he took stock of what was before him, and concluded he was going to like it here.

*

It was information received from another British squadron that enabled Bill to amend the search pattern by half. He presented his officer with the area to cover and time schedule. All John had to do was to allocate the pairings.

The SE's of Dick and Aubrey were the first to get a hit. The formidable German formation were fortunately flying East, probably back to their place of origin. The two SE's stayed behind, using what cloud cover they could. Although they had most likely been observed, they gambled they would be left alone.

The aerodrome came into view through the misty air, and Dick turned his bus away, not wanting to risk any contact. Aubrey hadn't seen the field himself, but matched the manoeuvre anyway. Adrian and the twins went up the next morning. The Bristol was fitted with its camera. They arrived over the field just after dawn, where the scout patrolled the airspace, as Jules took photos with practised efficiency. On the return leg they came across a pair of Albatrosses, who evidently also had an early start. They clashed two minutes later, in a brief dogfight. One of the Boche was quickly on the tail of the Bristol. The British two-seater was manoeuvring violently in sudden ducks and drakes, making it impossible to hit, but the incoming fire from the observer was appallingly accurate. The Fokker peeled off, not interested in pressing the issue. His comrade in the other machine, made only a token attempt to engage with Adrian. His first pass with the British scout confirmed to him that this was no amateur. Short of ammunition, he too left them unmolested. Adrian noted the colours and insignias on them, to pass on to Bill when they returned.

*

General Caddell cherished his time in the club. Here he could meet with his peers, drink or eat at his pleasure, or spend a convivial hour scouring the papers. The Marlborough Club in Pall Mall, was an exclusive and private London club, popular with civilian gentlemen and officers of the military. He absently noticed someone who sat in a leather winged armchair immediately opposite to him. He was mildly irritated, as there was plenty of other seating options in the room, which would not intrude on his privacy. "Good morning, General, it's a tad brisk this morning is it not?"

Caddell snatched his paper down to his lap, and saw a smartly dressed civilian type smiling benignly at him. He didn't recognise the man, who had obviously recognised the uniform. "Do I know you Sir?" he replied curtly. The stranger stood up, oblivious to the General's irritation "Forgive me General Caddell, my name is Wentworth, Willerby Wentworth, I believe you know my son."

Caddell thought for a second and then recognition came. "Ah, Adrian. Fine young man." He held out his hand "You must be The Lord Wentworth, I believe, lately returned from illicit journeys abroad I here."

Caddell gestured for some service. "They do a marvellous lunch here Wentworth. That would be the price I will pay, if you would care to elaborate on how the devil you and your good lady managed it."

After lunch, David sat reflecting on the tale of Wentworth's rescue. "That Sir was a brilliant campaign, and superbly executed. I would also say you must have had considerable military training yourself."

Willerby poured them both another glass of whisky. "Very astute off you David, except it's not of the past, which is why this, umm, encounter is not by chance."

Caddell kept his own council, to re-appraise the man.

"I have certain areas of expertise the Government feel is of some use, including military intelligence." Willerby leaned forward. "I am aware of the mission your men have been given regarding a certain German aviator."

Alarm bells began to ring in the generals head. "Unfortunately for us, our intelligence bods aren't all that good at keeping secrets, and if I know, then believe me, Berlin knows."

Caddell took the news well. "I will of course warn Captain Singh-Smythe. Anything else I should know?"

Willerby hesitated, "Just this, if I was on the other side, I wouldn't wait. Tell Singer to look out for a trap."

*

In Between his hours in the air, Leslie was roped into assisting Bill with assimilation of the information they we're getting on *Jasta* 11. Photographs, documents, paper cuttings and reports. Jules pitched in with converting all the intelligence receive in German. On the wall was a large map that was covered in string of different colours. Close ups of the Fokker overpainted for effect. Apart from the German newspapers, they obtained a report on the flying qualities of the Fokker Dr.1, which threw up some intriguing information.

Leslie found to his amazement, that he enjoyed this academic exercise very stimulating, as opposed to his lethargic efforts back at school. This had a purpose, and an end result, which made all the difference. Bill was very pleased with himself at the progress of his investigations, which to an onlooker might be interpreted as a smug or self-satisfied. That was changed in an instant, when a communique from the General had been passed on by John, confirming the German's awareness of the threat to their poster boy.

Reconnaissance confirmed the massing of German troops released from the Russian front. The days were getting busier with the lengthening of the days. They were usually protecting the slower two-seater's who had to fly into Boche territory to hunt for any, and all movement of interest. Trench lines, supply dumps, artillery parks, the list was endless. The demand for information was insatiable. Alternately, the enemy were just as keen to probe for areas of weakness in numbers and terrain, and so the intensity of activity increased. All of the pilots reported increased contact with enemy EA on both sides of the lines, resulting in the destruction and damage of considerable number of machines, mostly two-seaters.

Adrian took Leslie on his first active sortie. They came across an ageing LVG flying alone at two thousand feet. Adrian took the pair of scouts around to cut off his line of retreat, and led them into attack. The lumbering machine turned back towards his own lines, after seeing the threat from above. Adrian led his protege in behind, and signalled for Leslie to attack. The SE leaped forward and fired lengthy bursts that missed hopelessly. Leslie had emptied his Lewis without hitting a thing. He quickly took himself out of the fight to avoid the observers unnervingly accurate reply, and to reload the drum. Adrian took his place and ruthlessly dispatched the poor observer with his first dozen bullets. He waited for his partner to reload, and again invited him to finish the job. It took almost the entire drum of fifty bullets, but eventually he had scored enough hits to bring it down. He watched in fascination as the plane fell out of the sky, and smash into the ground behind the British lines. Adrian noted that the youngster was too mesmerised at his first victory and, he failed to keep watch of the skies. He will pull him up on it later, but the boy had been bloodied, it was a good start.

*

Bill was found in the mess playing chess with Peter. As always with his concentration he noticed nothing outside of what was developing on the board. John was lounging with Dick, Adrian, and Herbert mulling over what they should do now, knowing the Boche were lying in wait for Rogue flight to make its move.

Suggestions were being offered, many of which were improbable. The underlying consensus was that the idea should be abandoned altogether. Bill called over. "Fancy a game John?" he asked. "I think Peter here has had enough."

John was annoyed. "Bit busy here Bill, not in the mood," he said petulantly.

Bill didn't bite. "Oh, but I insist John. Playing chess is all about strategy, including avoiding traps you know. I think I have an idea," he said mildly. "Might need few more games to think it through though."

*

"That's a bit cold Bill, if you don't mind me saying," Adrian was shocked at the plan than Bill has formulated.

"Not if you think about it, that is from a mathematical perspective," Bill hit back, "it makes perfect sense." Bill had surmised that the Boche would use Richthofen as bait, then ambush and destroy the flight. Bill proposed using a relatively new squadron which also flew SE's, just arrived in theatre, to trigger the trap, with Rogue flying within their ranks. The problem was it was pitting new pilots with minimal combat experience against the finest that Germany had. Casualties would inevitably be high. He also calculated that although the *Jasta* itself had been historically mobile, it would make sense to have their in the air best to support the anticipated offensive

Bill's argument was that they were being thrown into the theatre anyway, and contact with *Jasta* 11 was inevitable. If they had Rogue flying with them, it would stiffen the ranks, and actually increase the survival rate instead. John had to admit that Bill's logic was hard to argue with. He duly ordered for the SE's to be painted in the livery of the squadron, so the Boche wouldn't be able to set them apart. He would explain it all to the squadron leader later, if he picked up on the fact he was going to have more machines in the air than he actually thought.

Without asking permission Leslie Ballard had arbitrarily had his machine repainted. John found out about this and rounded on him for his insubordination. he wasn't nearly ready enough for combat patrols yet.

"I'm sorry sir, I just assumed that I would be needed." Before he could get a word in, Leslie blurted. "Those boys there, are being sent out on the orders of the high command Sir, I'm a better pilot, which is why I'm here with you. If they think that is okay to send them out, you cannot expect me to stay grounded." John was seething, that's twice in one morning he had been verbally bashed. "You'll fly with me, no arguments."

For the next few days Rogue flight flew with the squadron out on patrol on the pretext they were escorting them as was their remit. There wasn't any mention of the identical markings of the machines to their own which was either overlooked or ignored. They did however soon learn to appreciate the quality of their guardian angels, who repeatedly showed their mettle in the fight.

Most of the Aerial contacts were for once mainly over British held ground. This gave the British the advantage for once, of being able to stay in the fight longer due to the shorter range, and any downed or damaged machines the pilot could walk from, would not now lead to captivity. The fight in the air became as much as attritional as that on the ground with substantial losses on both sides. The feedback from his men was that the German aviators were of variable standards, even in Richthofen's squad. The veterans that were left however were excellent, and very dangerous. These were the ones that the boys had to weed out, and eliminate if possible.

Dick decided to have a look in Bill Mellor's office, to find Bill and Leslie pouring over type written notes. They both looked up when he entered without knocking. "Ah Dickie m'boy, how goes it up there?" He greeted genially. Dick took a cursory look over the untidy heap of paperwork and Photographs covering both desks.

"Bit bloody crowded up there, whatever the trap was, I think events have overtaken any chance of getting to the man, especially with this attack looming." Dick sat down disconsolately.

Bill remained infuriatingly jovial. "*Carp diem* Dickie. Phase one is redundant its true, as we shall soon move onward." Bill irreverently clapped Dick on the back. "As you are here, you might want to pass on the news to the others,"

Bill graciously allowed Leslie to elaborate. "Bill here has projected the Hun and will make their move around the middle of March, don't ask me how he knows" He picked up file.

"Our friend the Baron has a taken a liking to flying alone, sometimes with only one or two others for company. He has a taste for targeting vulnerable two-seater's, mostly over Boche land of course.

"With that statement, Dick was all ears. "Now, we have here a pattern of times he likes to swan around the skies, usually after breakfast and lunch presumably in between meals." Leslie was getting theatrical by pacing the room, and raising his finger to make a point. "Now that the Boche will be coming over to play on our side of the fence, then so will his air force, and with it, the Baron himself"

*

A letter arrived unexpectedly on John's desk. He read it twice, and put it in his tunic for safe keeping. That evening John patently waited for the right time to get all assembled their attention. Herbert duly obliged in his usual manner by bellowing out across the room.

John stood up with the letter in his hand. "Apologies chaps, but I thought you might be interested in this letter received this morning." He opened the letter, already familiar with its contents. "A comrade of ours, sadly no longer with us has written to let you know, he is safe and well, and residing in America, Virginia to be precise. Doing very well with a garage business by all accounts. Anyway, I'll give it to Herbert here to pass around. In the meantime, Gentlemen, if you would care to raise your glasses."

There was a brief shuffle of chairs, with whispered voices echoing the name "Its Ernie". John raised his glass and said. "Absent friends," he then handed the letter to Herbert, who was quickly surrounded by bodies, all impatiently waiting to get a glimpse.

Herbert looked on to the crowd and sat down next to John. "He made it then."

Adrian finally got a hold of the letters and read it, before passing it on. After a few moments he waved Dickie over, inviting him to join him. "Read the letter yet?," he asked enthusiastically.

"Yes of course. Good to know one of us will survive the war," Adrian ignored him, and pulled at his sleeve. "Come with me, I have an idea."

They conversed quietly in low tones in one corner of the mess for some time. Dick was nodding in agreement at his friends' comments. "If I were you Addie, I would get your father to help us out with this one, but first lets go and sell it to John, while he's still in a good mood"

*

The assault began in the early hours of the twenty-first of March, starting with a furious artillery barrage. Thousands of Germans emerged from the low mist and fog, by the wire, cut previously. In minutes some of the

British first lines were overwhelmed, with thousands in full retreat. It took several days for the German advance to slow down, with supplies and re-enforcements coming up short. Above the carnage dozens of machines clashed in endless dog fights. The advance was supported with the Boche strafing and bombing the PBI below, with the RFC struggling to delay and harass the advance. The most important weapon in Rogue's arsenal in those days, was the camera strapped to the side of the 'Brisfit'. The developments on the ground were dynamic, and the General staff was desperate to get real time information, to enable them to reinforce where needed most, and nurture the limited resources to hand in those first few days. The SE's provided a protective screen around the twins, as they flew continually, sometimes going up six times a day.

Singer was shot down on the morning of the third day. A Fokker biplane jumped them from out of the sun, with others closely in tow. Singer's plane flew into a hail of bullets which resulted in petrol spewing out from a damaged pipe, soaking him from his head down, covering his overcoat. Some wires were also cut though, as the steering became sloppy and unresponsive. Ballard successfully chased the Hun off with a few parting shots. He thought it must be from the circus, as it had a bright ochre fuselage, with a huge black cross. The wings were a chequered blue and yellow. The Rogue flights scattered and turned to evade the other planes, turning the machines in tightly with wings vertical to repel the threat. The Huns didn't stay to press home the attack, but used their speed to dive back towards the own lines. Singer flattened out the glide slope and looked over the side for a suitable place to put down. He checked again to ensure he had switched off the petrol and glided towards an island of greenery that looked reasonably flat. He was fortunate that the undercarriage held together as the SE's wheels brushed the ground. Singer was thrown forward against his harness, as the resistance of the long grass brought the plane to halt in the shortest landing he had ever had. The tail of the plane rose up into the air, threatening to completely overturn, but fell back with a distinct thump to the ground. The smell of petrol was a reminder that there was still the real threat of fire or explosion. He quickly exited from the cockpit followed by a few seconds of walking as fast as his bulky clothes would allow, away from the wreck. He sat down to recover himself, and was soon surrounded by a number of New Zealanders arriving to assist. One of the privates naively offered him a cigarette, which on this occasion he tactfully declined.

*

The offensive petered out after a few weeks and failed to deliver the decisive victory the Germans had hoped for. In that short time Aubrey was also forced to land with his bus damaged, but he was fortunate to make it back to the aerodrome. Kiwi suffered engine failure, and became an overnight guest of the French. In all the time the twins were on reconnaissance duties, the Bristol remained unmolested by the enemy, thanks to the tireless efforts the pilots and ground crew.

It was at that time that the RFC morphed into the Royal Air Force. The specific day passed by without comment. The uniforms, and the planes they flew remained unchanged. One wag did remark that it seemed appropriate that the change took place on April fool's day!

One evening Jules and Mario put on a circus show to thank their comrades in keeping them alive in this phase of the battle. They decided to showcase their talents, none of the others had ever seen. A compendium of acts entertained the men, in and out outside the mess. They managed to obtain some props from stores, and delivered a show of juggling, fire eating and ending with an hilarious puppet show featuring the brass hats and royalty from both sides.

*

The pilots were assembled in the office the next morning, where Bill presented them with three areas of interest he had calculated they would make contact with Richthofen. He couldn't determine with any confidence as to whether he would have company though. They flew as one flight, as John had accurately determined that a pair alone, would not guarantee a positive outcome should a fight occur, and may well result in merely adding to the Baron's tally. The following days were ones of long patrols, trying to remain unseen, and avoiding contact with any hostile machines.

A month to the day, after the start of the spring offensive the flight spotted a pair of machines in the distance.

It was Dick who first confirmed them as hostile, and as they drew nearer, his animated gestures suggested it might be the distinctive red machine they had been hunting. Singer was right to leave Ballard and the Bristol behind on this particular day. This would be a fight of Aces, with the best machines in the air at that time. Four Se5a's came down onto the red triplane of Richthofen and an accompanying Fokker bi-plane. Adrian led the flight down to engage, leaving Singer sitting aloft, observing every move the red plane made. The two Germans made no effort to escape, rather they turned back towards the SE's, the triplane in particular turned flatly on its axis, and fired several short bursts, at more than one target. The SE's scattered to avoid further punishment, with each in turn giving his partner enough air space to fight. Peter used his airspeed to come up beneath the Boche biplane and executed a telling deflection burst immediately in front. The Hun appeared to fly though without any visible damage, nevertheless, the Hun took his bus down abruptly to put distance from the action. Peter's plane went initially down in pursuit, and then reversed course. His instincts had kicked in, before he remembered the mission. The three SE's were probing for a line of attack, like jackals around a lion. Singer looked down in dismay as the Baron turned and fired, reversed, and rose sharply in an astonishing series of manoeuvres. On several occasions he created enough of a gap to remove himself from the fray, but each time he turned back into the fight, to inflict further pain on his enemy. Dick waited patiently, as the red plane suddenly focused it's attention onto his comrades, and closed in with a short burst. Aubrey was out of his depth, with his machine having hits along the fuselage. His wings also had several large holes where the fabric flapped tellingly. He was just hoping to stay put until someone else could inflict a killing blow. The sweat poured from Adrian's brow, as he almost got a bead on him, but so far, he had failed every time. Adrian made the mistake of slowing himself down to get in closer, giving the Baron a clear sight of his cockpit. As he fired, another SE flew in on a tight turn between them with its belly exposed, which absorbed the bullets from Richthofen instead. It was Dick's machine, that had watched the encounter being played out, and Dickie only had enough time to put himself in between the two combatants in a desperate effort to save his friend!

Above, Singer watched and waited. The Baron had fended them off for a good twenty minutes in a magnificent ballet of airmanship. He flipped the SE over and pointed the guns at an empty area of space, and fired. A quick push of the rudder pedal, and he fired again. He roughly put the bus on its side, and watched with satisfaction as the triplane flew in to the second of his bursts. As he came in behind, Aubrey managed to inflict further damage on the Tri-plane with further damage to its rudder and tail plane.

Singer found himself just thirty yards or so behind, and was in the perfect position to apply the coup de grace. He hesitated for a few seconds, observing the large red machine in front flying straight and level, with no attempt to manoeuvre. Singer took himself up alongside the German, Richthofen looked towards him, and waved wearily. Blood was visible on his coat, with further traces along his fuselage. Singer gestured for him to follow him down, receiving a nod in acknowledgement. They were not too far from the airfield, so with the flight in tow he made for there.

Dick knew he had been hit, when he put himself in front of Richthofen in that critical moment. He didn't think it was too bad, and he couldn't fathom for now where he was struck. He shivered as a coldness came over him, and he had to concentrate on flying to overcome bouts of drowsiness.

Singer took them all down and landed a couple of fields away from the aerodrome, and the others followed his lead.

Richthofen remained in his cockpit not moving. "Addie, were going to give your idea a go. You and Aubrey help the Baron out of the cockpit, I'm pretty sure he's wounded." He turned to Peter. "Commandeer some transport, preferably an ambulance, and make sure only you drive it here, okay. Where's Dickie at?" Peter took himself at a pace, while the others managed to get Manfred out of his plane, and laid him comfortably on the grass. He was in pain, but conscious, and little confused.

Aubrey removed his leather jacket, and started to clean his wound. "You've taken a bullet to the shoulder, mate. Looks quite severe, but you'll live alright. Won't be flying for some time I don't think."

Manfred looked at Aubrey blankly, not understanding a word.

John waved Adrian over, just as he was going to see what was up with Dickie.

"Right Addie, this is your little scheme, perhaps you might like to tell the Baron here what you have in mind." Peter had managed to acquire an ambulance, and was navigating it slowly over the rough terrain, coming to a halt close by. A quiet conversation between the two former enemies came to a halt.

Adrian went back to John. "He's not buying it John, much to do with honour and loyalty. I'm just going over to find Dickie for a bit, and I'll try again."

He made his way over to his friends SE, and found him leaning on the fuselage. As he drew close he noticed Dickie looked pale and unsteady. "Bloody Baron is not having any of it Dick, says he would prefer captivity, you alright?"

Dick ignored the question. "Won't have it eh. Think it might be my turn for an idea Addie." Dick winced in pain, and grabbed at Adrian's sleeve. "Claude. Will you take care of him? Tell him of me?"

Adrian looked at Dick in confusion, and then noticed the blood. "Your wounded Dick. Let me get Aubrey, bloody hell you should have said something."

Dick released his grip, and looked up to the sky. "I'm dying Addie, no, no, it's okay. I can feel it inside. My son Addie, please, will you care for him?"

Adrian could only nod dumbly. "Now go get his clothes and headgear, and help me into his plane, the Baron dies today" Dickie winced in pain "Remember what Voss said, remember his words"

A few minutes later all the pilots looked on in astonishment as they watched the Fokker take off, and disappear into the thin cloud. He walked back to where the Baron now lay in the back of the ambulance. "Manfred, my friend, one of my men is wounded, badly wounded so I am told, at your hands. He is doing us the honour of taking your plane for its final flight. You will die today with honour as befits you."

Tears were now streaming down Adrian's oil smeared face. "All the arrangements have been made to get you to America. We know you have family there. What you don't know is that you have friends there too, friends of ours. You may live there in peace or, in time return to your homeland," He saw that Manfred now understood the generosity and sacrifice they had offered him. I have a message from Werner for you." Adrian leaned closer to the Baron. "Katie Helen Georgia." He slowly nodded his head in acknowledgement, and closed his eyes. "And you won't be flying anytime soon either, not with that arm. Get some rest, we have a long journey ahead."

Manfred pulled at Adrian's sleeve weakly. "His name, your friend in my plane. Please, his name."

*

The red machine bought a brief smile on Dickies face, as he felt the response from his light touches. He was a lot weaker now, and his eyes sometimes dimmed into greyness briefly, before recovering. It wasn't long before he came across an Se5a, which he thought was suitably poetic for his last patrol. He flew behind it as the pilot ahead began to jinx. The red triplane shuddered with multiple hits from another SE that had manoeuvred in behind him. behind. Dick let the controls go, and waited for the darkness to come.

Time had no meaning to him, as he briefly opened his eyes once more. The plane was somehow on the ground, and he felt, rather than saw people crowding around the cockpit. In front of his eyes, Claudette appeared, she had waited for him, and now had come to take him from here. The grey mist came over him once again, this time forever. He was with her now, and called out her name, as he died.

A New Zealander looking up at the plane called up his mate who was next to the cockpit. "What did he say?"

His friend replied, "Dunno mate, Kaput! I think."

*

A few days later Adrian watched the elaborate funeral being played out for the celebrated Manfred Von Richthofen. He silently prayed for his friend, and repeated a solemn vow to raise his son as his own. He will be told in time of the life of his friend. The good times they spent together, and the man who gave so much to his friends, his family and his country.

The one thing he will never know, would be the truth of the fate of Dickie Watson, and Manfred Von Richthofen. That secret will stay with Rogue flight forever!

THE END

Lightning Source UK Ltd.
Milton Keynes UK
UKHW011820111222
413752UK00008B/124

9 781803 810737